"ONLY MARRIED MEN NEED ROOTS...

"And I'm not married," Duncan Kincaid said. "Never have been...at least that's what the annulment papers said."

Cairo didn't want to discuss the annulment. "You never wanted to get married again?" she asked. "Have children?"

"I'm perfectly happy with my life just the way it is."

Cairo studied his eyes to see if he was telling the truth. "Are you truly happy?" she asked. "I got the impression from everything I read about you that you don't have a lot of money. You would have had more if you'd stayed married to me."

"Contrary to the excuse you used for getting the annulment...I didn't marry you for your money."

Duncan stepped in front of her. Close. Very close. He towered over her, strong and powerful. His muscles flexed under his shirtsleeves. "And you're not in the past anymore. You're here. Now. And I want to know why."

ATTENTION: ORGANIZATIONS AND CORPORATIONS
Most Avon Books paperbacks are available at special quantity
discounts for bulk purchases for sales promotions, premiums, or
fund-raising. For information, please call or write:

**Special Markets Department, HarperCollins Publishers, Inc.,
10 East 53rd Street, New York, N.Y. 10022-5299.
Telephone: (212) 207-7528. Fax: (212) 207-7222.**

PATTI BERG

Bride For A Night

AVON BOOKS
An Imprint of HarperCollins*Publishers*

This is a work of fiction. Names, characters, places, and incidents are products of the author's imagination or are used fictitiously and are not to be construed as real. Any resemblance to actual events, locales, organizations, or persons, living or dead, is entirely coincidental.

AVON BOOKS
An Imprint of HarperCollins*Publishers*
10 East 53rd Street
New York, New York 10022-5299

Copyright © 2000 by Patti Berg
Library of Congress Catalog Card Number: 99-96451
ISBN: 0-380-80736-X
www.avonromance.com

First Avon Books paperback printing: May 2000

Avon Trademark Reg. U.S. Pat. Off. and in Other Countries, Marca Registrada, Hecho en U.S.A.
HarperCollins® is a trademark of HarperCollins Publishers Inc.

Printed in the U.S.A.

WCD 10 9 8 7 6 5 4 3 2 1

One

Duncan crawled deep into the limestone tunnel, the cold seeping through his heavy denim shirt, while the solid barrier of rock pressed against his back and squeezed his shoulders. With each movement the passage grew tighter, forcing him to lie on his belly and grip onto any small outcropping of rock to pull himself along, inch after inch.

Cool, dank air filled his lungs when he sucked in his next breath, and for the first time inside the tunnel, he felt moisture on the walls and floor. A moment later the passage widened, and in the light shining from his head lamp he could see the crawlspace take a sudden vertical turn, dropping straight down into nothing.

Surprised laughter burst from his throat, the reverberation echoing about the chamber until it disappeared down the hole—a narrow shaft so much like the ones he'd found in the last seventeen tunnels he'd explored in this barren part of southeastern Montana. This one could come to a dead end, too, but he had no intention of giving up. He was following a dream, and he wouldn't quit easily.

Not this time.

The precipice jutting out over the shaft was barely wide enough for him to stand on, the ceiling a good six and a half feet above it, allowing him just enough room to straighten his spine, flex his constricted muscles, and study his surroundings. The only two ways to continue were to go back the way he'd come or climb straight down, and he didn't believe in moving backward.

Within seconds, he was back in action, taping a reflective arrow on the wall of the cave and securing his rope to the sturdiest rock he could reach. When his climbing gear was ready, he tossed the rope over the edge and rappelled into unexplored territory, hoping this shaft would lead him to the mysterious cavern—and the city of gold.

For ten years he'd wondered about the city. Was it a myth? A legend? Rumors he'd heard years before had caught his interest, but he hadn't given them much credence until he'd found an old journal in a rugged Rocky Mountain canyon. The sheaf of papers had been wrapped in oilcloth and leather, and was clasped against the skeletal chest of Angus MacPherson, a nineteenth-century mountain man who'd lived a bold and adventurous life, if there was any truth to his stories. The Scotsman had gone on one escapade after another, and Duncan had read the tome so often that Angus had pretty much come to life, roaming dark caves by his side. Hell, he even had conversations with the grizzled old goat.

Did I ever tell you about the blizzard of 1837?

"At least a dozen times," Duncan answered, as he pushed away from an overhang, making sure his rope didn't catch on a jutting rock as he made his way further into the pit.

Might have died if I hadn't trailed an old she-bear into her den. Too bad the place wasn't big enough for both of us. I suspect she would have been better company than the bats or the sound of my own gruff voice. Still, that old girl, tough as she was, kept my belly full and my body warm all winter long. If it weren't for her, I would surely have died, and I never would have found the city of gold.

The city of gold. Duncan's sixth sense told him he'd finally found the right tunnel. After five months of searching, after ten years of scrimping and saving to fund his own expedition, he knew he was close to the legend that many people in this part of Montana had been seeking for years. Fortunately for him, they were looking north of the town of Sanctuary instead of south, and Duncan was bound and determined to keep what he knew a secret—from everyone, especially his colleagues.

They already considered him an oddball. The archaeology journals and even his first employers, the renowned archaeologists Helen and George McKnight, claimed he'd become nothing more than a caricature of an archaeologist, a modern-day Indiana Jones who thrived on adventure rather than the pursuit of knowledge.

Hell, they were probably right. Analyzing pottery fragments, fossils, and the remains of ancient vegetation had never caught his interest. It was the dream of finding new worlds that had drawn Duncan toward archaeology. He liked the search, the fear and excitement of the unknown.

That's what drove him now.

With Angus's journal tucked in his backpack for company, Duncan dropped further down the shaft and into a cavern that seemed to stretch forever. He hung in midair and took in the magnificence of his surroundings. Milky white stalactites glistened in the light from his helmet and pale yellow stalagmites rose from the cavern floor like towering cathedral spires. He'd been in hundreds of caves, and their magnificence always amazed him. But he had a special feeling about this one, as if Angus was hanging beside him on the rope saying, "Get cracking, Dunc. This is the place."

He hadn't felt this kind of excitement since he'd come across an undiscovered tomb in the Valley of the Kings, since he and Cairo . . .

What was he thinking? Cairo was history.

He pushed his ex-wife out of his mind and released his descender, dropping slowly to the rocky surface. When his boots touched ground, he uncinched his harness, pulled his own journal from his pack, and made some quick notes about his journey. Measuring and making detailed drawings would have to wait until later. He was in a hurry to explore.

Flicking on a hand-held flashlight, he walked about the cavern, which resembled the hub of a wagon wheel with tunnels leading away from it like spokes. Multicolored flowstone waterfalls swept down the walls like giant stairsteps, and impassable thickets of bamboo-like formations blocked the entrance to some of the tunnels he could see. The only sounds about him now were the crunch of his boots on the rocks, the dim and distant drip of water, his own heart-beat, and the ever-present wind, which seemed to draw him toward a jagged, forbidding-looking passage.

After marking his way, he stepped through the hole. The tunnel twisted and turned, and he moved cautiously, half expecting the floor to vanish in front of him if he made even one false move. He'd gone barely fifty feet when he thought he'd hit another dead end, but then he saw one more rift in the rock and squeezed through, at last finding himself in an even bigger cavern.

The light from his helmet illuminated the walls. "Damn." The whispered word rushed from his lips and grew louder as it reverberated in the massive room. Everywhere he looked were vividly painted pictographs, exactly like Angus had said.

I've never seen the likes of it. The walls were covered with drawings of painted warriors and big-breasted women, and I'll be damned, they were standing at the entrance to a great golden city.

Duncan stared at the colorful wall, at warriors and goddesses wearing feathered crowns, their necks, arms, and ankles encircled with gold and silver bands, gazing at pyramids and temples built amid stalactites and stalagmites.

Duncan moved closer, afraid his eyes were

deceiving him, but the pictures were real, and almost beyond belief.

"Mayan." He said the word out loud, as if uttering it would make the impossible easy to accept, and it echoed back to him again and again. He'd seen drawings like these in the scrubland of the Yucatán Peninsula and the rain forests of Belize, Guatemala, and El Salvador, but never anything *this* far north. As many times as he'd read the mountain man's journal, he never expected a find like this.

He spun around, his discovery so mind-blowing that he needed to tell someone. But he was alone, except for the cold wind moaning through the tunnels.

I swear that cave is haunted. Screams came out of holes in the walls, and that icy air chilled me to the bone. I thought for sure I'd walked straight into hell when a phantom rose up from the ground, a big, white, evil thing with arms reaching out. I damn near thought it was going to swallow me whole.

A horrendous howl and a rush of cold wind flooded the cave, whipping about, stirring up dirt and fine powdery silt that shrouded everything in the cavern.

Duncan stepped into a deep crack in the limestone wall and waited for the wind to die down. When the wailing ceased, when the swirling banshees disappeared down a tunnel and the last of the dust settled, a massive, milky white stalagmite loomed before him, twisted and deformed and looking every inch the ghoul.

Suddenly all was calm and far too quiet. A shiver raced up his spine, as if something foreboding lurked nearby.

Then, without warning, an earsplitting scream burst through the silence.

The wind?

A woman?

Ten years he'd waited for this moment and right now he wanted to do nothing more than inspect the pictographs. He hoped he hadn't heard that blasted scream, but there it was again, shrill, piercing—a cry for help.

"Ah, hell!" He raced back through the tunnel, and when he reached the end of the passage, his gaze followed the beam of light bouncing about the main cavern until he saw a curvy female body suspended high above the rocky floor.

Damn if the cave wasn't full of hidden treasures.

Her gear was stuck, something he could relate to. He'd been hasty and careless with his rigging once before and ended up in the same predicament. His own experience told him the woman wasn't in immediate danger, otherwise he would have climbed right up to help. Besides, she looked awfully good hanging there, with her long, jeans-clad legs scissored around the rope and her red shirt hugging her body so tightly that he could see the outline of full, sumptuous breasts. Even in the dimly lit cavern he thought he could see her hardened nipples pressing against—

"Damn it, Duncan! Quit staring at my body and get me down from here."

The all-too-familiar voice struck him with the force of his old memories. The last person he wanted to see right now was his ex. "What are you doing here, Cairo?"

"Dangling."

"That's obvious. Now, why don't you explain what isn't so obvious, like how did you find me, and why the hell did you bother?"

Cairo McKnight angled her dusty face toward him and flashed a glare that could turn a man to stone. "Just get me down, Duncan. I'll explain everything later."

Later? Sure she would, Duncan thought cynically, in the same way she'd responded to his letters asking why she'd filed for an annulment—by marking them "Return to sender" and dropping them back in the mail unopened.

Well, he had no intention of letting Cairo McKnight avoid him this time. She was a woman at the end of her rope, literally and figuratively, and no one could save her but him.

He leaned against the cold limestone wall, folded his arms over his chest, and glared back at her. "What's it been, Cairo? Four years? Five?"

"Five years and one month," she said, her voice tinged with anger as she struggled with the rope.

"You've been counting the days?"

"Every blessed one."

"You missed me, then." It was a statement, not a question.

"Missed you?" Cairo's laughter ricocheted around the cavern, the burst so sharp and hostile Duncan feared the sound might split a stalactite in two or cause the ground beneath his feet to open up and swallow him.

"Sure I missed you, Duncan, the same way I'd miss a brain tumor after it was removed. The way—"

Duncan laughed, interrupting her tirade. "I'm glad to see you're still the same sweet girl I married."

"And you're still the same arrogant, frustrating—"

Cairo's words were bitten off by her scream as she plummeted down the rope. He could see terror in her eyes, could feel the fear in his throat, and once again he ran toward the scream.

Cairo latched onto the rope, feeling the burning friction through her gloves as she stopped her sudden descent. She held on tight, giving silent thanks to Allah and Isis and every god and goddess she could think of for letting her live—once again.

Beneath her, the cave floor seemed to spin, so much like the tangle of jungle had done a few months before, when the plane she was in had made its death dive. All she could think about then was Dylan, about her precious little boy being raised—as she had been—by her aunt, instead of by the mother who loved him, or by the father who didn't even know he was alive.

Dylan's father. She closed her eyes for a moment to still the spinning, then opened them again. Her child's father—Duncan—was coming toward her now, hoisting himself up hand over hand until he reached her, and as he'd done so many times before, he pulled her into the safety of his arms.

She felt secure in his embrace, and for the moment she didn't want to think about the way he'd abandoned her after their wedding night, the hurt she'd felt back then or the anger she still harbored. Instead she wondered if this big, strong, unreliable man could be a good father, if he would run after Dylan if he was hurt, if he would hold him and soothe him and take care of him, day and night.

The bristle of Duncan's whisker-coated cheek brushed against her face, and she felt his warm breath trace her ear as he whispered, "Are you all right?"

Nodding, she closed her eyes again, resting in his arms while her breathing and her heart-beat calmed. Once upon a time she'd loved this man with every part of her; now she felt nothing but indifference. He was the father of her son, and her precocious little four-year-old needed a father desperately. She hadn't realized that until the plane had crashed, until she struggled to free herself from the twisted, burning wreck and thought of all the others who'd perished, men and women with children left at home—children who no longer had parents.

She didn't want the same thing for Dylan. Yes, Phoebe would be there for him. Wonderful Aunt Phoebe, who was always there—but she wanted even more for her son. She wanted him to have the kind of family she'd never had, a mother *and* a father who loved him—the kind of family Duncan had had.

But she thought of Duncan's adventurous spirit, and sadly, his irresponsibility. That irresponsibility had made her annul their marriage, had kept her from telling him about their child. If things had been different, he would have been at her side as she struggled to raise their son—but could she have trusted him?

Now she didn't know for sure. That was part of the reason she'd come to Montana—so he could prove his worth.

"Ready to go down now?" Duncan asked, bringing her back to the fact that she was hanging a good thirty feet above a cavern floor.

She twisted her head and their helmets clicked together. His pale blue eyes burned into hers, and she forced herself to smile. "Thanks for coming to my rescue."

His lips tilted into a grin. "Old habits die hard."

He didn't wait for a retort and she couldn't think of one as they began their descent. They moved slowly, while she tried to concentrate on her reasons for coming to Montana, but instead she found herself watching Duncan's hands next to hers on the rope, powerful hands that she couldn't help focusing on. Hands that had skillfully guided her through unexplored tombs, that had tenderly comforted her when her parents didn't have the time. Hands that had been the first ones to caress her, stroke her, and drive her mad.

And then had blown her a kiss good-bye.

Remember *that*, she reminded herself. And remember that you have a purpose for being here—not just for Dylan, but for your business. She needed a real life Indiana Jones to bail her out of trouble, and Duncan came close to that image.

She pulled out of his arms the moment her feet settled on solid ground, not wanting the closeness that would make falling under his spell far too easy. She'd been entranced by him as a teenager, had spent years fantasizing about him, dreaming of his kiss, his touch, and like a lovesick schoolgirl, had run off with him to Las Vegas and ended up his bride—for a night.

Then he'd left her. Damn him!

It had taken too many tears, too many years to get over him, and she had no plan to live through that again.

She ambled around the cave, focusing on the splattermites rising from the ground, the twisted helictites and flaming red soda straws that were everwhere she turned. She began to wonder what Duncan was doing here. His interests didn't lie in geology, so she knew something far more exciting than calcium formations had attracted him. If she didn't have a son to get back to or a business to get back on track, if her life hadn't been changed by the events of the last five years, she could easily stay down here and find out what had brought Duncan to this intriguing place. But staying here wasn't part of her plan.

Behind her, she could sense Duncan's fiery gaze watching her every move and then his voice broke the silence. "I'm still waiting, Cairo. What are you doing here?"

She took a deep breath and turned slowly, ready to ask him—a man she'd never wanted to see again—to do her a very big favor. She aimed her helmet's light directly at him. "I want to hire you."

His eyes darkened. Narrowed. She could see his jaw tense, and then he laughed harshly. "I worked for the McKnights once. I'm not interested in doing it again."

"This isn't for my parents; it's for me. I'm sure that's not much of an incentive, but the money is far better than anything you've ever made as an archaeologist."

He rubbed his fingers over the black stubble on his chin, staring so intently into her eyes that she thought for sure he was trying to look inside her mind to see what she was hiding.

"I work for myself and by myself," he said, and turned away, as if the subject was closed.

Thank goodness he'd stopped studying her. Duncan had always had a way of looking at her with those hypnotic blue eyes of his that could make her divulge all her little secrets. And right now, she didn't want him to know about Dylan.

He pulled a camera from his pack and started snapping pictures of flowstone, gypsum flowers, and popcorn formations, seemingly disinterested in her presence and her offer of a job, but she wasn't about to give up. She needed Duncan's expertise far too badly. Sixteen tourists had died on that plane when it crashed, sixteen people she'd been hired to lead, to watch over, to make sure they were safe—and she'd failed. The people she'd taken on previous expeditions wouldn't give her references after the accident and now she couldn't book more than two or three people on a tour. If Duncan would lead one, just one, she might regain her credibility. And it would be the perfect opportunity to see if he had grown up over the years.

She walked across the cavern and stood in front of the jagged tunnel Duncan was staring at. "It's a good job," she said. "Something right up your alley."

"Not interested."

"It's in Central America."

He put the camera in front of his face and snapped a picture. "I'm perfectly happy in North America." Stubbornness was part of his character, but she'd never seen him quite so adamant, as if he had some reason to despise her instead of the other way around.

Maybe she had annulled their marriage without his consent, but he'd left her for some crazy adventure in Egypt. And then he'd ended up in jail—damn him! She'd had every right to end their so-called marriage. He was an irresponsible fool! As for keeping Dylan a secret, maybe she'd been wrong to do that, but she hadn't known she was pregnant when she'd filed annulment papers and besides, he'd proved he was a lousy husband. How could she possibly have thought he could be a decent dad?

"What's the real reason you're here?" Duncan asked, taking a few steps to his left so he could snap a picture of the tunnel behind her. "Management rarely travels to the middle of nowhere or crawls through a cave to talk with a prospective employee. You could have used a telephone."

"Considering our past, would you have talked to me or returned my call if I'd left a message?"

"No, Cairo," he said slowly, deliberately, staring at her over the lens, "I seriously doubt I would have called you back."

"I didn't think so. That's why I'm here now."

He snapped another picture. "So how'd you

find me? I haven't made my whereabouts public."

It was her turn to look away, to walk about as if she were disinterested. Two could play at that game. "I know how you work," she said, skimming her fingers a fraction of an inch above the ancient formations. "I spent five summers dogging your footsteps when I was a teenager and know just how methodical you can be. You stay away from paved roads and even unpaved ones. If you had a choice between spending the night in a five-star hotel or in a tent, you'd take the tent every time." Cairo remembered that she'd once felt the same way, especially during those nights she'd spent with Duncan under a full Egyptian moon. Quickly she brushed the thought aside. "Finding your camp wasn't difficult. Maybe you've forgotten how good a tracker I am."

He pinned her with his blue-eyed stare. "You're wrong, Cairo. I haven't forgotten a thing."

She hadn't either. She hadn't forgotten their wedding night and the way she'd quivered inside when his callused fingers splayed over her belly. And long before that, she remembered the sweet taste of wine on his lips the first time *she'd* kissed *him*, and the fact that she'd been only fifteen, while he was twenty-two. She could still recall the look of surprise on his face, the hint of desire that flashed across his eyes before he laughed off what had happened and made her swear it wouldn't happen again.

But she didn't care to remember those moments. Instead, she plucked the camera from his hand and put her eye to the viewfinder so she could hide her troubled expressions—anger mixed with a desire she thought she'd overcome. "I've tried forgetting all about you," she admitted, "but it seems that every time I pick up an archaeology magazine, your photo stares back at me. And how could I possibly ignore the captions? *Duncan Kincaid—adventurer extraordinaire.*"

One of Duncan's thick black eyebrows rose. "Mostly hype, I assure you."

Cairo aimed the camera in his direction. "I said I read the articles; I didn't necessarily believe every word."

A touch of amusement softened the hard planes of his face, and she captured the moment on film. Then she turned away, weaving in and out of a zigzagging line of stalagmites, catching occasional glimpses of Duncan standing in the middle of the cavern, observing her every move.

"Do you like your nomadic existence?" she asked, as she disappeared behind a crystallized column. His love of adventure had been one of the reasons she'd fallen head over heels for him, but it was also the thing that had torn them apart. She wished—for Dylan's sake, she assured herself—that he had harbored some thoughts of settling down.

The animosity in his response shook her. "Only married men need roots. I'm not married. Never have been . . . at least, that's what the annulment papers said."

She didn't want to discuss the annulment. "That's a part of history that's better off dead and buried."

The moment she rounded the next column, Duncan stepped in front of her. Close. Very close. "It's no longer dead and buried." He towered over her, as strong and powerful and unbending as the massive stalagmites. "You're not in the past anymore either. You're here. Now. And I want to know why."

She stared at his shoulder, at the muscles flexing under his shirtsleeves as he folded his arms across his chest. "I'm waiting, Cairo."

"I told you. I want to hire you."

"For what?"

"To help me lead an archaeological tour into Central America."

"You want me to be a tour guide?" He laughed, but she couldn't miss the indignation in his voice. "You're out of your mind. No respectable archaeologist leads tours."

"I do."

"Since when?"

"Three years. Four. I lost count."

"Your parents must be having a field day with that. As I recall, you were destined to work at their side."

"I tried," she said honestly. "Turned out I didn't have much interest in sifting through sand."

"You're a lousy liar, Cairo. I've never known anyone with your kind of curiosity about the past. I've watched you spend hour upon hour searching for the smallest fragment of antiquity. It's in your blood. You don't lose that overnight."

You do when you have a child to raise, she wanted to tell him. You do when you've been hurt by parents who were too obsessed with their work to give you the time of day.

But she shrugged off thoughts of her past. Instead she said, "I keep my hand in it. In fact, my tours always include a side trip to a dig. That's one of the reasons I want you to go with me on my tour of Belize next month—"

"Belize?" He laughed. "Is this an archaeological tour, or a week of fun in the sun?"

"A little of both," she admitted. "I don't need

any help while we're snorkeling or touring the Jaguar Reserve. What I do need is someone who knows the jungle and Mayan ruins."

"I can give you the names of a dozen archaeologists who could go with you."

"I want more than just an archaeologist. I want . . . well . . ." She looked at the smirk on Duncan's face. "I need someone who knows his way around boa constrictors, can hack through the jungle with a machete—"

"You're perfectly capable," he interrupted. "If I remember correctly, you had a pet cobra named Jagger and once told your parents you wanted a crocodile for a Christmas present."

Cairo sighed, partly in exasperation, partly because he remembered far too much about her. "Look, Duncan, I've led this kind of tour before, and trust me, the tourists want a man guiding the way, not a woman."

"You'll have to find someone else."

"I can't. There's not enough time. Besides . . ." The word slipped off her tongue and over her lips before she could stop it. Maybe he'd just ignore it.

"Besides what, Cairo?"

Damn! She faced him eye to eye. "Your name is printed in the travel brochure. People are expecting Duncan Kincaid, adventurer extraordinaire."

Humor spread across his face and laughter erupted, filling every corner of the cavern and smacking Cairo's ears. "Looks like you've got yourself in one hell of a mess."

"You'll help me get out of it, won't you?"

"Why should I?"

"For old times' sake."

"You had our marriage annulled. You ignored every letter I sent you asking why. You—"

"Please?" she asked softly.

"No."

Duncan's fingers wrapped around her upper arm and tugged her toward the rope.

"Don't be so impulsive," Cairo pleaded, as Duncan took the camera from her hands. "Give it a little thought. I know you can use the money."

He fastened her harness around her, hooked her up to the ascender, and slapped the rope into her palms. "Climb."

"I'm not quite ready to leave. I'm not ready to give up yet, either."

"You're leaving," he said flatly. "So am I, but I'm *not* changing my mind."

She felt a very feminine expression cross her face, as if some repressed kind of womanly wile had taken over to persuade Duncan.

"Don't look at me that way, Cairo."

"What way?"

"You know damn good and well. You did the same thing in Egypt every time you wanted something from me. Well, I was crazy back then. I'm not crazy anymore and I'm not going to fall for your theatrics ever again."

"Then why are you leaving with me? Wouldn't you be better off to stay down here and let me go home alone?"

"I'd be better off if you'd never come back into my life, but since you have, I'm going to escort you right back out and make sure you leave."

"I'm not that easy to get rid of, Duncan."

Heat radiated in his narrowed pale blue eyes, as he stared down at her. "Tell me something I don't already know." A knot formed in her throat, the kind of knot she hadn't felt since they'd stood face to face in the honeymoon suite at the Luxor in Las Vegas, when he'd slipped the straps of her white cotton sundress over her shoulders and pressed a searing kiss to the hollow of her neck.

She drew in a deep breath and turned her head away, but not for long. Duncan touched her, his index finger curling under her chin as he made her face him again. His thumb brushed lightly over her lower lip, and she thought for sure it would tremble and give her nervousness away. But he dropped his hand all too quickly.

"I don't want your job, Cairo. I don't want or need your money, either." He shoved the rope that she'd released back into her hands. "Now, *climb.*"

She didn't argue. Instead, she ascended the rope, thinking she should head back to Sanctuary and give up her quest. Being around Duncan much longer could easily lead to unwanted trouble and God knows what else.

Unfortunately, giving up was the last thing on her mind.

Two

Hell, yes, he could use the money! Duncan reminded himself as he moved through the narrow tunnel, but he wasn't about to earn it by working for his ex, no matter how provocative she was, no matter how amazing she looked crawling in front of him with her curvy bottom, beckoning him to follow her . . . anywhere.

Cairo McKnight was the epitome of a flirt, a siren who'd teased him for five years, then ripped his heart out not long after he'd married her. No, he wasn't going to fall for that again.

Never.

Why had she come back into his life? If her

27

plan had been to make him miserable, she was doing a slam-bang job of it.

How did she know he needed money? A lot had been written about him, but he couldn't remember even seeing his finances mentioned. More than likely she'd investigated every twist and turn of his life since they'd last seen each other, and if that was the case, she already knew that his bank account had dwindled down to barely four figures. She probably also knew about the money he'd forked out for his father's rehab, for exercise equipment and physical therapy, and all the other things that hadn't been and still weren't covered by insurance. But, hell, if she hadn't returned—unopened, damn her!—the letter he'd sent, telling her about the head-on collision, about his mother's death and his father's spinal cord injury, she wouldn't have had to investigate him.

If she'd read even one of his letters, they might still be married. But no, she'd ignored them, and before that she hadn't bothered coming to see him in that godforsaken Egyptian jail. Maybe he'd made some big mistakes where Cairo was concerned, but she hadn't even given him a chance to explain.

Hell, it was probably a good thing that she hadn't. The last thing he wanted was to be tied down to a maddening woman like Cairo. Even if she did have the sexiest bottom and the sexiest eyes and the sexiest smile and the tightest, hottest—

The light on his helmet plowed into her sexy bottom and smacked the hardhat against his forehead long before he realized she'd stopped crawling. He reached for her hips, touching the firm curves that felt pretty damn good underneath close-fitting jeans. When he was able to tear his eyes from the saddle-stitched seam that raced over her derriere and between her legs, he could easily see the slow turn of her head and the frown in her eyes.

She reached behind her, lifted his left hand from her hip, and dropped it off to the side. Her gaze slid to his right hand, still resting comfortably on the pocket of her jeans.

Her frown deepened, and he tugged all five reluctant fingers away.

"Is something bothering you?" she asked, her frown turning to a tight-eyed, questioning glare. "You've been mumbling to yourself for the past five minutes."

"Just trying to figure out what you're up to."

"I told you."

"Yeah, right, you want me to entertain a bunch of rich, pampered tourists who couldn't tell the difference between a real archaeologist and movie character any more than they could tell the difference between a Mayan ruin and a plaster façade built on some movie studio back-lot. So why did you track me to Sanctuary when it would have been much easier to fly into Hollywood and hire some good-looking stud to pose as me?"

"Because it's too damn hard to find any other man on the face of this earth who could act as arrogantly as you do, who could strut around pretending to be the greatest archaeologist alive, when everyone else knows that he's nothing more than a two-bit adventurer who's the laughingstock of the archaeological world."

"Well, that's pretty straightforward."

"You want me to tell you I've heard how respected you are? You want me to tell you that every museum from here to Timbuktu is anxious to finance your next project?"

He shrugged and felt one side of his mouth pulling upward, smiling of its own accord. "No need to lie."

"I didn't think so."

She started to crawl again.

"So," Duncan said, "did you hire an investigator to find out what I've been up to since the last time we talked?"

"No, "she said, not bothering to stop or turn around. "Like I said before, I read about you in magazines, even on the Internet, but it was an old friend of yours who told me you were in Montana."

Impossible. He'd made a point of keeping his whereabouts a secret from everyone but his dad. "Who?"

Her voice quivered when she spoke. "Jim Gregory."

"Jim?" Duncan felt a sharp pain in his heart for his friend who'd died in a Bolivian plane crash. "He's dead."

Cairo stopped moving and Duncan watched her shoulders slump before she tilted her head to look at him. "I know," she said softly. "I was sitting next to him when the plane went down."

In the light from his helmet, Duncan could see the moisture in her eyes. She bit her lower lip. "He was talking about you right before . . ."

Duncan wanted to tell her she didn't have to talk about the accident, she didn't have to recall any of the events leading up to it if she didn't want to, but he knew from helping his dad recover from his own nightmare that it was better to let her say anything she wanted, without interruption, without sympathy.

"Jim talked my ear off in the plane," Cairo continued. She sat down on the tunnel floor, facing him as she spoke. "He talked about Copán and your trek through Honduras, even the time the two of you braved the jungles of Colombia."

"Not the brightest thing we ever did," Duncan admitted, making himself comfortable on the cold, hard-packed dirt. He'd been in a hurry to get out of the tunnel. Now he was held by Cairo's words.

"Jim told me Colombia was your idea, and so were all the other foolish things you did together."

"He was responsible for his share."

"That's not the way he told it. In fact"—a smile brightened her face—"he said you were the craziest son-of-a-bitch he'd ever known."

"I imagine you agreed with him."

Cairo stared at the ground between them. "I never even told him I knew you."

For someone who'd talked a blue streak when she was younger, she'd grown terribly secretive. "Why not?"

"I liked listening to him talk, and I figured if he knew you and I had a past, he'd clean up the stories to make you look better."

"I imagine the stories you heard were already whitewashed. We had some good times together."

Her head rose, and their eyes met. "With women?"

Duncan wasn't about to touch that question,

wasn't about to tell Cairo that there'd been several flings in the past five years, but all had been meaningless. Instead, he told her, "We did a lot of exploring. We got in and out of trouble a few times, and then we parted company. Did he tell you about that?"

"He said you'd asked him to go on some wild goose chase in the badlands of Montana and that he'd told you that you were out of your everlovin' mind." She grinned. "Jim's words, of course, were far more colorful. "

Duncan laughed. "He was a colorful guy."

"That's what I liked about him."

"Everyone liked that about Jim." He remembered a hot night in Guatemala City, and the last drinks and laughs he and Jim had shared. "He said he had a new girl," Duncan added. One with a nice ass, great tits, and hot lips, Jim had told him. Duncan's gaze trailed Cairo's body, and he thought about the way she'd looked and felt and moved on their wedding night. Suddenly, his throat went dry. "You weren't Jim's girl, were you?"

Cairo shook her head, and unexpected relief rushed through him.

"Jim was sitting in the middle seat, and his girlfriend—Angelica—was on the aisle." Once again she bit her lip. "God, it was so awful. Jim died, Angelica died, so did the people in my tour group and the pilot." She drew in a deep breath, and let it out slowly. "I should have smelled the liquor on the pilot's breath. I should have checked him out, but my regular pilot didn't show up and this guy was the only one I could find at the last minute. I should have called everything off, but we were having a good time, and then Jim and Angelica showed up and asked if they could bum a ride if there were any empty seats, and—"

Duncan cupped a hand to her cheek, feeling a tear against his palm. "Don't blame yourself, Cairo."

"There's no one else to blame. I've got people suing me right and left. My insurance premiums skyrocketed, and they would have been cancelled if I hadn't fought like hell with the carrier. One stupid, careless mistake on my part took the lives of eighteen people, and now the business I worked so hard to build is about to go under."

"Is that why you concocted the story about me being your tour guide?"

She looked up at him through thick, damp lashes. "It seemed like a brilliant idea at the time." For a moment he thought she might be making up the story just to change his mind. He thought the tears might be false, but he could feel the quivering in her body, and he knew she was telling the truth. "I really do need you, Duncan."

He thought about the annulment of their marriage and the way Cairo had ignored all his attempts to get in touch with her. He thought, too, about the city of gold, how long he'd waited to go on this search, and how close he was to making a great discovery. He took one more look at her eyes, which pleaded for him to take her up on her offer. And then he shook his head. "I already gave you my answer."

"I know you did, but you've got a bad habit of doing just the opposite of what you say."

"Not this time."

She smiled as if she didn't believe him. The hell of it was, he didn't quite believe himself, either.

Cairo squeezed between the boulders that had come close to blocking her view of the cave, and stepped out into the fresh evening air. She took a long, deep breath, inhaling the scent of pine and sagebrush that dotted the rocky bluff where she stood. A few puffy clouds skittered across the wide blue sky, casting shadows across the far-reaching prairie that had turned golden in the summer sun.

"It's beautiful here," she told Duncan, when he exited the tunnel and began concealing the opening with loose sagebrush. "I can see why you like it."

He stood at her side, and for a moment it seemed as of they were standing atop a pyramid, looking over the burning sands. "Do you ever want to go back to Egypt?" she asked.

"Someday, maybe, but my interests have changed over the years."

"To what? Stalactites and stalagmites?"

"Possibly."

"I take it you're not going to give me even one little hint about what you're searching for."

"If I did, you might want to stick around." He grinned. "We both know that wouldn't be a good idea."

"You're anxious to get rid of me, aren't you?"

"I'm only anxious to get back to work."

Stubborn. Pigheaded. He hadn't changed a bit in five years. She turned on her heels and scrambled down the rocky cliff. Boy, had she been wrong to think Duncan could head a tour group, that he would ever consider helping her out. Coming here had been absolutely crazy!

"Slow down, Cairo," Duncan called out to her, "or you're going to slip and fall."

He might be unreasonable, but he hadn't lost his protective streak. If he showed that kind of concern for Dylan, she could forgive him for anything. But would Duncan react that way with Dylan? she wondered. Would he know how to handle a gifted child, a boy with the body and emotions of a four-year-old, but with an I.Q. that bordered on genius? A boy whose middle name should have been trouble?

"Did you hear me, Cairo? Slow down."

She heard him dimly but her mind was crowded with too many other thoughts, like guilt for keeping Dylan a secret. At the very least she should have sent Duncan one of the birth announcements Phoebe had designed or maybe an invitation to one of Dylan's four birthday parties. But she'd sent him nothing. She hadn't called him, either.

Oh, God, what would she do if Duncan tried to take Dylan away from her when he learned the truth?

She moved a little faster, her boots slipping and sliding in a mixture of dirt and shale.

Dylan needed a father. She'd realized that as the plane was going down, when her greatest fear had been for her son's future.

But would Duncan be willing to stop his ceaseless wandering if he had a child? Would he love Dylan the way she loved him?

"Damn fool woman," she heard Duncan mutter behind her, his footsteps getting closer and closer, as if he was going to grab her, spin her

around, and know immediately what was tor-
turing her.

She didn't want that. She just wanted to get
back to Sanctuary, away from Duncan for a little while so she could rethink her plan.

She leaped across a wide break in the half-
baked Montana soil, and the narrow path on
the other side gave way beneath her. A second
later she was on her belly, sliding feet first
down the hill. There wasn't time to scream or
be scared or close her eyes to keep the dirt and
rocks from pelting her face and blurring her vi-
sion, but she somehow managed to grab onto
something prickly that made her fingers and
palms sting.

And then she felt Duncan's hands latch on to
her wrists, felt him pulling her upward, holding
her close.

"I told you to go slower," he barked. Thank
goodness he hadn't said anything warm and
comforting, or she might have cried.

She tried to respond, to tell him she had to
get home, but her mouth was sandy and dry.
At least it was until Duncan touched a wet cloth
to her lips, wiping them gently before doing the
same to her eyes, careful not to rub the grit in
deeper.

"Here, drink some of this," he said, holding
a canteen to her lips.

The water was cool, but she tasted sand when she swallowed. The next sip was better. She opened her eyes slowly and realized she was sitting in his lap, that his arm was around her. He removed her helmet and cradled her head against his shoulder. Her face was only inches from his, and for the first time that day he had his helmet off and she could see so much more of him in the light from the setting sun. His pale blue eyes were startling against his deeply tanned skin, and there were a few wrinkles at their corners that hadn't been there in the past. He looked older, wiser—and even though it didn't seem possible—much more handsome than he'd looked five years before.

Sitting in his lap was a huge mistake. She started to move but he tightened his grasp. "Hold still, Cairo."

"I'm fine now. It's getting late, and—"

"And you've got half a cactus stuck in your hands."

Her gaze traveled to her upturned palms, to the blood oozing from the few dozen puncture wounds. She hadn't felt the pain since he'd dragged her to safety because too many other thoughts had taken precedence, but now her skin burned and the scorching pain radiated up her arms. She rested her head against the strength of Duncan's chest, took one look at the bottle of antiseptic, and closed her eyes. "Just do it fast and get it over."

Duncan's chest rumbled with laughter, and she knew that he was enjoying every second of her suffering as he poured the vile, torturous liquid over her palms and pulled out the prickly thorns.

"So, Cairo," he said, and she opened her eyes to watch him expertly tie off the gauze he'd wrapped around her hands, "who gets you out of trouble when I'm not around?"

She aimed a scowl straight at him, but the laughter didn't leave his face, and this time when she pushed out of his lap, making her injured hands hurt even more in the process, he didn't stop her.

She swept her helmet from the ground. "Don't give yourself too much credit, Duncan. Trust me, you haven't always come to my rescue."

Three

They'd walked nearly a mile through rugged wilderness, a place so remote that Duncan saw little reason to worry about people finding his cave. Still, he'd taken precautions. Not far from his camp he'd cordoned off two survey areas and salted them with bones to make people think he was a dinosaur hunter. When he went in search of tunnels that might take him to the city of gold, he'd wiped out his footprints if they left too deep an imprint in the sand.

Still Cairo had found him.

A smile touched his mouth as he watched her long blond ponytail sway back and forth, brushing like a pendulum over her dusty backpack. Her helmet, as well as a flashlight, was clipped to the belt around her waist, and she'd put on a green Oakland A's baseball cap, tilting the brim low to keep the setting sun out of her eyes.

She'd worn a cap just like it the first time he'd seen her in Egypt. Her hair had reached her waist back then, instead of stopping halfway down her back, but it was still the color of the Sahara sand. She'd been younger then, barely fifteen, with chubby cheeks and a flat chest. He was twenty-two and she was a nuisance who dogged his every footstep, but damn if he hadn't liked her spirit, her enthusiasm, and her unwavering interest in anything Egyptian. He'd even found himself missing her when she went back to the States for school.

Hell, he had the feeling he'd miss her when she left his camp and disappeared from his life—again. But that was the way it had to be. There'd been an all-consuming passion between them, and maybe a bit of it still remained, yet neither of them had the staying power to make a relationship work. He'd proved that when he'd left her, and she'd proved it when she'd annulled their marriage.

They were better off apart. Far apart.

Cairo stopped in front of him, and he stopped too. As much as he wanted her out of his life, he wasn't in such an all-fired hurry that he couldn't take a moment to admire the view of her long, shapely legs and the profile of her pretty face. The light breeze blew through her hair as she bent down and trailed her fingers through the sandy soil.

Tearing his gaze away became physically impossible. Her red shirt plunged, baring a slender neck, the lightly tanned skin of her chest, and as she leaned over, he could see the swell of her breasts, luscious breasts, breasts he'd once drizzled champagne over.

A lump caught in his throat and he took a swig of cool water from his canteen.

The brim of Cairo's cap rose and he could see her gaze shift toward him as she lifted a mud-crusted shell from the hole she'd dug in the dirt. "Dylan will love this."

"Who's Dylan?" Duncan asked, unwilling jealousy welling up inside him. "Your boyfriend? Husband?"

Cairo's eyes darted back to the shell in her hand. She laughed nervously. "You know, I don't have either; he's just a friend."

Like hell! Duncan thought, but he wasn't going to pursue it. Besides, she'd be out of his life in an hour.

She cautiously brushed mud away from the shell, not once looking up. "He's got a collection of Mesozoic shells, but nothing like this nautilus."

Her voice quivered as she spoke, and damn if he didn't want to know why.

"Spend a week or two out here and you can find a lot more than that. Thescelosaurus, Edmontosaurus, Triceratops."

She looked up again, right through a fringe of thick lashes. "Is that an invitation to stick around?"

Duncan shook his head, refusing to fall in her trap. "It's just a comment."

She smiled. "That's what I thought. Either way, I'll be in Belize in a little over a week." She tucked the nautilus into the side pocket of her backpack. "Ever been to Belize this time of year?"

"It's hotter than hell, and no one in their right mind would go in September."

Her lapis-blue eyes brightened and her smile widened, that same maddening smile that had snared him years before. "I always liked living on the edge, doing crazy things. You do, too. That's why I thought you'd want to go with me."

"I've got plans of my own."

She winked. "So you told me." She flipped her ponytail back over her shoulder and continued down the trail.

Damn! She was getting under his skin again, just as she'd done all those years ago in Egypt. They'd been nothing more than friends those first few years, but by the time she'd hit eighteen, he knew he wanted to initiate her into the fine art of making mad, passionate, sweaty, no-holds-barred love.

He'd wanted her badly but he'd ended up waiting for three miserable years, until she was twenty-one. And then, like a fool, he'd felt some compelling need to marry her first. He'd spirited her away from her graduation party in San Francisco to some neon-lit chapel in Las Vegas where she'd willingly stood beside him in front of Reverend Love and answered "I do" to every question she was asked.

Obviously she'd lied to Reverend Love ... and to him.

Maybe he'd lied, too. Maybe all he'd felt was lust—the same feeling that hit him now as he watched her walk away.

How could she have made a mistake like that? Cairo chastised herself as she beat a hasty retreat from Duncan's questioning eyes. She wasn't ready to tell him about Dylan, yet her little boy's name had slipped so easily over her lips, and Duncan's curiosity had risen in an instant. At least he'd thought Dylan was her boyfriend or husband, not her son. And she hoped he'd keep thinking that way.

Duncan skirted past her as they neared a roped-off area she'd seen on her trip to the cave. She slowed her pace, stopping to look at the loose dirt and rocks. "Is this your dig?" she called out.

Duncan was a good twenty paces beyond the cordoned area when he stopped and turned around. He laughed. "Would I leave good tools lying around? Would I mark an important site in a way that would attract attention?"

"You would if you were trying to keep people away from what you were really looking for."

A slow smile touched his face as he moved toward her. He wiped perspiration from his brow with the back of his hand, and for the first time that day she noticed the way the ends of his blue-black hair curled when wet. His stride was slow, methodical. The man oozed sexual magnetism that could send a seismograph right off the Richter scale. The first time she'd seen him he'd been walking out of an ancient tomb and the sunlight slashed across his eyes. The blue was so pale that he looked like a man from another world, a god moving toward her, hypnotizing her, seducing her. He'd do the same thing now, if she'd let him.

She turned her head away, not wanting to be mesmerized by this blue-eyed devil. Still, she felt the strength of his seductiveness when their arms touched as he stood by her side, staring at the unkempt dig. "I've been out here for five months, and until today, no one's followed me into the caves."

"So this dig is just a camouflage?"

He nodded. "It, and another one near here, are laced with a few dinosaur bones and some fossils."

"So what's in the cave that you're trying to keep a secret?" she asked.

He stared straight ahead, not looking at her, but she saw the tilt of his lips, saw the dimple in his cheek deepen, saw a faraway gaze in his eyes. "I haven't found anything yet."

Cairo laughed. "People who don't know you might believe that, just like they might believe this is a real dig. But I know you, Duncan." She thought back to all those summers when they'd been inseparable. "You once told me I knew your mind almost as well as you knew it. I think I still do."

"So what am I thinking?"

"That you've found something bigger and better than anyone could imagine. That you've just brushed against the edge of the find and you can't wait to get back because the most miraculous part is still waiting to be discovered."

He didn't say a word for the longest time, and Cairo wondered if he planned to tell her the truth. Finally, he looked toward her. "I haven't found a thing," he repeated.

"You used to tell me everything about your digs."

"That was a long time ago. As for telling you anything now, what's the sense?"

"Maybe I could help you?" she asked, her curiosity about what he'd found getting the better of her.

Duncan laughed. "You're a tour guide, Cairo, not an adventurer or an archaeologist. Besides, you're heading to Belize."

She gritted her teeth, irritated by his stubbornness, and took a quick glance at her watch. "Yeah, and I'd better get out of here. I've got work to do, and Dylan's expecting—"

"Dylan?" One of Duncan's black brows rose. "Your friend's in Sanctuary with you?"

"My aunt's in Sanctuary with me and I promised her I'd be back for dinner."

"What did you promise Dylan?"

"A phone call." Cairo found herself rubbing her temples, trying to drive away the headache that was building. She had to be more cautious. One more error like that and Duncan was bound to ask more questions.

She slipped around Duncan and beat a hasty retreat for camp, but he was hot on her trail. "You might as well slow down, Cairo."

"Why?"

"Contrary to what I told you earlier, you're not going anywhere tonight."

"You've spent the past few hours telling me how anxious you are to get rid of me, and now you say I can't go. Do you mind telling me why?"

"Because once the sun goes down, you won't be able to see the trail you drove in on."

"All I have to do is head straight north."

"Yeah, you could do that, but if you do you'll drive right over the edge of a cliff, and I don't think one prickly cactus will stop your fall."

"You could drive your truck and I could follow."

He shook his head. "I'm not leaving camp till morning. That's when you head for home and I head back to work."

"I have to go, Duncan." She'd promised Dylan and Phoebe that they'd go out on the town and see some real honest-to-goodness cowboys. Of course, it would take an hour to drive back to town and it would be far too late to keep her promise; still, she wanted to be with her son. She definitely didn't want to be with Duncan. "I can't stay here."

"You're staying, whether you want to or not."

Staying the night with Duncan was a bad idea. A really bad idea. What if her son had a nightmare during the night and needed her? What if she mumbled Dylan's name in her sleep?

She took a quick look at Duncan and couldn't miss his satisfied grin. Oh, no, she couldn't stay, not when she thought he was an irresponsible cad one moment and a breathless wonder the next.

Heaven forbid, she remembered their wedding night and the heart-shaped bathtub filled to the brim with bubbles and two warm, slick bodies. She remembered the cool satin sheets and Duncan introducing her to the delights of chocolate mints that melted at body temperature and tasted—and felt—so blissfully wonderful when they were licked away.

And she remembered the warmth of his embrace, and their whispered promises to love each other forever.

No. She couldn't spend the night with Duncan. He was far too dangerous, far too seductive, and she didn't want to wake up in the morning and find that he'd left her all alone. Again.

Four

Duncan kicked a beer can halfway across the camp, which, to Cairo, seemed like the perfect thing to do, under the circumstances. She would have done the same thing if she'd gone away from her home for a few hours and returned to find that it had been ransacked and that her car had been wrapped up like a mummy with toilet paper.

At least the olive-green tent hadn't been knocked down, she thought, as she swept an empty bottle of cheap wine up from the dirt. She tucked it under her arm, plucked two crushed beer cans from the hood of Duncan's truck, and looked around for anything remotely resembling a trash can.

Her parents' camp in the Valley of the Kings had always been immaculate, tended by a minimum of two servants at any given hour—a lot like those you'd see in an old black-and-white movie about the upper-crust English on African safari. Duncan's camp, on the other hand, lacked any refinement, just the ten-by-ten tent, a makeshift shower with a water tank perched above it on a wooden scaffold, and a fire pit, all of it walled in on two sides by a thick border of pine and brush, and most of that was strewn with Duncan's clothes.

"You really should keep your campsite neater." She laughed at the situation, only to have Duncan hit her with a scowl as he tore jeans, shorts, and shirts from the surrounding shrubbery. His clothing added a degree of color to the camp when it waved in the wind, but it didn't look like he was in the mood to appreciate the esthetic value of his underwear flapping against the sunset.

"Damn kids," he muttered, tossing his cot and sleeping bag back into the tent along with his clothes.

"You don't like kids?" It seemed the perfect question to ask, considering her reason for being here.

"Of course I like kids," he shot back. "But I'd like to get my hands on the ones who did this.

Hell, it's the fifth time this month someone's come out here and torn up the place."

"It's summertime," Cairo said, ripping toilet paper from his battered blue pickup. "They're probably bored."

"You want to know what happens when kids get bored?"

Cairo grinned as she looked at the mess all around her. "I can see for myself."

"They do a hell of a lot more than this, Cairo. Sometimes they get in a car and take a joyride. Sometimes they drink too much and get in head-on collisions with other cars. And you know what happens then? Someone gets killed."

He swept an empty cigarette pack up from the ground and crushed it in his fist. Cairo watched the anger slowly drain from his face as he leaned against his truck, but his jaw stayed clenched as he stared across the prairie at the purple and orange sunset.

Cairo moved to his side. She was silent a moment, watching the early evening shadows spreading across the land, and the sadness in his profile. "Who died?" she asked softly.

"My mother."

She couldn't miss the sorrow in his voice, and she, too, felt a deep sadness for the woman she'd always wanted to know. "I'm sorry."

His sorrow suddenly turned to anger. "It was five years ago. You had a chance to be sorry then."

"But I didn't know."

"You would have known if you hadn't returned every goddamned letter I sent to you, if you hadn't ignored the messages I left with your parents."

"I never got any messages."

He laughed. "Whether you did or not doesn't matter anymore." He pushed away from the truck. "Like I said, Cairo, it was five years ago, just like the annulment you hit me with. It's all ancient history and I don't feel like digging it up."

Cairo followed him, placing a hand on his arm. She thought for sure he'd jerk away, but he stopped instead. He didn't look her way, instead he slipped a hand over her fingers and took a long, deep breath. "Since neither of us is driving tonight, do you want a beer?"

She nodded, letting the other conversation drift away. There would be plenty of time to think about what he'd told her, plenty of time to realize that he'd needed her five years ago, just as she'd needed him, and neither had been there for the other.

God, how could things have gone so wrong?

* * *

Cairo pulled toilet paper from Duncan's pickup, wadded it into a ball and tossed it in the trash bag, while Duncan opened the camper shell, dragged the ice chest onto the tailgate, and pulled two cold beers from inside.

Taking one of the cans, she popped the top and rested her bottom against the tailgate. She wondered if he wanted to talk about his mother, or the accident, but he remained silent, pensive. She was afraid he'd again bring up the annulment of their marriage, so she ended the silence with a much safer subject. "Why would someone come this far just to TP a tent?" she asked. "And why five times in a month?"

"I think they come out of curiosity about what I'm doing." He settled next to her on the tailgate. "Messing up the camp is probably their way of blowing off steam when they realize they've learned nothing."

"Why wouldn't they be happy with the dinosaur bones you've left for them to find?"

"They're not interested in anything prehistoric."

"Then what *are* they interested in?"

"A myth."

He took a long, cool drink of beer.

"A myth? That's all you're going to tell me?"

A grinned tugged at the side of his mouth.

"If you want to know so badly, you're gonna have to figure it out on your own."

She loved a challenge. Unfortunately, she wouldn't be sticking around Montana long enough to figure it out.

She sipped the beer and pushed all thoughts of the myth from her mind. The anger she'd harbored the past five years slipped away, too, and she found herself concentrating on the closeness of Duncan's hip, his arm, his shoulder.

She unconsciously licked her lips, remembering her first beer, stolen from Duncan's ice chest when she was fifteen, remembering, too, the way he'd held her head and pressed a cool cloth against her brow when she'd gotten sick after downing three in a row. Earlier that evening she'd stolen a kiss and even now she remembered the warmth of his breath and the hesitant touch of his mouth. Out of the corner of her eye she caught the way Duncan's gaze settled on her lips, his pale blue eyes turning dark, intense, and dangerous.

Her heart began to beat far too fast, and she suddenly realized her emotions were taking a very wrong turn. She pushed away from his truck. *Get a grip,* she warned herself, and pulled her cell phone from the backpack she'd tossed on the hood of her rented Dodge. "I've got a call to make," she said in a rush of words.

"To Dylan?" he asked, still watching her mouth.

"Of course, not. Just my aunt."

"Phoebe?"

"You remember."

"I told you, Cairo," he said, his eyes continuing to focus on her lips. "I've forgotten very little."

He downed the last of his beer and dropped the can into a bag in the back of his truck. "I'm going to take a shower."

As he walked toward his tent, her eyes roamed to the water tank and to the tight confines of the makeshift circular shower designed for one. "Is there enough water for two?" she asked.

Her question was innocent enough. Dust and dirt covered her from head to toe. But Duncan turned around and she could easily see the mischievous spark in his eyes. "If you want a shower, we'll have to take one together."

She dragged in a deep breath, remembering the last time they'd showered together, right before he'd left her with a promise to return.

Damn him! There was no way she'd get in the shower with him now.

"If you've got a bucket," she said, trying to

keep the anger out of her voice, "I'll take a sponge bath."

He shrugged. "If that's what you want." He didn't hesitate a moment, he just turned away and continued toward the tent.

Cairo looked at the shower again, and thought about the solar-heated water and how good it would feel on her itchy skin. "I don't suppose you'd consider using the bucket and let me have the shower?" she called after him.

He had a grin on his face when he turned toward her, but he still shook his head.

"I didn't think so."

She hadn't expected him to walk toward her, slowly, deliberately, looking intently at her mouth. Her body tensed as his hand moved close. As if in slow motion, he touched her hair, his fingers weaving through the strands. She took a deep breath and steadied herself, afraid she would fall into his arms when she didn't really want to.

All of a sudden he drew his hand away, and her legs wobbled beneath her.

"Sagebrush," he said nonchalantly, holding a twig in his fingers. "Must have gotten stuck in your hair when you fell."

She nodded mechanically, working her way out of the trance he'd easily put her in.

"Why don't you make your phone call," he

said, and flicked the prickly stick to the ground as he once again headed to the tent.

She watched him move, his gait long and powerful. And then she willed herself to look away. Duncan Kincaid wasn't an easy man to ignore, but she sure as heck planned to try.

She dug a business card for the Heavenly Haven Inn from her backpack and punched in the phone number. She listened to the ring on the other end. Once. Twice.

Duncan walked out of the tent with his shirt off, and Cairo caught her breath at the sight of his hard, flat stomach, a chest liberally sprinkled with black hair, and skin the color of burnished copper. Suddenly she was in Egypt again, a fifteen-year-old schoolgirl spying on a twenty-two-year-old grad student as he dived into the waters of a palm-shrouded oasis. She'd never seen a man naked before, never even imagined that a man could be so beautiful. But Duncan was—every darkly tanned inch of him.

Putting him out of her mind seemed an impossibility—until she heard her son's sweet little voice. "Hello."

"Hi, pumpkin." Suddenly she wished she was in Sanctuary with Dylan. Talking with him on the phone was never as special as holding him close, cherishing her little boy's laugh, his rosy cheeks, pale blue eyes, and mop of raven black hair—eyes and hair so much like his dad's. Every time she looked at Dylan, a part of Duncan looked back at her. As much as she'd wanted to rid herself of memories of Duncan, she'd never been able to.

"Are you on your way home?" Dylan asked, and she wished she could tell him yes.

"Not yet, honey. Did you miss me today?"

"Well . . . a little bit, I suppose. Aunt Phoebe and I had a lot of fun. We went shopping, and to the park, and we rented a movie."

"Something good?"

"*The Mummy.*"

"Didn't I tell you that you couldn't watch that movie for a couple of years?"

"Well, yeah, but I kind of forgot to tell Aunt Phoebe. She thought it would be too scary for me, just like you did, but she's the one who got scared. I told her the bugs crawling out of people's mouths were only make-believe, but she screamed anyway and then the lady in the room next to us started pounding on the door and the people who own the Heavenly Haven Inn came running up the stairs and right now Aunt Phoebe's trying to calm them down."

"In other words, the entire place is in total chaos."

"That's right. C-H-A-O-S," Dylan spelled out. "We learned that word last week."

"Um-hmm, we sure did." Cairo remembered the panic her son had started in Phoebe's art gallery not long after he taught his hyacinth macaw how to say "fire."

Dylan wasn't an easy child—lovable, yes, but easy? No. And all too often she was traveling when Dylan pulled his shenanigans, and poor Phoebe had to do the explaining on her own.

"You didn't do something to make Aunt Phoebe scream, did you?" Cairo asked, although she already had a good idea what the answer was going to be.

"Well . . ."

Cairo didn't like the sound of Dylan's *well*. He was far too smart for his own good—not to mention hers and Phoebe's—and often far too playful.

"What did you do?"

"Well, there was one part in the movie that was really scary and Aunt Phoebe was just staring at the TV like she was in a trance or something. And, well, do you remember that rubber cobra you gave me when I wanted a real one?"

"I remember."

"Well, I sneaked up behind Aunt Phoebe and dangled the snake over her shoulder. That's when she screamed, and then she grabbed the cobra and threw it across the room, and, well, something broke."

Speak calmly, she reminded herself. Ask questions, lots of questions. Keep his mind active, and whatever you do, don't get upset. "What broke?"

"The window."

"The window?" she repeated softly, mentally calculating the cost, adding that to the donation she'd made to the Mendocino Fire Department for the false alarm. "Can you explain to me how a lightweight rubber snake can break a window?"

"It wasn't the snake's fault. Aunt Phoebe also threw the remote control she was holding. Did you know she used to date an Oakland A's pitcher? That's who taught her how to throw."

Phoebe had probably dated half the team twenty-six years ago, and then she became a surrogate mom to Cairo and pretty much gave up on men. But that had nothing at all to do with the current topic, and Dylan knew it. He was trying to change the subject, but Cairo wasn't quite finished.

"Is Aunt Phoebe still talking to Mr. and Mrs. Tibbetts?"

"Yes, and I don't think they're very happy."

"Would you be happy if a total stranger broke one of our windows at home?"

"I guess not."

"Would you like to be scared the way you scared Aunt Phoebe?"

"It was only a play snake."

"A very real-looking play snake," Cairo reminded him.

"Am I in trouble?"

"What do you think?"

"That you're gonna make me do chores to pay for the window."

"Right. What else?"

Dylan was silent a moment. He'd been through this routine too many times to count, so thinking of the punishment shouldn't take long. "No TV for a week?"

"Try again."

"Two weeks."

Cairo smiled. "Anything else?"

"Do I have to apologize?" She could practically hear the look of agony on his face.

"Yes, to Mr. and Mrs. Tibbetts *and* to Aunt Phoebe. In fact, why don't you apologize to the Tibbettses right now, and tell Aunt Phoebe I'm on the phone and need to speak with her."

Again he was quiet, and Cairo could hear the gears in his far-too-intelligent brain churning. "You're not coming home tonight, are you Mommy?"

"Not tonight, pumpkin."

"Why?"

"It's getting late and the sun's going down. I'm not close to a road, and if I leave now, there's a chance I could get lost."

"Like my daddy?" Cairo heard fear in Dylan's voice, and she wished she could hold him in her arms right now.

"Don't worry, honey. I'm not going to get lost and I'm not going to leave you. I just can't drive the car in the dark. But I will be home first thing in the morning."

"Promise?"

"Promise."

"Okay," he said on a long-winded sigh. "I'll get Aunt Phoebe now."

Cairo heard the phone hit what she assumed was the table, followed by a moment of silence before the triple clank of it hitting the floor and bouncing twice. She heard the clatter of Dylan's boots as he ran across the room yelling at the top of his lungs for his aunt.

Suddenly all was quiet, and guilt swept through her. Telling Dylan that his father had gotten lost in the Amazon jungle was the only lie she'd ever told her son, but she hadn't known what else to say. Honesty had been out of the question, and right now she didn't even want to think about telling either Dylan or Duncan the truth. Neither one would understand her reasoning. They'd both be mad at her, and Duncan would probably want to string her up.

Oh, she'd made such a mess of things.

"Cairo?" Her aunt's voice sounded strained, concerned. "What's wrong? Dylan said you're not coming home tonight."

"I'm fine, Phoeb. It's just too dangerous to drive home in the dark, and Duncan insisted I stay at his camp till morning."

"You found him, then?"

Cairo let her eyes stray to Duncan's truck, to the tailgate where he sat, his muscular chest looking awfully good as it glistened in the setting sun, while he loosened the strings on one of his hiking boots. "Yes, I found him."

"And now you're going to spend the night with him?"

"He has a tent. I have the back seat of the car."

"Back seats are terribly uncomfortable, Cairo. I spent many a night in the back of my '66 Mustang—by myself. Miserable way to spend the night, especially when there are other options."

"There *are* no other options. Duncan's not the least bit interested in me any longer, and I'm not interested in him. Besides, you know that's not the reason I'm here."

"So you've told me."

Doubt rang loud and clear in Phoebe's voice

and resonated in Cairo's head, especially when she watched Duncan remove the boot and set it aside. He slipped off a thick white sock and tossed it over his shoulder into the bed of the truck. And then he rubbed the back of his neck with the same strong hands that had caressed every inch of her body.

"Cairo? Are you listening to me?"

Phoebe's voice drew Cairo's mind back to the present, but her eyes stayed fixed on the slow movement of Duncan's fingers. "I'm sorry. What did you say?"

"Have you told Duncan about Dylan?"

"Not yet. I'm still not sure that I should."

"We've been through this at least a hundred times in the past five years. You've wavered back and forth about telling him, and now, when you're finally face to face, when you finally have the opportunity, you're not sure?" Phoebe's voice rose an octave or two as she finished her diatribe. "What in heaven's name are you waiting for?"

"I'm afraid, Phoeb. I don't want Dylan to have a father like mine."

"You were stuck with two lousy parents. It's not that they aren't good people, it's just that Helen and my brother are self-indulgent intellectuals who weren't meant to have children. Fortunately for me, they had you."

"Duncan is self-indulgent, too. And irresponsible."

"You knew that before you married him, but it didn't seem to matter at the time. You ran off with him without even telling me. You had sex with him. You got pregnant by him. Irresponsible or not, you obviously liked something about him."

Cairo watched the way the muscles bunched in his arms and shoulders when he drew his other foot up to the tailgate and started to untie the strings on his boot. A lock of raven-black hair fell over his brow. Oh, yes, there were definitely a few things she'd liked about Duncan Kincaid. She'd been thinking about all those things when Dylan had been conceived; she sure as heck hadn't been thinking about his reliability.

"You're forgetting a few things, Phoeb. He abandoned me and I annulled the marriage."

"But you still love him." Cairo laughed out loud at the insanity of Phoebe's words. She couldn't possibly still love him, not after everything that had happened.

Duncan chose that moment to look up. A smile just barely touched his lips as he slid off the tailgate and walked across the camp, his bare, bronzed chest almost glistening in the setting sun. She forgot to breathe as she watched him. Her heart kicked up its pace.

Those feelings were nothing but lust, but they didn't go away when he disappeared into his tent.

"The only thing I feel right now, Phoebe, is confusion. I'm running out of money, and if my next tour isn't successful, I'm going to lose everything I've invested. On top of that, I want Dylan to know his father, but I'm not sure I can trust Duncan with him."

"You're not being fair, Cairo. People can change in five years. You've gone from a wild child to a sharp businesswoman and a terrific mother. Maybe Duncan's changed, too."

"That's why I'm here. That's why I want him to go with me to Belize. I just need a little time to find out for sure, and then I'll tell him everything."

"And how much more time are you going to want after Belize? You've got two separate issues you're dealing with, Cairo, but the most important one is your son, and if you don't deal with it soon, your little secret's going to raise it's ugly head and bite you on the butt."

For the longest time Phoebe chattered on and on about rubber snakes, broken windows, innkeepers, and the crazy lady in the room next door who'd come running when Phoebe screamed. Cairo liked the light tinkling sound of Phoebe's laughter, the way she switched subjects so easily, a trait she'd passed down to Dylan.

Still, she only half listened to Phoebe's talk about Sanctuary and the restaurant where she and Dylan planned to go for steak and to see real honest-to-goodness cowboys. Instead, she focused her thoughts on telling Duncan the truth, because Phoebe was right. He had to be told soon.

Phoebe was discussing the merits of Wranglers over Levi's, when Duncan stepped out of the tent with nothing but a plush navy blue towel wrapped around his hips. Low on his hips.

Duncan had a unique way of making her forget any sensible thought she ever had.

"I have to go, Phoebe," she said abruptly. "This call's costing a fortune."

"You will be home tomorrow morning, won't you?"

Duncan slipped behind the thin, off-white vinyl shower curtain and pulled it closed. A moment later he flung the navy blue towel over the rod.

"Definitely. Kiss Dylan good night for me."

"I will. Have fun tonight," Phoebe suggested before hanging up.

Fun? How could she possibly have fun? Duncan Kincaid was standing under pulsating water—all by himself—and the only thing rubbing against that hard, sexy body of his was the shower curtain.

No, she wasn't going to have any fun. In truth, she felt she would accomplish nothing important this evening, and end up spending the night feeling very, very frustrated.

Five

♡ Phoebe tapped the end of her charcoal
pencil on the sketch pad in front of her,
matching the beat of the country song
playing on the jukebox. She didn't know beans
about country music—but she kind of liked
what she was hearing.

She kind of liked what she was seeing in this
place, too.

She studied the men bellied up to the old-
fashioned, brass-railed bar at the far end of the
restaurant. Unbeknownst to them, they'd become the perfect male models for her current
work of art. Spurs jangled on the backs of
scuffed boots. Their Wranglers were worn but
looked awfully good stretched over muscular

thighs and slim hips, and their broad shoulders strained the fabric of their shirts. The rest of the trappings surrounding them were mere background to the picture she'd paint when she got back to Mendocino. All that really mattered in her current sketch were the men.

"Whatcha drawin'?" Dylan asked, kneeling on the booth's shiny red vinyl seat and leaning forward with his elbows planted right next to the sketchpad.

"Cowboys," Phoebe answered. "Lots and lots of cowboys."

Her nephew tilted his head and looked at her like she'd lost a marble or two. "Maybe I should go ask them to turn around so you can draw their faces instead of their backs."

Phoebe swept her palm over Dylan's baby soft cheek and smiled. "We don't want to disturb them, honey. Besides, an artist should look at a subject from all angles—don't you agree?"

"Well . . ." he began, scrunching his eyes into a frown, thinking far too hard for a child of four. "Wouldn't it be better to draw what you like?"

"Exactly."

"Then why are you drawing their backs?"

She'd explained a lot of things to Dylan in the last couple of years, but talking about the birds and bees or the appeal of the opposite sex—whether they were standing backward, forward, or lying down—was going to be Cairo's territory, so she went in a different direction. "What else do you see in the sketch?"

Dylan tilted his head one way and then another as he studied her drawing. "Spurs."

"Are they all the same?"

"No."

"What about the pockets on their jeans?"

"They're different, too. So are their belts and the colors of their shirts and the way they're standing."

"That's right." Phoebe moved a crayon from the top of Dylan's sketch pad and put a finger on the object he'd been intent on drawing since they'd finished their hamburgers nearly half an hour before. "A casual observer might look at your picture and say, 'You're drawing a pyramid.'"

"But it's more than that," Dylan declared.

"Of course it is. Which just goes to show that you shouldn't judge anything on first glance. You've got to study the complete picture."

"Okay," he answered, as if her psychoanalytical answer to his original question had bored him.

He slurped up a mouthful of his Roy Rogers, sorted through the pile of crayons he'd dumped in the middle of the table, grabbed an orange one, and went back to coloring the sun over the top of the pyramid.

With Dylan pacified for the moment, Phoebe turned her gaze back to tight, heavenly looking buns. That was, after all, the reason she'd picked this place for dinner. It had a family-style restaurant at one end and a bar at the other, and the crazy lady renting the room next to Phoebe's at the Heavenly Haven Inn had told her this was the perfect place to see and meet cowboys, unless she wanted to rent a horse and ride around the range where, unfortunately, cattle outnumbered men.

The second idea hadn't interested Phoebe in the least.

Putting her pencil back to her paper, she filled in a few less important details, like the etched mirror behind the bar that had a bullet hole right smack in the center, and the half-dozen brass chandeliers hanging from the pressed tin ceiling.

Smoke filtered through the air, adding a special atmosphere to the picture, especially when it swirled through the bit of light skittering across the hardwood floor when the street door opened.

A wheelchair-bound man rolled slowly into the room, and her pencil came to a halt as she watched his movements. He looked about the saloon as if searching for someone, and she could almost feel the heat of his silvery-eyed stare when his gaze slowed on its journey past the booth where she and Dylan sat.

Fascination set in when he turned his wheelchair toward the bar. Phoebe leaned back in the booth and sipped on her daiquiri, never taking her eyes off the man as he made his way to the far end of the room. Two men moved out of his way, and another man slapped him on the back, said a few passing words, then headed out the door. She knew that it wasn't polite to stare, but she just couldn't help herself.

He ordered a beer, his husky baritone voice carrying across the room. The bartender leaned against the bar, probably telling a bawdy joke, and Phoebe could hear them chuckle. Their laughter brought a smile to her lips. If Dylan wasn't with her, she'd sashay across the room and join in the fun. For now, she was content just to watch.

The bartender handed the man a bottle, and he tilted it to his lips taking a long, slow drink. The light shining over the mirror behind the bar illuminated his face. She could see the healthy color of his tan and the powerful muscles in his shoulders, arms, and chest. His hair had once been dark, probably even black, but now it was dusted with silver. He wore a navy polo shirt and it didn't take a genius to see that his stomach was flat and hard. His legs were long, and encased in khakis they looked healthy and strong. Yet there he sat, staring at a bottle of beer, all alone, and unable to walk.

Phoebe sipped the last of her drink and pushed the glass to the center of the table. She flipped to a clean piece of paper in her sketchpad and began to draw, starting with the wheels, the spokes, the footrests, and the brown loafers he wore. Taking her time, she sketched his legs and the way he leaned against the leather back of the armless wheelchair, making sure she captured the entire picture, the strength of his upper body, the legs that he rubbed occasionally, as if he were in pain.

When the man reached for his second beer, Phoebe started another drawing, capturing the way his eyes flicked down to his left hand, to the gold wedding band he wore. Capturing his mood was harder to do. He intrigued her far more than any man had in a very long time.

Dylan's cheek brushed her arm, pulling her attention away from the bar. For a moment she thought he was tired, that he was going to rest his head on her shoulder and fall asleep. She even thought she should take him home and put him to bed, but he peeked at her drawing instead.

He pointed a pudgy little finger at the face she had sketched. "He's got eyes like mine."

Phoebe took a good look at her drawing, at Dylan's pale blue eyes, and shook her head. "They're light, like yours, but his are silver, not blue."

"I still think they look the same. My mom says my eyes are silver sometimes, especially when the sun shines in them. She even told me that I have eyes exactly like my daddy's. Did you ever see my daddy's eyes?"

"No, I never did."

"You don't think that man in the wheelchair could be my daddy, do you?"

Phoebe shook her head again. "I don't think so, honey." But she took another hard, long look at the man. "He's a little older than your dad, probably old enough to be your grandfather."

"Well," Dylan said with a long-winded sigh, "I don't have a daddy and I don't have a grandfather, either. Maybe he'd like to have a grandson, someone like me, since we have eyes that look alike."

"It doesn't work that way, Dylan. You're not related, so you can't just snap your fingers and make him your grandfather."

Dylan shrugged. "Well . . . I think I'll go ask him anyway."

Dylan slid under the table quicker than a flash of lightning. An instant later he dashed across the bar with Phoebe hot on his trail. But she was too late. Way too late.

The cowboy boots Cairo had bought Dylan right before the trip slipped on the floor and Dylan came to a skidding stop right in front of the wheelchair. Even from ten feet away, Phoebe could hear Dylan loud and clear. "My name's Dylan," he said in a rush of words. "My dad's lost somewhere in the Amazon, which is really terrible, because I think every little boy should have a dad. On top of that, I don't have a grandpa, either, so would you like the job? My mom says I'm precocious. But I don't think that's a reason not to want me for a grandson."

Phoebe gently cupped her hand over Dylan's mouth. "Sorry to bother you," she said, dragging her nephew into her arms.

The man in the wheelchair laughed, making it awfully hard to miss the twinkle in his silver eyes. Eyes really quite like Dylan's.

"It's no bother," he said.

She took a few hesitant steps backward. "Well, we'll leave you alone now."

The last thing Phoebe wanted to do was leave him alone, and she gave him nearly three whole seconds to ask her to stay and have a drink, or to sit and talk, or something, but he just took a sip of beer and stared at her and Dylan over the top of his glass, like they were both total lunatics.

So much for dramatic entrances, she thought.

She carried Dylan back to the table and finally took her hand from his mouth. She could feel deep furrows forming between her eyes as she looked down at her nephew. "Don't *ever* do that again."

"I didn't do anything bad, and gee, Aunt Phoebe, you didn't give him a chance to answer my question. Maybe he *wants* a grandson."

"Well, we'll never know, because we're not going to be talking to him again."

"I wouldn't be so sure of that if I were you," Dylan said looking over her shoulder. Even before Phoebe twisted around, she had the oddest feeling that the man was coming toward her.

His eyes bore straight into her. He wasn't smiling. He wasn't frowning, either, so she couldn't tell what was on his mind. But he pushed on the wheels and continued moving toward their booth.

Cupid must have been standing somewhere nearby, because Phoebe thought for sure an arrow pierced her heart. She felt all fluttery inside, like a senseless schoolgirl, until a totally unexpected hot flash raced from her chest, up her throat, and blazed in her cheeks. Perspira-

tion sprang up on the back of her neck and between her breasts.

Oh, God! Not now.

She reached for her daiquiri, needing something cold and slushy to drink, but the glass
was empty. There wasn't even one chunk of ice,
but it still felt cool and she held it to her burning face.

The man with the silvery eyes must think her
a crazy woman, she thought, but he still rolled
toward her—slowly, very, very slowly.

Graham Kincaid pushed the wheels on his
chair not much more than an inch or two at a
time, and with every bit of progress he made
across the barroom floor he wondered, "What
the hell am I doing?" He hadn't been with a
woman in five years. He hadn't flirted with a
woman other than his wife in thirty-three years.
What made him think he could flirt now?

He stopped in the middle of the saloon and
took a drink of beer, hoping it would give him
the confidence he needed to get to the far end
of the room.

This is insane, he told himself. It's just one
woman, and you've faced tougher challenges in
the last five years—like losing your wife.

He twisted his wedding ring, then stopped.
He didn't need to be thinking about Jill right

now, or the fact that he couldn't bring her back. He thought about taking off the ring, but he didn't know if he was ready to play the part of a single man.

Why did he have the feeling that the pretty blond woman in the gauzy flowered dress could make him want to put the ring away? Maybe it had to do with the laugh lines at the corners of her big green eyes, eyes that sparkled even in the dimly lit room, or the way she'd smiled when she'd latched onto her son—a precocious kid who wanted a grandpa.

Grandpa? Hell, until that moment he hadn't thought of himself as old. He was only fifty-three, for God's sake.

He rolled a little closer, and he watched the woman twist her long, curly blond hair into a knot. She held it on top of her head and her breasts rose beneath the clingy fabric of her dress. Oh, man, five years was a long time to be without a woman.

But this woman had a kid sitting next to her, and the last thing he needed was a child to bounce on his knee, considering the fact that he couldn't bounce anyone on his knee.

He was only a few feet from her now, so close he could smell her perfume, so close he could hear the little boy whispering in her ear, "He looks like he'd be a really cool grandpa."

Sanity returned in an instant. Graham pushed on the left wheel, spun his chair around, and didn't stop moving until he was outside in the cool night air.

He took a long, deep breath and stared at the array of neon signs on Main Street and the emptiness of the sidewalks.

Well, Graham, he thought, you've just managed to come up with the lamest excuse in the world for not getting involved with a woman ... she has a kid.

He sat outside all alone in his wheelchair and laughed out loud. He could come up with a million excuses for not getting close to a woman again, but there was only one real reason: he was afraid of someone finding out that he wasn't much of a man.

Six

Telling Cairo she had to stick around all night had been a mistake. Duncan knew it the second she walked out of the tent wearing one of his shirts—and nothing else. She looked too damn good in that big white shirt, silhouetted against the black night sky. Cairo was danger spelled with a capital *D*, and he knew he should have escorted her back to town, but he'd always been a fool where Cairo was concerned.

She was five feet nine inches of very curvy womanhood, and five years had only made her curvier. Considering the way her long wet hair hung over her shoulders and dampened the front of the shirt, and the way the wet cotton clung to her breasts, he had a damn good idea he might continue to be a fool.

"Thanks for taking such a short shower," she said, pulling a comb through her tangled hair. "I was far too dirty for a sponge bath."

Water dripped from her hair and landed right on the very tip of her breast. That spot on his white shirt suddenly turned pink, very pink, and a lump caught in his throat. He should probably offer to help with her hair, sit behind her and comb out the tangles, but he was a fool, not a madman. He was better off sitting on an upturned tree stump feeding kindling into the fire and getting it good and hot so it would quickly dry out the shirt she was wearing.

So he could breathe again.

"I may have used too much water washing my hair," she told him. She sat on the flat-topped boulder he'd rolled from the prairie to the fire pit, and the shirt rode up her leg so high he could see she wasn't wearing anything at all underneath his shirt, only skin, and Cairo had great skin.

He jerked his head away and stared into the fire, which wasn't quite as hot as Cairo.

"Don't worry about the water," he said, trying his hardest to pick up on the slight thread of conversation. "I'll get more in a day or two. I get by on very little when I'm alone."

"Do you get tired of being out here by yourself?" She bent over at the waist, tilting her head toward him, and let her hair fall over her right shoulder. She ran her fingers through the layers, and he could almost see each individual strand drying in the heat of the flames.

"Being alone's not so bad, once you get used to it." He wasn't going to tell her that he had conversations with the ghost of an old mountain man just to pass the time.

He opened the ice chest that he'd set by the firepit and pulled out a package of wieners. "Hungry?"

"Starved."

He put two franks on a wire skewer and held it over the flames, turning the handle slowly.

She sat up straight and stared at the fire. "I really am sorry about your mother. I remember you talking about her and your dad, how close the three of you were. I'd always wanted a family like that."

"I was pretty lucky." He turned the skewer, watching the skin on the hot dogs start to sizzle. He thought for a moment about the weekend campouts his family had gone on, about playing Monopoly late at night and trying to keep the paper money from blowing away when a wind came up. He could even picture his mom in their kitchen. How he and his dad had enjoyed her cooking. "She made the best peanut butter cookies," he said.

Cairo smiled. "Remember the care packages she used to send to Egypt, the way we'd dig through the box looking for the cookies?"

"I remember."

"She sent me the recipe. Did you know that?"

Duncan shook his head.

"It was inside the card she sent for my sixteenth birthday. She wrote the nicest note, and"— Cairo laughed—"she accidentally signed it, 'Love, Mom.' Then she lined through 'Mom' and wrote Jill, but I always thought of her as 'Mom" after that."

Cairo put the comb down on the rock beside her and warmed her hands before the fire. "I still have the card. I even make her cookies at least once a month. Sometimes I think all of Mendocino can smell them baking, because people never fail to drop by for a chat just as they're coming out of the oven."

He'd always associated Cairo with Egypt, dressed in khaki shorts, a white T-shirt, hiking boots, and an Oakland A's baseball cap. Somehow he couldn't picture her with flour on her nose, standing in the middle of a big country kitchen, beating batter in a bowl. As much as he liked that image, he liked the khaki version better.

"When did you move to Mendocino?"

"A year ago. I had a couple of really good years when I started the tour business, so Phoebe and I pooled our money and bought an old house overlooking the ocean. It's the perfect place for her to paint. It's a great place for kids."

He grinned. "Are you planning to have a family sometime soon?"

She laughed off his question, and then he remembered her telling him way back when that she didn't want kids, not till she was older and ready to settle down. Her own parents had ignored her. He'd seen that every summer. She called them Helen and George and they never called her anything but Cairo—the name they'd picked simply because that's where she was born. He never saw them put their arms around her. Never heard them say I love you, things his own parents had done day in and day out. No wonder she'd envied him.

He twisted the skewer that had been motionless for far too long. The wieners were charred and puckered in places, but he placed a bun around the first one, pulled it off the tine, and handed it to Cairo.

"Mmm, it looks delicious," she said, avoiding the mustard and catsup he handed her.

He pulled the second wiener off for himself, loaded it and the bun with a wild squirt of mustard, and took a bite. It tasted like smoke and he heard the skin crackle when he chewed. "I never was much of a cook."

"I never complained. Actually, I preferred your cookouts over an open fire to the French cuisine my parents' chef always fixed. Nasty stuff!" She took another bite of her hotdog. "Give me a burned frank any day."

He watched the way the firelight sparkled in her eyes, and suddenly he was back in Egypt, falling in love with Cairo all over again.

He wondered if there was any way they could ever regain what they'd lost, if she could ever forgive him for the mistake he'd made.

Hell, then he'd have to completely forgive her. And he wasn't quite ready to do that.

He shoved another wiener on the skewer and stuck it over the flames.

"How's your dad?" Cairo asked, as she peeled a chunk of blackened skin from her hot dog and tossed it into the fire. "It must have been awful for him when your mom died."

"He was in a coma when she died." Duncan plowed his fingers through his hair, hating the memory of those days. "He was in the car, too."

"How's he doing now?"

"Better than a lot of people who suffer spinal cord injuries."

Cairo touched his leg. He'd wanted that kind

of comfort when he'd been at the hospital and the cemetery, when he'd cried because he'd lost his mother and nearly lost his dad. He'd cursed Cairo for years because she hadn't been there for him. He'd thought he'd hate her touch if he ever saw her again, but he'd been wrong. Her fingers felt good on his thigh, warm and soft and gentle.

He took a drink of beer and watched sparks and ashes from the fire flicker up in the air. "It seems like a million years have gone by since the accident. My mom was dead by the time I found out, and my dad was hanging on by a thread. The doctors didn't think he'd make it, considering how many bones were broken in his body, but he's tougher than anyone ever imagined. He came out of the coma not remembering a thing. He still doesn't remember the accident, he just remembers waking up, not being able to move, and then me hitting him with the news that Mom was dead. Working through that loss was tougher on him than getting his strength back, or finding out that he'd never walk again."

He felt her fingers tighten, saw tears at the corners of her eyes. "I'm so sorry Duncan, for your mom, your dad . . . for you."

"Somehow you get through it," he said. "I got Dad into counseling, then rehab and physical therapy. And two years ago, in spite of his wheelchair, he took a trek with me to Honduras. Things are looking up."

"Were you with him the whole time?"

"He needed me and I needed to be with him. I gave up a lot of job offers, and I'll admit there were times when I wanted to walk out and have my own life, but I couldn't."

"You've changed," she said softly.

"I didn't have a choice."

Silence surrounded them as he fixed his second hot dog. The night was warm, like so many nights in Egypt when he and Cairo had talked and laughed. This night was different, though. The old familiar comfort had disappeared, and he didn't know if they could ever get that feeling back.

But he sure as hell liked having her near.

Tell him. That steady refrain had played over and over in Cairo"s head for nearly half an hour, making her a nervous wreck. She knew she should tell Duncan about their son, but she couldn't bring herself to do it. What if he got angry? What if he wanted to take Dylan away from her?

Oh, hell! She'd assumed he was still irresponsible; maybe it wasn't fair to assume the worst now.

Tell him!

First she needed some courage, so she lifted Duncan's beer from the ground and absently took a sip. He turned his head and watched her tilt the can to her mouth. "Would you like a can of your own?" he asked.

"No, yours is fine."

She took another sip and started to set the beer back on the ground, but Duncan reached for it first. His fingers touched hers lightly. They were warm and gentle, and she could feel his thumb making soft, lazy circles over her knuckles.

She could see firelight dancing in his darkened blue eyes. His Adam's apple bobbed. This was exactly how it had been that night they'd partied far too hard in San Francisco.

She'd never seen him anywhere but in Egypt, and then one night he showed up at the San Francisco apartment she shared with three other girls. Music played loudly on the stereo, she and her college friends were dancing and laughing, and she barely heard the knock. When she opened the door, he stood there looking sexier than ever in his tan corduroy jacket, white shirt, blue jeans, and dark brown cowboy boots. He'd smiled and handed her a single pink rose, and she'd dragged him inside to meet her friends.

They'd sat in front of the fireplace sharing

one beer after another, and then he'd kissed her. She could still feel the way his hand cinched around her waist and pulled her against his hard, unyielding chest. She could taste the beer on his tongue, smell the smoke in the room, and see and feel the misty fog rolling in when he pulled her out to the rickety balcony.

"Marry me," he'd whispered against her lips. "Marry me tonight, Cairo."

A few hours later they were on a plane for Las Vegas, and a few hours after that they were man and wife. At least for a night.

Cairo drew her fingers from the beer can, away from his touch, and stared again at the fire.

Tell him! The refrain hit her again, and she knew she couldn't put it off any longer.

"Have you ever thought about having a family?" she asked.

"Once or twice."

"Lately?"

"Not for five years." He laughed, a bit too cynically. "There was a time when I thought the two of us would have three or four kids. Not right away, of course. You were too young. Hell, you were just a college sophomore. On top of that, there were too many places I still wanted to explore, and . . ."

His words trailed off and his head jerked

around. He frowned as he stared deep into her eyes. Oh, God, he'd figured it out. He knew she had a child, knew she'd kept Dylan a secret.

She never should have come here, because just like Phoebe said, this whole thing was going to bite her in the butt.

"What's going on, Cairo? I haven't seen or heard from you in five years and suddenly you go to a hell of a lot of trouble to find me. Then you tell me you've bought a house that's perfect for kids. Are you going through some kind of overly maternal phase, or something?"

"I've been going through that for a long time, and since the plane crash—"

"Look, Cairo, having sex with you sounds awfully tempting."

"Sex? When the hell did I mention having sex?"

"Okay, let me get this straight." He shoved up from the stump he'd been sitting on and stalked halfway across the camp. Then he turned around, his arms folded angrily over his chest. "You don't want to have sex with me. Right?"

"Right!"

His jaw tensed. "So, what you're saying is that you want me to go to some kind of clinic, hide away in a cramped little room where I can drool over old copies of *Penthouse*, do my thing in a sterile glass, pass it over to some doctor, then walk away?"

"What on earth are you talking about?"

"If you want a kid, Cairo, you should do it the right way. Get married. Screw your brains out until you get pregnant, then raise your kid in a normal family."

That did it! "I did get married. I did screw my brains out, and—"

"And then you annulled our marriage! Damnit, Cairo, you didn't even give me a chance to explain."

"What was there to explain? You said you'd stay in San Francisco until I finished the semester, but you didn't."

"The opportunity of a lifetime came up."

"You could have called me. You could have written."

"I was in jail!"

"Yeah, that's right. You were in jail, and I was in San Francisco, suddenly married to a con."

"I was wrongly accused of plundering ancient artifacts. And just in case you haven't heard, I was acquitted, but before that happened, I was so damn glad I hadn't been executed on the spot that I wasn't about to complain about not having access to a phone or the local postal service."

"You wouldn't have been in jail if you hadn't

run off on some asinine wild-goose chase."

"I like those asinine wild-goose chases! As a matter of fact, that's the *only* thing I like anymore! I don't want a wife, I don't want a home, and I sure as hell don't want kids—with sex or without!"

He grabbed a long-handled shovel from next to his tent and tossed a couple of blades full of dirt on top the fire. "It's late and I'm tired. The sun should be up around six. You can leave then."

Cairo refused to touch the tear that had slipped down her cheek. At least the air between them had been cleared. She no longer needed to wonder if she'd made the right decision about keeping Dylan's birth a secret. Duncan had made his feelings perfectly clear.

So why did it hurt so much?

Seven

Dylan's head rested heavily on Phoebe's shoulder as she carried him from the park. For nearly an hour they'd sat on the lawn that stretched down to the rocky perimeter of a fishing pond. She'd always liked quiet evenings like this.

She loved Cairo and Dylan, too. Lately, however, she'd felt the need to have a man in her life. Why this sudden urge had grabbed hold of her in the middle of menopause was something she couldn't figure out, but it had hit her a few months back that she wanted to wake up in the morning with someone special by her side. She wanted that perfect companionship that only a lover can provide, the half-smile at the remembrance of a night of passion, and the gentle squeeze of a hand that says I love you.

Maybe someday I'll have that, she thought.

Right now, however, she had a heavy head on her shoulder and no prospects of a lover.

The man in the wheelchair would have been nice.

No, no, no, she chastised herself. He was a complete impossibility. Again and again tonight she'd checked out the eyes in her sketches, and Dylan was absolutely correct. They looked exactly like his.

Coincidence? She didn't think so. Dylan had a father living near this town and there was a strong possibility that Duncan had family living near here, too. Silvery eyes—or pale blue ones—that looked mysterious and otherworldly weren't all that commonplace. Maybe the man in the wheelchair was related to Dylan in some way.

Oh, wouldn't that be just dandy? Cairo was trying to keep Dylan a secret from Duncan, which meant he needed to be kept a secret from Duncan's family, too. Cairo would just die if she found out her aunt was consorting with a member of the Kincaid family.

So much for thoughts of having a silvery-eyed man in her life.

She strolled along Main Street on her way

back to the Heavenly Haven Inn. The night was quiet, and except for a few bars in town, the street had completely rolled up for the night.

She turned up Tenth Street and hung a right on Eden. The road was lined with two- and three-story turn-of-the-century homes, beautiful lawns, and spreading shade trees, such a sharp contrast to the fairly barren prairie that surrounded the town. As she neared the Heavenly Haven Inn, a salmon and green Victorian with stained windows and etched glass everywhere, she heard the sound of an engine behind her, the faint noise of tires rolling slowly along a freshly graveled road.

She looked over her shoulder. A fairly new van, white and shiny, moved at a snail's pace down the street. Someone was following her.

She picked up speed. So did the van.

She ran, holding Dylan tightly against her chest. Oh, God, she shouldn't have been walking so late at night in a strange town. It seemed peaceful enough, but . . .

"Stop. Please."

The voice came from the van and she could see the white hood and chrome bumper and big tires out of the corner of her eye, but she wasn't about to stop.

She raced up the B&B's walkway and did not stop until she was inside with the door slammed and locked behind her. Only then did she peek through the lacy curtains covering the etched oval window.

The van had parked on the wrong side of the street, close to the path leading to the house. The headlights lit up the road ahead of it and she could see a dark figure sitting behind the wheel.

She heard a creak behind her and jumped. Every muscle in her body tightened.

"Is there a problem?"

Thank God. It was only Mr. Tibbetts peering out from the door of his apartment.

"I was walking back from the park and a van started to follow us. It's parked out front."

Mr. Tibbetts tightened the ties on his black satin robe and walked into the entry. Stepping around Phoebe, he peeked through the window. "I've never seen that van in the neighborhood. Maybe I'd better call the sheriff."

Phoebe looked out again. The side doors on the van slid open, and even from a distance she could hear the hum of a motor. All of a sudden she saw a wheelchair balanced on top of a ramp begin to come out of the van.

"Wait, Mr. Tibbetts. Please don't call anyone. I know him . . . sort of."

"You're sure?"

"We met earlier tonight."

Mr. Tibbetts's eyes narrowed suspiciously. "Tell you what. If you want to talk to him, why don't you let me and Irene look after Dylan for a few minutes while you go outside?"

"Are you sure it won't be any trouble?"

"No trouble at all. We're just watching TV."

Phoebe smiled. "Thanks. I won't be long." Mr. Tibbetts pulled Dylan out of her arms, and Dylan's head flopped heavily onto his shoulder. "He'll sleep through anything, " she added. "So don't worry about keeping the sound down."

Mr. Tibbetts stood at the front door until she was out on the porch. He closed it behind her and she could see him part the curtains again. He wasn't nosy, just concerned, and when she smiled, he dropped the fabric and disappeared.

The ramp with the wheelchair on it was level with the yard, but the silvery-eyed stranger kept his distance. "I didn't mean to frighten you," he said.

"Well, you did." She sat on the steps, gathering her long flowery skirt around her legs. "Were you following me all night?"

"No, I was driving around trying to figure out why the hell I left you at the restaurant."

That sounded kind of nice. "Did you come to any conclusions?"

"I decided I already had enough trouble in

my life without adding a woman to the mix. Then I saw you walking through town and decided what the hell was wrong with adding a little more trouble to what I've already got."

"Do you always make such rash decisions?"

"This was a first and I'm about to make a second." She watched the way his chest expanded beneath his polo shirt as he drew in a deep breath. He had great pecs. Nice shoulders. Beautiful eyes. "Go out with me tomorrow night. Dinner. Dancing. A night on the town."

Phoebe eyed the wheelchair and did what came so naturally. She said the first thing that popped into her head. "Dancing?"

He grinned, a look that brightened his entire gorgeous face. "I do a mean twirl on the dance floor."

"I bet you do."

"Let me show you."

She loved his sense of humor. She loved the sparkle in his eyes. Dylan's eyes. And she thought of Cairo.

"I can't."

"Why?"

"Do I really need an excuse?"

"No, but I'd like one. You're the first woman I've asked out since the sixties. Took a lot of guts to do it, too. So, what's wrong? Are you leaving town tomorrow?"

"Maybe. I'm not sure yet."

"Then say *maybe* you'll go out with me, rather than you can't."

"I don't know a thing about you. You could be a serial killer."

"The van's a dead giveaway, isn't it?"

She couldn't help but laugh.

"Tell you what," he said. "I know where you live, so why don't I stop by tomorrow night at seven-thirty? If you're not here, even if you just don't want to answer the door, there won't be any hard feelings."

Phoebe shook her head. "I have a better idea. *If* I decide to go, I'll meet you for drinks, maybe dancing, but let's skip dinner this time. *And*, if I do show up, I'll probably bring a friend."

"Fair enough." She heard the hum of the lift again as it started to rise. When it came to a stop, he smiled. "By the way, I'm Graham-not-a-serial-killer-Kincaid."

Kincaid. The last name rang out loud and clear. She knew that first name, too. Duncan's father. Dylan's grandfather.

Cairo was not going to be the least bit happy about her choice of dates.

"I'm . . . Gertrude." *Gertrude?* Surely she could have come up with a better spur-of-the-moment name. "My friends call me Gertie."

"Nice to meet you." He smiled. Oh, man, she

liked his smile. "If you want to bring your little boy tomorrow night, I don't mind. He reminds me of my son when he was that age."

Great. That's all she needed! "Actually, he's my friend's little boy. We're just visiting Sanctuary for a day or two, but *if* I meet you for drinks tomorrow night, I'll find a babysitter."

He backed his wheelchair into the van, making all the maneuvering look effortless. "Tomorrow night, then. Seven-thirty."

"Where?" Phoebe asked, as if meeting him was a foregone conclusion.

"The Desperado at the far end of town. It's a big place that used to be a livery stable. You can't miss it."

She stood, wrapped her fingers around the newel post, and smiled like a smitten teenager. "I'll be there."

"Good. I like a woman who makes rash decisions."

Cairo lay on the back seat and stared at the headliner in the rented four-by-four, the same thing she'd been doing for the past three hours. Sleep wouldn't come. Instead, she thought about the anger in Duncan's voice, the cold glaze in his eyes. She'd had that same look in her own eyes a few weeks after their marriage, when she hadn't heard a word from him and then learned, from her parents, that he was in jail, arrested for being a grave robber.

She'd cried buckets of tears when her parents had phoned her in San Francisco and suggested an annulment. She'd told them no, but a week later, when the attorney they'd hired had shown up at her apartment, she was more than ready to sign the papers he'd already drawn up. Duncan had married her fraudulently, the record stated. He'd married her for money.

She laughed out loud, the sound bouncing through the Dodge. Her parents spent money on their digs, fine living, and Cairo's education. But they'd made it perfectly clear that she should marry a wealthy man, because they intended to will all that belonged to them to archaeological museums. Whether or not Duncan had known their intentions, Cairo wasn't certain. But since she'd no longer wanted Duncan in her life, the attorney said the claim of fraud would work, and it had. Her marriage was nullified—and a little over a week later, she found out she was pregnant.

"Have an abortion," her parents had told her. "We've raised one child. We won't take care of another." But abortion was out of the question. It might be fine for some people, but not for her. She was carrying Duncan's child, and in spite of the anger she'd felt, she wanted at least part of Duncan to hold on to.

And damn if she hadn't held onto his memory for five long years. She'd told herself she didn't want him back in her life, but thoughts of all that they'd shared came to her most every night, whether she was lying awake or dreaming.

She'd been kidding herself that Dylan and her business were the only reasons she'd come looking for Duncan. In truth, she'd come on her own behalf, too. She'd needed to know if he still felt anything at all for her. Now she knew, and the answer was no.

Duncan didn't want a child. He didn't want a home. And he definitely didn't want her. That meant that tomorrow morning she could head back to Sanctuary, pack up her son and aunt, return to Mendocino . . . and get on with her life.

She closed her eyes, tired of thinking about the past and the future. Right now she just wanted a few hours of dreamless sleep.

Snap!

The noise outside made her jump. She quit breathing and listened to footsteps, someone running, someone moving through the brush. What—who—was out there? Had the teenagers returned, thinking the camp might be empty so they could have another party?

Again she heard footsteps, closer this time, heavier. She heard breathing, a distinct snorting, and pulled the sleeping bag up to her nose and tried not to move.

Something bumped against the car, again and again and again, rocking it back and forth. She forgot to breathe. She felt her muscles tense inside. Suddenly a light flashed across the windows, and the car was struck again, one hard blow against the side.

The car rocked again from one abrupt jolt, and she thought for sure it was going to roll over on its side, but it stayed upright, and then the ground beneath it began to vibrate.

Suddenly, all was quiet, and she drew in a deep breath.

Something tapped against the window. She forgot her fear and jerked up, ready to charge out of the car and yell at her tormenter. Instead, a blinding light blazed through the window.

She screamed so loud it hurt her ears and throat.

"Jesus, Cairo!" She recognized the voice, although all she could see were circles of light.

"Duncan?" She blinked several times as she shoved open the door. "What the hell are you doing? Trying to scare me to death?"

"I was trying to save your ungrateful hide."

"From what?"

Duncan laughed, and she wanted to hit him. "I thought I heard a car, but it was nothing more than a big old bison bull who must have thought this Dodge of yours was a lonely female."

"Please don't tell me it was trying to mate with my car."

Duncan looked at the back of the vehicle and she twisted around. Two big dents stared back at her. The scratches in the red paint looked like gigantic dollar signs. Her insurance would cover the damage, but her premiums would probably climb sky high, and these days she couldn't afford any added expense in her life.

She flopped against the car and closed her eyes. "Can anything more possibly go wrong today?"

"It's possible." Duncan's arm brushed against her shoulder. She felt his fingers weave through hers. Her every nerve stood on end—from fear, from anger, from his touch. "Relax," he said. "The buffalo's gone, and the coyotes rarely attack people."

She managed half a smile. "That's comforting to know." She took a deep breath, trying not to think too much about the warmth of his hand or the way his thumb absently stroked her skin.

He was only being protective, and as soon as her trembling disappeared, he'd let her go. Just as she started to calm, he jerked her away from the car and strode toward his tent.

"What are you doing?" she asked.

"You're sleeping with me the rest of the night."

Cairo pulled back, but stopping him was like stopping a train. "I don't think that's such a wise idea."

She smacked against his chest when he turned and came to a sudden halt. He put his hands on her shoulders and looked at her like he had when she was fifteen and he was twenty-two, like he wanted her and was determined to fight his feelings.

"It's nearly three in the morning," he stated. "I'm tired. I want to go to sleep, and that's not possible with you out here in your car and me in my tent."

"Why?"

"Because no matter what's come between us, there's still a huge part of me that wants to protect you. Okay?"

"No, it's not okay," she said, afraid of her own emotions, afraid of his. "I don't trust you."

His eyes narrowed. "I don't want to sleep with you, if that's what's got you so damned bothered."

"You made that perfectly clear five years ago."

"And I thought I made it perfectly clear a moment ago that all I want to do is have you sleep in the tent so I can keep an eye on you."

"Fine," she spat out, feeling childish but excited at the same time. Passionate outbursts were far better then silence.

He tugged her toward the tent. "You can have the cot," he said, when they got inside.

"What about you?"

Duncan opened an old army chest and took out a blanket, which he threw on the canvas floor. "I've slept in worse conditions."

Cairo climbed into Duncan's sleeping bag, still warm from his body. The scent of his aftershave clung to the flannel, and it felt cozy and nice.

He, on the other hand, looked miserable lying on the floor. She pulled the pillow from beneath her head. "Here, you take this. It's only fair."

His pale blue eyes studied her a moment, and then he managed to smile. "Thanks, but you keep it."

He turned off the flashlight, and a thread of moonlight shone though the tent flap. Cairo twisted onto her side, tucking her arm under her head, and let her eyes adjust to the near darkness.

She could see Duncan lying on his back, his arms folded beneath his head. His eyes were wide open and he was staring at the top of the tent.

"Do you have any idea how many times you've saved my life over the years?" she asked.

"I don't keep track of things like that."

"Well, I quit counting when I could no longer do it on two hands."

He didn't turn his head, but his gaze shot toward her and she could see the flash of a smile before he stared again at the roof.

"Do you remember the time I ran away from my parents?" she asked, no longer wanting to sleep.

"Which time?"

"When they insisted on taking me to see Aida at the Cairo Opera House."

The smile returned to his lips. "I remember. You sneaked out of the hotel and headed for the City of the Dead."

"It was much more interesting than sitting through an opera." She fluffed the pillow under her head. "I knew you were following me."

"Someone had to."

"There was a time when I thought my parents paid you to be my bodyguard."

"No one ever paid me to watch over you. I

did it because I wanted to, because someone had to make sure you didn't do anything too stupid."

"Why didn't you walk with me, instead of lagging behind?"

He closed his eyes, and even in the nearly dark tent she could see his lashes resting against his skin. "You've got a great walk, Cairo. I like the way your hips sway when you move. I like watching your ponytail swish back and forth." He drew in a deep breath. "You were just a week away from your eighteenth birthday—"

"You remember that?"

"I remember. It was hot and sultry and you looked so damn beautiful in that slinky silver dress you were wearing. But you were just a girl and I couldn't touch you."

"I wanted you to."

He laughed. "That's the night I realized how much I wanted you. Of course, I'm not the only one who wanted you that night."

"You mean the street barker?"

Duncan nodded.

"He didn't want me, not for himself. Don't you remember the way he latched on to my arm and suggested I could make some very good money working at a discreet location in Tahrir Square?"

"I haven't forgotten. I haven't forgotten the black eye I got, or the bloody nose, or your ripped dress. And I haven't forgotten the woman who jumped on my back and started hitting and kicking me so I'd leave her man alone."

"She put a curse on you. Did you know that?"

"I couldn't understand what she was saying. There must have been two hundred people cheering her on."

"Well, she said something like, 'May all your days and all your nights be plagued with misfortune, and may all your happiness be tromped on by beggars and camels.' She was speaking pretty fast and I'm sure I didn't translate it correctly, but I think that's the gist of it."

"And then she spit on me."

Cairo laughed. "She said a dab of spit would seal the curse."

Duncan turned his head toward her. "You don't believe in curses, do you?"

Cairo rolled onto her back and stared at the ceiling. "No, unfortunately."

"Why unfortunately?"

"Because I'd rather think that a curse tore us apart instead of something else."

"Such as?"

"Such as you waking up after our wedding

night and realizing you'd made a mistake."

"The only mistake I made was leaving you. Even if there were some mumbo-jumbo to take away the curse, it's too late to wipe away the hurt we caused each other."

"Ignoring it won't make it go away."

He was silent far too long. He didn't need to speak for Cairo to know what was going on in his mind. She understood completely, but finally he told her what she feared. "The timing's bad, Cairo. I've got something going on here that I don't want to give up, and you're going to Belize."

He stared at the top of the tent again, and she wished with all her heart that he'd ask her to forget Belize and work by his side instead. At the very least, she hoped he'd ask her to return after the tour.

But neither question came. Instead he rolled over on his side, turning his back to her. "Good night, Cairo."

The early morning sun shot through the opening of the tent and slashed across Cairo's just opening eyes. She yawned, stretching inside the warmth of Duncan's sleeping bag. Cool morning air chilled her cheeks and nose, making her want to stay bundled up, but she had to get home.

She slipped out of the bag, catching the scent of coffee wafting into the tent from outside. The white shirt she wore was wrinkled, and she attempted to smooth it out as she stepped from the tent.

She expected to see a fire burning in the pit, with Duncan sitting beside it, but the fire had been put out and the pot sat on a rock beside it.

Duncan was gone. She didn't see him by the truck, in the shower, or anywhere near the perimeter of the camp. The back of his truck was locked, but peering inside she could see that his helmet was gone as well as the rest of his gear.

He'd returned to the cave without saying goodbye. Considering the conversation between them earlier, how could she have expected anything else?

Ripping her hastily rinsed clothes from the makeshift clothesline, she went back into the tent, stripped out of Duncan's shirt, and climbed into her own things, not caring that they smelled musty and still felt damp.

She climbed behind the wheel of her four-by-four, shoved in the keys, and turned on the engine. She hadn't gone more than fifty feet when she noticed the reflection in the windshield. Stopping the car, she reached over the dash, and latched onto a piece of lined notebook paper. "Dear Cairo" caught her eyes, and she leaned back in her seat to read.

Dear Cairo,

You were sleeping so soundly that I hated to wake you just to say goodbye. Hope Belize is a big success.
Drive safely.

Duncan

She crushed the note in her fist. Any hope she might have had of rebuilding their relationship had just been dashed.

Putting her foot on the gas once more, she stared into the rearview mirror at the cliffs growing smaller and smaller as she drove away. She refused to think about her past. Dylan was all she had now.

Eight

"Mommy!" Dylan dropped the controller for the Super Nintendo and ran across the room, flinging his little body into Cairo's arms. "You're home! You're home!"

"I promised I'd be here." She kissed his cheeks and forehead, cuddling him close. He felt so wonderful and she loved him so darn much, and it seemed like she'd been away from him for years instead of just one miserably long day and night.

How could she possibly have considered sharing this little bundle of love with Duncan Kincaid?

She'd spent far too many minutes on the drive crying because he'd left her again, and then she got mad. Really mad. Last night she'd tried to explain about Dylan, and he'd ended up turning her words around and making it sound like she wanted him as a sperm donor! On top of that, she'd tried her hardest to put the past behind them, to make amends, and he'd told her that whatever he was looking for was far more important than a relationship with her.

She'd been crazy, absolutely out of her mind, to think he would help her out in Belize or be a good father. The man was nothing but a waste!

Phoebe peeked her head out of the adjoining bedroom, her hair wrapped in a fluffy white towel, her body draped in a hand-painted silk robe, one of her latest artistic creations.

"Welcome home," Phoebe said, as she walked into the cozy living room, picking up a toy here, a game there, and dropping them into a plastic mesh tote bag at the end of the sofa. "Did you have a nice time?"

"My car got bulldozed by a buffalo. I slid down the side of a hill and did a pretty good number on my hands. My climbing gear got stuck and then I almost plummeted sixty feet into a bunch of jagged rocks. Other than that, I had a great time."

Dylan's eyes had widened. "A real buffalo?" he asked.

"Yes, a real buffalo. It's actually called bison, B-I-S-O-N, but it's okay if you call it a buffalo."

"I suppose I should call it by its real name. I'd hate it if someone called me Dudley or something like that." He wiggled out of Cairo's arms. "Did you bring me anything?" he asked.

"You bet. Something really great."

"A new Nintendo game?"

"Not exactly."

"A bicycle?"

"You're not big enough yet for a bicycle." Cairo unzipped her backpack, dug around inside, and pulled out the nautilus she'd found. She held it in the palm of her hand. "What do you think it is?"

Dylan frowned. "It isn't exactly a toy, but it still looks pretty cool." He cautiously lifted the shell in his chubby little fingers. "It's a seashell," he whispered.

"It's not just a seashell. It's a nautilus," Cairo told him. "It's from the Cretaceous period."

"C-R-E-T-A-C-E-O-U-S. Did I spell that right?"

Cairo nodded. "Do you remember how long ago that was?"

Dylan concentrated. "Sixty-five million years?"

"That's right. Sixty-five to, oh, about one hundred and fifty million years ago."

"Cool. Can you take me to the place where you found it so I can look for more?"

Cairo would have to be dragged kicking and screaming before she'd go back, but she gave Dylan a simpler answer. "Not this trip, honey."

"I bet I could find a lot more, then we could sell them to a museum and make lots of money. Then we'd be rich and you wouldn't have to go away on any more tours."

"I like my job," she said. "The only thing I don't like is leaving you, and pretty soon you'll be big enough to go with me."

"When I'm big enough, can we go hunt for my dad?"

"Maybe." She hated to keep up the lie about Duncan getting lost in the Amazon, but she had no other choice now.

Dylan raced across the room, his boot heels clomping on the hardwood floor—a noise she was sure the innkeepers must love. He pulled his special keepsakes box—a pencil container he'd decorated with sea shells and driftwood—from his Tarzan backpack, dumped the contents on the table near the window, and dug through the rocks, marbles, and feathers, adding the nautilus to his other treasures.

Phoebe sat in an overstuffed chintz chair and sipped at a glass of iced tea. "So, how was the rest of your evening?"

"Mediocre."

Cairo slumped in the chair next to Phoebe's, and her aunt leaned close and whispered. "Did you tell him about Dylan?"

Cairo peeked at her son, who was engrossed with his valuables, then whispered back, "I tried, but my words got twisted around. Duncan's not going to Belize with me and he's not going to know about Dylan. Ever!"

She reached into her backpack and pulled out an envelope. "I stopped by a travel agency and changed our airline reservations. We're flying home tonight."

Phoebe plucked the envelope from Cairo's hand and tossed it over her shoulder. "Wrong. You may not be all that keen on Sanctuary, but Dylan and I rather like it here. In fact, we've already sketched out our itinerary for the day."

"I paid a penalty to change those tickets—"

"You should have checked with me first."

Phoebe picked a sheet of yellow construction paper off the coffee table and Cairo could see Dylan's neat cursive writing—one of many things he'd mastered at too early an age—in multicolored crayon. "Here's the agenda Dylan and I put together at breakfast this morning. First"—Phoebe eyed Cairo's hair and clothes—"that is, right after you get cleaned up, because you look and smell like you've been locked in a tomb for the past hundred years, we're going to the Dairy Queen for lunch. After that, we're checking out the art center and the museum. Dylan wants to go swimming in the lake, and after dinner—at a place of *my* choosing—he's going to spend the evening with the Tibbettses, while you and I go out on the town."

Cairo looked at her watch. "We're going to do all this in one day?"

"As long as we stick to the schedule."

Cairo peeled off her baseball cap and ran a hand through her hair. "Lunch . . . yes. Museum, art gallery and swimming . . . I'm game if we can do it all in one afternoon. But going out on the town isn't my idea of a good time, and you know it."

"You haven't been out on the town in years, not since Andy Webster took you to San Francisco for the Black and White Ball."

"And I had a miserable time."

"Only because you didn't like Andy Webster. However, you loved the ball, if I remember correctly. And since you won't have a date tonight, you should have a wonderful time."

"In Sanctuary?"

"That's right. In Sanctuary. Besides, going out tonight has everything to do with me and very little to do with you."

"You've met someone?"

"Don't say that as if it were impossible."

"You know I don't mean it that way. It's just, well, this town's so small and I never dreamed there'd be any available men." Cairo stared at her aunt, at the faraway smile on her face. "Please tell me he's a few years older than jail bait, because the last young man, and I do mean *young*, broke your heart."

Phoebe smiled. "But it was worth it. If it wasn't for him, I wouldn't have gotten into male nudes, I wouldn't have sold half-a-dozen of them to the women around town, and thanks to that beautiful naked body of his, we were able to get a new roof and dual-pane windows on the house."

"Okay, Chad did have a gorgeous body. And the paintings were wonderful, but please tell me you're not just attracted to the body of the man you're seeing tonight?"

"He's got terrific shoulders, not to mention gorgeous hair—which you'll be happy to hear is partially gray."

"That's it? You don't know anything more about him, yet you agreed to go out on a date?"

"I agreed to *meet* him, and I told him I'd be bringing a friend."

Cairo sighed. "I hope you at least know his name."

Phoebe's gaze made a sudden dart down to

Dylan's agenda and cleared her throat. "His name's Graham. Graham . . . Kincaid."

Cairo felt her mouth drop open as she stared at her aunt. The appropriate words—if there were any—wouldn't even form on her tongue.

Phoebe's eyes slowly rose. "I have the oddest feeling he might be Duncan's father."

Cairo rubbed her temples. She felt a tremendous headache coming on.

"He's got silvery eyes," Phoebe said. "In fact, they look a little like Dylan's."

Cairo couldn't miss the way Phoebe's entire face lit up. She was totally and completely taken by the man.

Still, all Cairo could do was rub her temples.

"He wants to go dancing," Phoebe chirped. "He said he's a marvelous dancer."

"Oh, thank God." Cairo felt a tremendous weight lift off her chest. Even her head felt better. "Duncan's dad can't dance—so it can't possibly be him."

Phoebe picked up a tall glass of iced tea and stirred, the spoon clinking against the crystal. "Well . . ." That word always precedes trouble. Suddenly the ache in Cairo's head intensified. "Graham told me he was really good at twirling around the dance floor, and I'm sure he was telling the truth, because, well, when we first saw each other last night, he did a really fast about-face in his wheelchair and rolled right out of the restaurant." Phoebe took a sip of iced tea.

Cairo plopped her head against the back of the chair and stared at the ceiling. For years she'd wanted Phoebe to have a good man in her life, but why in heaven's name did it have to be Duncan's dad? She let out a sigh. "Do you like him?"

"He's got a nice smile and a great sense of humor. Other than that, I don't know a thing. That's what tonight's all about—to get to know each other."

"And where do I fit into the picture?"

"Moral support."

"You've never needed moral support in your life."

"I've never dated a man in a wheelchair before."

"Does that bother you?"

"Not at all, but I think it bothers him, and then there's the fact that he wears a wedding ring. I should have asked him about it but—"

"He's a widower. Five years now," Cairo said, briefly relating the tragic story and feeling guilt and shame for not being at Duncan's side when he'd needed her the most.

But Duncan didn't want her at his side anymore. He'd made that perfectly clear in his note this morning. And the last thing she wanted right now was to meet another Kincaid. "I can't go with you, Phoebe."

"I'm sure I know why, but I'll ask anyway. *Why?*"

Cairo looked at her son, engrossed now in one of the Super Nintendo games she'd brought along on the trip. "I'm not going to see Duncan again," she whispered, "and I'm not going to tell him about Dylan."

"You don't have the right to keep it a secret."

"I have every right. He's only interested in work. I saw that firsthand this morning."

"Give him a chance."

"I can't."

"I hate to lecture, but not telling Duncan is wrong. It's been wrong for five years and it's going to be wrong until you tell him. And then there's the fact that every time Dylan asks about his father you tell him a lie—and that eats away at you. It's high time you tell both of them the truth."

"I need some time to think about it."

"You can do that tonight, while we're out with Graham."

Arguing with Phoebe was useless. "And how are you going to introduce me?"

"Well, definitely not as Cairo. You're probably the only woman in America with that name and Graham's bound to put two and two together. Of course, if you'd just told Duncan the truth last night, we wouldn't be having this problem now."

"I could just stay home."

"Not on your life. The Tibbettses are going to babysit, and you're going out! And I've already solved the name problem. Graham thinks my name is Gertrude—"

"Gertrude!"

"That was the first name that popped out of my mouth. Of course, I told him everyone calls me Gertie. Do you think you can call me Gertie?"

"I suppose." Cairo didn't like where this was going. "I imagine you've come up with a name for me, too?"

"Ingrid. I always liked that name. You'll be Ingrid, I'll be Gertie, and we'll just go out and have a rip-roaringly great time."

"Have you thought beyond tonight, Phoeb?"

"Of course I have. First thing tomorrow you're going to go back to Duncan's camp and tell him the truth, because I really don't like the name Gertrude—or Gertie, for that matter— and I'm not going to play this game forever. Second, do you think a forty-eight-year-old woman who's going through menopause can get away with wearing white at her wedding?"

Nine

Duncan was lured by the city of gold, and it drove him onward, in spite of the risks, through a succession of tunnels, crawling at times or squeezing through spaces where he feared he might get stuck and never be found again.

He was following a map he'd discovered on a cavern wall early that morning, a colorful drawing mixed amid dozens of others, making it nearly impossible to see. Over the years he'd learned to examine everything, no matter how minute.

What was it he was missing, though, about Cairo? He'd been agonizing over that thought since the middle of the night. That trip to Belize weighed heavily on her mind, but there was something more going on.

Of course, it didn't matter anymore. He'd left her a goodbye note early this morning and he'd meant it. He had too much work to do and didn't have time to go around rescuing damsels in distress—or to fall in love with Cairo all over again.

You're a fool, Dunc!

"Go to hell, Angus."

I'm already there.

Duncan laughed out loud, the sound bouncing off the limestone walls. He was hearing that old goat of a mountain man far too often lately.

You know, Dunc—

"Go away."

I've got a story to tell you first. I had me a sweet little woman once. Pretty thing. Hair as black as night and eyes the color of whiskey. That woman knew how to love, and she taught me a thing or two when we were crossing the Atlantic that made me, of all people, blush. But damn if she didn't cry when I left her. I said I'd be back. We all say that, don't we? But sometimes you get a powerful hankering to find something new. That's why I kept traveling west. Why the hell I didn't take her with me is anybody's guess. It gets powerfully cold out here at night, and that little woman had a hell of a way to keep me warm. It gets lonely, too, and talking to her was a hell of a lot better than talking to myself.

Duncan laughed again. He and Angus were two of a kind. Fools!

He shoved Angus to the back of his mind, but Cairo wasn't about to stay out of his thoughts. With every step he took through the tunnel she was there in front of him, her long blond ponytail swinging back and forth, her hips swaying provocatively in that shirt she'd been wearing last night, her naked body—the one he'd pictured underneath that shirt—doing a real number on his mind.

Would it be all that bad going to Belize? he wondered. He hadn't had a real vacation in years, and a tour like Cairo was planning wouldn't take too much effort on his part. He could kayak on the barrier reef, maybe do some whitewater paddling, and at night he and Cairo could find some little night spot with a good band and cool drinks. And they'd dance—close, real close.

The humidity inside the tunnel made it easy to think of hot sultry nights, of Cairo's warm body, but the steep, unstable floor of the passage brought him back to reality. All of a sudden his feet came out from under him and he slid down a slippery tube, stopping only when his feet slammed against solid rock.

Steadying himself, he took a deep breath and

gazed at a room unlike any he'd ever seen. Crouching two-headed stone serpents representing Venus and the sun circled the chamber. Their faces looked threatening, and Duncan wondered if they'd been placed there to keep people out—or in.

He moved slowly, skirting the stalagmites that seemed out of place in the cavern. A stream of water, not more than six inches wide, snaked across the floor, and disappeared beneath a sight he hadn't expected.

In the center of the room rested a sacrificial altar, its sides carved with the likenesses of many Mayan rulers, just like one he'd seen in Copán.

He moved closer, careful to avoid the open pit in front of the altar, and touched the faces that had been frozen in stone. Each ruler, wearing his own special ornamentation—earflares, feathers, bracelets, and anklets—sat cross-legged upon a block of stone carved with the intricate hieroglyphs that told the ruler's name. Duncan could easily recognize 18 Rabbit, Smoke Monkey, and Moon Jaguar.

He touched the altar and imagined the sweet scent of ceremonial incense swirling about. He could easily imagine men with their bodies painted red and white, wearing masks representing Chac, the god of rain and lighting. And behind the altar, he could picture the man of privilege, decorated in brightly colored plumes and jade, preparing to make a sacrifice in honor of royal ancestors.

In Copán they'd often sacrificed jaguars. But what, he wondered, had they sacrificed here? He knew an incredible amount about the Maya. What he wanted to know, however, was why they had come to Montana, and how many had traveled thousands of miles north from Central America?

Had it been just a small band of artists and craftsmen? Were there more men than women? Had any members of the nobility come? What about farmers and merchants?

And why had they disappeared?

Maybe the answer was in the magnificent temple façade carved in the limestone wall behind the altar. Just like those he'd seen in ancient Mayan cities, it loomed over everything else. The steps on the temple were chiseled with glyphs that probably told a story—but glyphs were Cairo's specialty, not his.

Maybe he should have asked Cairo to come here with him, to join his search. But she wouldn't have come. She had a trip planned to Belize. He was on his own in this expedition.

On his own, and all alone, except for the

ghost of an old mountain man, and the lore of an ancient underground room.

He touched the deeply carved glyphs. The ancient Maya were stargazers, people obsessed with time, with chronicling their history, so he knew there was a record of what had transpired hidden somewhere in these caves. But how could he unlock their secrets?

For ten years he'd dreamed of making a find like this. For the past five months he'd spent every waking and breathing moment thinking about standing at the edge of a great discovery, of photographing his find, documenting every inch of it, then turning it over to a museum so others could find out even more. Yet the thrill wasn't as overwhelming as he'd expected.

He felt empty.

He hadn't felt that way yesterday, not even when he and Cairo argued. The emptiness had left him the moment he heard her cry for help, and returned when he'd walked away from her this morning.

He needed her by his side.

Too bad she was hell-bent on going to Belize, because he was hell-bent on not leaving here.

Those darned Mayans of yours believed in sacrifice, Dunc. What about you?

Sacrifice? Maybe it was time he stopped putting his own interests first. Hell, Cairo said she needed him. He couldn't turn his back on her now.

But somewhere along the way, she was going to have to sacrifice a little, too—if they were going to be in this together.

"I really am sorry about the display." Cairo uttered those words at least three times after Phoebe and Dylan made a mad dash out of the museum, and headed for the pizza place down the street, but the curator didn't seem at all appeased, not even with the fact that she was helping him put the tepee back together. "My son gets terribly curious at times."

"You should keep a better eye on him."

"I try my hardest, but—"

"My children were never allowed to run free, especially in a public place, most especially when there were valuables around."

"He's not allowed to run free, either. It's just that he has this unique habit of disappearing—very quickly. It's not because he likes to get in trouble, he's just interested in how things come apart and go back together. I'm sure he would have had this tepee put back in its original condition in no time at all if we hadn't caught him tearing it down."

The curator looked at her over the top of his glasses. "Have you tried a leash? I've heard they do wonders for kids who like to run away."

Cairo was offended by the suggestion. "I'd never put my son on a leash."

"It's just a thought."

Cairo backed away from the tepee, afraid her talent for constructing American Indian dwellings wasn't much of a talent, and that the display might collapse at any moment. As she'd done so many times in the past year, she opened her purse and dug out her wallet. "I'd like to leave a donation for the museum. It's a nice place."

The curator wiped his brow and pressed his hands against his back. Bending over repairing tepees obviously wasn't in his job description. "Why do I have the feeling this isn't the first donation you've offered to a museum?"

Cairo smiled, glad that he'd relaxed a bit. "The Exploratorium in San Francisco is one of our favorites. In fact, Dylan did such a fine job taking apart one of their energy displays that we now get a fully guided tour whenever we're there."

He laughed. "If you really want to make a donation, a couple of dollars will do. Why don't you give it to Lori up at the front desk."

Cairo shook the curator's hand. "Thanks for being so understanding."

He went off, his Hush Puppies squeaking on the hardwood floor, before disappearing into another part of the museum. Cairo hoped he wouldn't find anything else that Dylan had gotten overenthusiastically interested in.

At least now, with Phoebe and Dylan off to order pizza, she could spend ten or fifteen minutes enjoying the quiet peacefulness of the small-town museum. It was fairly empty except for a few teenagers, a middle-aged man and woman who were walking hand-in-hand past the exhibits, and the petite redheaded woman standing at the desk where postcards and a few books were displayed.

"Are you Lori?" Cairo asked.

"Yes. May I help you?"

"I'd like to make a small donation to the museum."

"That really isn't necessary. Your little boy isn't the first one to get in trouble here and I'm sure he won't be the last."

"I'm sure this won't be the last donation I make, either," Cairo said, tucking a twenty into Lori's hand.

"Would you like a receipt?"

"That would be nice. Thank you." Cairo looked about the room while Lori wrote out a voucher. It was awfully nice of people to continually give her receipts marked "Donation" when they were actually for damages, because she couldn't legitimately claim mishaps on her taxes.

"Here you go," Lori said, and stepped from behind the counter. "I saw you looking at our pioneer photos earlier. Would you like me to give you a tour?"

"I'd love one."

"My grandparents donated a lot of these pictures," Lori stated, clasping her hands behind her back while she walked along the wall, as if she were afraid to touch anything. "My great-great-great-grandfather came here in the 1870s to open a saloon." She pointed to one of the pictures. "That's him, the one with the biggest mustache. There were a lot of soldiers here at the time and rum was a hot commodity."

Cairo smiled. "You know a lot about the area?"

"A lot of fact, a little fiction. Stories have a way of growing over a century."

"Sometimes the stories are more interesting."

"They abound in this town. Talk to any of the old timers and they'll willingly give you an earful."

"What about you?"

"That's one of the reasons I volunteer. I grew up thinking this town was rather dull, so now I add a bit of color to the scenery whenever I can." She pointed to a photo of a gaunt and dour-faced pioneer woman dressed in black with a lacy white collar. Her hair was pulled severely back from her face and she wore a deadly scowl. "This is Augusta Marsh, another one of my relatives, although some of my family members refuse to accept the fact."

"Why's that?"

"Augusta had a reputation that wasn't exactly sterling. She owned a boardinghouse—at least, that's what she told the good citizens of the town. By day it looked respectable. By night, the liquor flowed and men from all over the territory dropped by Augusta's place for a visit. From the looks of her picture, I don't think she was personally entertaining any of the clientele, but she became very rich all the same."

Cairo laughed, enjoying Lori's tales. "Who's this?" she asked, pointing to an elderly man whose white beard covered most all of his chest. He wore an old-fashioned coonskin cap and a fringed coat and breeches—a true Davy Crockett if there ever was one.

"That's Angus MacPherson," Lori told her. "He was a mountain man who traveled through town a few times. I imagine he stayed in Augusta's boardinghouse when he did."

"The name sounds familiar." Cairo stared at the old tin-type, thinking she might have seen one like it in another museum, but it was only the name that rang a bell.

"Angus is pretty much a local legend or, I should say, he created a local legend."

"It seems like every Western town has one or two."

"Oh, but this one is special. Angus claimed he had found a golden city buried deep beneath the ground, somewhere not too far from here."

Bingo!

Golden city? Angus MacPherson? Suddenly Cairo remembered stories Duncan had told her about a grizzled old mountain man, a crazy fellow who claimed he'd stumbled on a city of gold.

Now Duncan had stumbled on it as well, or at least he was getting close. She was sure of it. And he was keeping his discovery a secret. He hadn't even wanted to share his search with her, just a little more proof that what they'd once had together was over.

"Hunting for the city is a ritual," Lori said, drawing Cairo's thoughts to the present. "As soon as the weather's good, people head out of town with their picks and shovels, determined to make a find. That's been going on for the last hundred years—but no one's found a thing."

"Angus MacPherson didn't leave any clues?"

"No." Lori walked to a small display case.

"This is all we have of Mr. MacPherson's." Cairo looked at the knife—an original Bowie, if she wasn't mistaken. The coonskin cap was worn, hunks of fur had fallen away, but the stitching had been good and the leather was still holding together. A small diary was opened to the words *Sanctuary, August 1879.*

"There were stories that he had another journal besides the one in the case," Lori told her. "From what I've heard, Angus wrote all about his adventures, but there's nothing about a golden city in this one."

"Maybe the other journal is buried with him."

"Oh, no. Very little of Mr. MacPherson's belongings were buried with him. His remains, plus the things you see in the display case, were found near Bozeman about ten or eleven years ago. The journal you see there," Lori said, pointing to the old leather-bound diary, "was near his body and the man who found him saw a few entries about our town. It seemed Angus preferred this place to anywhere else he'd ever lived, so the man brought him here to be buried."

"And the town paid for it?"

Lori shook her head. "No, the man who found him paid for it himself. He said he felt some kind of attachment to Angus. It sounded sort of strange to me."

"Is he a local citizen?"

"No. A paleontologist, I think. He was here just long enough to bury Mr. MacPherson, then he left for quite a number of years. He came back a few months ago. Some people thought he might be looking for the city of gold, but I hear he's looking for dinosaurs. They're common around here, you know. Their bones, at least. We're hoping to get a T-Rex one of these days. It would be a nice addition to the museum. On top of that, it would take a little bit of the focus off Mr. MacPherson's journal. You can't imagine how many times it's disappeared from the museum—only to reappear a day or two later. Teenagers, I'm sure, hoping to find some clue to the city."

"Do you think there's a clue in the diary?"

"I've read it through at least a dozen times." Lori laughed. "I've yet to find any mention of any city except this one."

"Have you looked for the city yourself?"

"We all did when we were kids. My husband talks about it occasionally, especially when the bank account's looking pretty grim."

"It's a bit like looking for the pot of gold at the end of the rainbow," Cairo said. "A fantasy."

"Oh, I'm sure it's all fantasy. But you know what, some of the best times I've ever had were spent out on the prairie, hunting for that legend. Lately I've gotten too set in my ways. I've forgotten how much fun a little adventure can be."

Lori went on and on about the city, about the fun of the search, and Cairo just barely heard her words. She was too busy thinking about Duncan, his need for fun and excitement, and how that sense of adventure could drive you away from the ones you love.

Ten

"Here he comes," Phoebe said, feeling dizzy and overly warm as Graham rolled toward her booth, looking even sexier than she remembered. She slid her hands over her sleek purple silk dress, wishing for a moment that she hadn't worn something so form-fitting, so low in the back and so high in the front, but considering the way Graham's eyes were shining as he slowly made his way across the room, she knew she'd made the right decision.

"Now, don't forget, I'm Gertrude," she reminded Cairo, "but you should probably call me Gertie. And you're Ingrid, you're in town researching museums for a book you're writing, and you have a son named Dylan."

"This isn't going to work, Phoeb."

"Think positive."

"That's easy for you. You've never had a doubt in your life."

Phoebe aimed a frown at her niece. "I'm on the verge of embarking on the craziest relationship of my life—well, at least I'm hoping to embark on a relationship—and you think I don't have a few worries?"

Beneath the table, Phoebe felt Cairo squeeze her hand, and then she smiled. "You have nothing to fear, Phoeb. You're beautiful and Graham's going to fall head over heels in love with you . . . much to my dismay."

Cairo slid out of the booth. "Where are you going?" Phoebe asked.

"To the little girl's room. You and Graham need a few minutes alone, and I need to get up the guts to go through with this."

"You're going to come back, aren't you?"

"I'll be back," she said, smiling softly. "Don't worry."

Suddenly Cairo was gone, Graham was close, and Phoebe was very glad that Cairo had disappeared. Why she'd wanted her niece there in the first place was anybody's guess because, truth be told, she wanted Graham all to herself.

"This is for you," he said, rolling right up next to where she sat and handing her a single red rosebud. "It's a peace offering, to make up for scaring you last night."

Phoebe took it from his hand, casually brushing her little finger over his skin, feeling an unexpected thrum in her heart. She lifted the delicate flower to her nose and inhaled its sweetness. "Thank you."

The smile that touched his face said so much more than "You're welcome."

"I was afraid you might not come," Graham said. She liked the deep timbre of his voice. She loved his honesty.

"I'm not the least bit frightened of your wheelchair, if that's bothering you."

"You noticed." A dimple formed in his right cheek when he grinned. "Some people like to pretend that I'm not sitting in this thing."

"I notice a lot of things about people. I've noticed a lot of things about you in particular. And yes, I noticed the wheelchair." Her eyes trailed to the brown loafers he wore, to his khaki slacks and the crisp pleats in each leg. She noticed his left hand resting on the wheel, and the wedding ring he hadn't removed. Finally, her gaze settled on his eyes. "Can you walk at all?"

He shook his head. "I've given it a shot, but

my ankles won't support me, even when I'm wearing braces. The break in my spinal cord was incomplete, so there's hope that I'll walk again." He shrugged, as if it didn't matter all that much. "I get by just fine the way I am, but I still keep trying."

Phoebe reached out and put a hand on his leg. "Can you feel my touch?"

She halfway expected him to flinch, to move away, but he only smiled as he shook his head. "My legs don't feel a thing, but the rest of me knows your hand is there and it feels pretty damn good."

"I spent most of the night thinking about touching you."

"Are you always so direct?"

"Always." She took a sip of the daiquiri she'd ordered earlier. "When I was eighteen I danced naked at Woodstock."

"I assume you've got a point to make," he said, smiling, "in addition to making me want to see you dance."

"I just want you to know, right up front, that my body isn't quite the same as it was thirty years ago, but I don't let that keep me from doing what I enjoy."

"I play basketball," he told her. "Thirty years ago I ran from one end of the court to the other, now I roll. I still love the game."

She couldn't help wondering if Graham had unique ways of doing all the things he enjoyed. She felt a rush of heat in her cheeks, and this time it wasn't a hot flash.

Before she could say another word, Cairo slipped back into the booth and Phoebe almost turned to her and said, "Go home." But since she'd made such a big deal about Cairo joining her tonight, she decided to be polite.

"Graham Kincaid, this is my friend Ingrid Jorgensen." Phoebe watched the curiosity dancing in Cairo's eyes as she was introduced to her former father-in-law for the first time.

"Nice to meet you," Graham said, shaking Cairo's hand and holding it much longer than he needed to. It wasn't jealousy that struck Phoebe, it was fear that her charade had just hit a major snag.

"You look familiar," Graham said, furrows forming between his eyes as he looked at Cairo. "Have we met before?"

Phoebe felt her niece gingerly kick her under the table.

"I don't believe so," Cairo answered.

"Ingrid has one of those familiar-looking faces," Phoebe interrupted. "People are always saying she looks like somebody's sister, or girl-friend—"

"You look like my son's ex-wife."

Cairo coughed and grabbed her margarita, tilting the glass to her lips to hide her face.

"Your son's name isn't by any chance Thor, is it?" Phoebe asked, horrified at her ability to lie so easily.

"Thor?" Graham questioned, while Cairo shot Phoebe a withering glare.

"That's who Ingrid was married to. Thor Jorgensen. A big, tall Norwegian. He looked like a Viking."

Graham laughed, shaking his head as he looked at Phoebe. "No, my son's name is Duncan—a big, tall guy with Scottish ancestry."

"Speaking of Duncan—" Phoebe managed to say before being interrupted.

"We were speaking about Thor," Cairo declared.

"Actually," Phoebe continued, ignoring her niece's more-than-justified protest, "I believe we were talking about Graham's son." She turned to Graham. "You said Ingrid looks like his *ex*-wife. Does he have a *current* wife?" Cairo kicked her a little harder this time, and Phoebe just turned to her and smiled.

"No current wife," Graham answered. "Just an ex, and I don't think he's given up hope of getting her back."

"Oh?" Phoebe put her elbows on the table

and leaned closer to Graham. "What makes you say that?"

"He still carries pictures of her in his wallet."

Phoebe nudged Cairo's leg this time. "He must have really loved her."

"I suppose. I don't know what the hell happened between them and Duncan won't talk about it." Graham laughed. "They were only married one night. Can you believe that? Cairo—that was his ex's name, went back to college and he went to Egypt. If you ask me, neither one of them had any idea what's needed to make a relationship work."

"Maybe they'll get back together someday," Phoebe said, hopefully. "Sounds like Duncan's still in love with her, considering that he's still carrying around those pictures."

"Maybe he's a packrat and doesn't like to throw anything away," Cairo added.

Graham frowned and Phoebe followed suit. "That's not very romantic," Phoebe said.

"I haven't felt too romantic since . . . since *Thor* and I broke up. He was extremely irresponsible, but, hey, you're here to have fun, not talk about broken marriages." A smile finally touched Cairo's face. "Why don't we talk about something else. Better yet, why don't the two of you dance." She turned her eyes to Graham.

"Gertie tells me you do a mean twirl on the dance floor."

Graham grinned, and oh how Phoebe loved that dimple in his cheek. "That's the worst line I ever threw out at a woman," he admitted. "I wasn't much of a dancer thirty years ago, and I doubt that I'm much better now."

"Too bad." Phoebe slid out of the booth and grabbed his hand. "I'm going to make you live up to that line of yours whether you want to or not."

"If you're game, so am I."

Phoebe felt a small twinge of guilt at leaving Cairo alone at the table, but the feeling didn't last long. A tall, good-looking cowboy walked over to the table as she and Graham were headed to the dance floor. Over her shoulder, Phoebe could see Cairo trying to say no but not having any success turning the guy down. A minute later, she was doing a fancy two-step that took Phoebe totally by surprise.

"Are you going to watch Ingrid all evening, or have a good time with me?" Graham asked, and a moment later she was in his lap and he had a nice, strong, oh-so-wonderful hand pressed to the small of her back. Wearing that almost backless dress had been a brilliant idea.

Her eyes were mere inches from Graham's. Their lips were within touching distance. He smelled like Old Spice, and she was totally and completely hooked.

"I suppose I should have told you that my idea of dancing means holding on to each other," he said.

"I knew there was a reason I liked you."

Phoebe slid her hands around his neck, and basked in the lightheaded joy she experienced as he twirled the wheelchair around and around, moving expertly between the other people out on the floor.

"You know what, Graham?"

"What?"

"Dancing has never felt so good."

Duncan kicked off his mud-crusted boots when he walked into his dad's darkened house, and left them on the service porch with his bag of laundry. He took a quick walk through the house looking for his dad, and felt relief that he wasn't at home. He'd come to town to find Cairo, and he didn't want to spend time explaining the situation to his father.

He was tired. He was dirty and a hot shower sounded awfully good, but he grabbed the telephone book, plopped it down on the kitchen table, and flipped the Yellow Pages open to motels. There weren't all that many places in Sanctuary, and if Cairo was still in town, he should know within the next ten minutes.

While he waited for someone to answer his first call, he snatched a cold beer from the refrigerator, popped the top, and took a drink.

"Do you have a Cairo McKnight registered there?" he asked when someone answered the phone.

"One moment, please."

The El Dorado had a grand total of fifteen rooms. Duncan knew because he and his dad had stayed there when they'd first come to Sanctuary. It seemed to him that the proprietor should easily remember the names of every guest. Then again, Duncan was in a hurry and he was feeling a bit disgruntled. He needed to find Cairo.

"No, sir, there's no one registered by that name."

"Try Phoebe McKnight."

"Just a moment."

Maybe it would take longer than ten minutes to call every motel in Sanctuary.

"No one by that name, either."

"Okay, try one more." This was a long shot. "Cairo Kincaid."

"Is that you, Mr. Kincaid?"

Damn! Now he was going to have to have a conversation with someone. "Yes."

"I thought the voice sounded familiar. How's the dinosaur hunting going? Found anything yet?"

"I'm still looking," he said, as patiently as he could.

"Good. You find a tyrannosaurus rex and we might get a little more business in town. We could sure use more guests here at the El Dorado."

"I'll do my best," Duncan added. "So, Mr. Potter, do you have a Cairo Kincaid registered?"

"No, no, I don't think so."

"Well, thanks for checking."

"No problem. Tell your dad hello for me."

Duncan hit the reset button, drew a thick line through El Dorado and moved on to the next motel on the list.

Forty-five minutes later he'd shaved, showered, gotten dressed, and hopped in his truck. Cairo was nowhere to be found, which probably meant just one thing: she'd left Sanctuary—and him—for good. The only thing left for him to do was to head downtown, get a good steak and another beer, and try to wipe Cairo out of his mind—again.

Duncan parked his truck on a side street and walked toward the Desperado. From the number of trucks and cars parked outside, it looked like half the people in southeastern Montana had converged on the place, a converted stable on the edge of town that had a huge dance floor, where a person could easily get lost, and a decent band on Friday and Saturday nights. Inside, it was crowded and smoky, the music was loud and he had to wedge himself between two groups of people so he could get to the bar and order a beer.

With the cold bottle in his hand, he leaned against the bar, hooked the heel of his cowboy boot over the rail, and looked around, hoping he might spot his dad. Instead, he saw Cairo—looking like she was having a hell of a good time . . . without him.

Damn her!

She had her long blond hair pulled into a bun on the top of her head, but wisps of it were falling about her face and one long lock curled over her shoulder—a bare shoulder. She was wearing the most damnably sexy white blouse he'd ever seen. The sleeves, the inch or two that existed, slid over her shoulders and just barely cupped the top of her arm, in much the same way the rest of the stretchy fabric molded over her breasts and stomach. Tight, too tight, letting everyone see just how curvy she was. Her blue denim skirt came down to her calves, but it was slit indecently high up the front, like she wanted to call attention to the greatest pair of legs in Sanctuary, or maybe even Montana.

To top it off, she was doing the two-step with a guy who looked like he could single-handedly take on the Green Bay Packers—and win. Her cheeks were flushed and she was smiling and nearly every man in the bar was watching her make a damn spectacle of herself.

Jealousy wasn't his style, but it was running through every fiber of his body.

Finally the band stopped and Duncan made a mad dash to the dance floor. He was bound and determined to pull Cairo away from the jock and into his arms, but he wasn't fast enough. A guy with a beer belly and a silver buckle the size of Montana and Wyoming put together grabbed her hand.

Reluctantly Duncan found his way back to the bar and sipped at his beer, watching the way her boots moved, the way her hips swayed, the way she twirled and smiled—and he wanted a piece of the action.

He was faster on his feet the next time around, and latched onto Cairo's arm during a lull in the music. Damn, she nearly took his breath away when he spun her around and saw the wild, having-a-fantastic-time smile on her face.

"Mind if I have the next dance?" he asked.

Her smile melted into a frown. That look said a hell of a lot more than "no." In fact, it said far more than he wanted to know. She was mad that he'd left her that morning, and she wasn't going to let him off the hook very easily.

"You'll have to stand in line."

"Line?"

She looked over his shoulder and Duncan turned around. The four men standing at the edge of the dance floor didn't seem to like the fact that he was trying to horn in. He looked into Cairo's flushed, beautiful face. "I take it you're not interested in giving me cuts?"

"Nope."

"How about going someplace quiet, where we can talk, and forget about dancing?"

"We did that last night and you made it perfectly clear this morning that we wouldn't be talking again. *Ever.*"

"A slight slip in judgment, something I've thought about all day."

"Then think about it a little longer, Duncan. Right now I'm going to dance." The music started again and she smiled softly and pointed to the jock she'd been dancing with earlier. "That's Jerry. I've promised him three dances in a row, right after Tony, who's after Bill, who's after Greg. Like I said, Duncan, you'll have to wait your turn."

"I want all the dances after that."

"And five years ago you said you wanted a lifetime. You have a tendency to change your mind."

"I want to dance, Cairo. *And* I want to talk. I'll wait all night if I have to."

He felt a hand on his shoulder and saw another beefy hand pull Cairo away. Greg, the cowboy at the front of the line, had already wrapped her up in his arms and started to move to the music.

Duncan guessed he deserved the torture he was going through at the moment, but he sure as hell didn't like it.

Determined to get a dance sometime during the night, he took his designated place in line right next to Jerry the jock. "Pretty, isn't she?" Jerry said.

Duncan simply answered, "Yeah."

"Great dancer," Jerry added.

"Yeah."

"You know her?" Bill, the beer-belly, big-silver-buckle guy asked.

"We used to be married."

Bill's eyes widened. "No shit?"

"Yeah, no shit."

Tony, a skinny guy with a cast on his foot that ran halfway up his calf, peeked around

Jerry's hulk of a body. "You actually want to dance with your ex?"

"Yep."

"Hell, I send my ex a quarter of my paycheck every month just to keep her away from me, and you're standing in line waiting to dance. You crazy or something?"

Yeah, he was crazy all right! He stepped out of his place in line and headed for the dance floor, determined to dance with his ex. Cairo's eyes narrowed as he neared, but he ignored the frown on her face and slapped a hand on Greg's shoulder.

"Mind if I cut in?"

Greg hit him with a fiery stare that could melt a column of steel. "She already told you to wait your turn."

Duncan merely smiled, and squeezed Greg's shoulder a little tighter. "Cairo's been known to say a lot of things she doesn't mean."

"You two know each other?" Greg asked, looking from Duncan to Cairo.

Anger flashed in Cairo's eyes. "No!"

"There she goes again." Duncan grinned, enjoying every moment of Cairo's discomfort. "Hell, one little disagreement and she pretends we've never met." Duncan's fingers eased away from Greg's shoulder and slid around Cairo's waist as Greg moved away. He pulled her against his chest in spite of her protests.

"Let go of me, Duncan."

"You *do* know him!" Greg declared.

"Of course, she does," Duncan said. "Now, tell me Greg, do you really want to get between a man and his wife?"

"Wife?"

"*Ex*-wife!" Cairo struggled, but Duncan held her close.

"Wife. Ex-wife," Greg membled. "Doesn't matter to me which you are, I ain't about to get in the middle of this."

"Smart thinking," Duncan added, as he waltzed Cairo to a dark corner of the room."

"We need to talk," he said, his lips close to her ear. "And don't tell me later."

She sighed, and he felt some of the tension ease from her body. "We don't talk anymore. All we seem to do is argue."

He pressed his cheek against hers, and whispered, "All right, no more arguing. Just answer one question."

"If I can."

"Why did you marry me?"

He felt her muscles tighten again. She tried to pull away, but he kept her close, giving her only enough room to look into his eyes.

"Answer me, Cairo."

"I was lonely."

"That's not the answer I want to hear."

Her eyes narrowed. "Then why don't you just put an answer in my mouth?"

He smiled, and wove his fingers into her hair. "Tell me you loved me."

He felt her breasts rise and fall against his chest, heard a soft sigh escaping from her lips. "I did . . . a long time ago."

"What about now?"

"Too many things have come between us."

"It's not too late to get them back. I want to be together again. I want to know what you've been doing the past five years. I want to know about your tour business, your life in Mendocino. I want—"

"And I want to know if *you* ever loved *me*."

"I never *stopped* loving you."

She stared at him as if she didn't believe his words, as if she might start crying at any moment, and then she slipped out of his arms. "I have to go."

"But we need to talk."

"No one knows that better than me. Just give me five minutes, Duncan. Maybe ten." She backed away slowly, then turned and disappeared into the crowd.

Suddenly Duncan was hit with the fear that

Cairo might not come back. His throat tightened, and he wondered if Cairo had known this same kind of fear when he'd left her the morning after their wedding.

Eleven

Phoebe rather liked lap dancing, especially with Graham.

"Having a good time?" he asked, twirling the chair for at least the thousandth time, making every nook and cranny of her body feel dizzy—deliriously dizzy.

And like a rollercoaster ride, he suddenly came to a screeching halt.

"What's wrong?"

"Remember that son of mine I was talking about?"

"Of course I do. Duncan."

"He's here."

Oh, Lord! Duncan was supposed to be in the middle of nowhere, crawling through a cave with dirt and bugs and ancient things. He had no business coming back to Sanctuary—not now.

Phoebe scrambled out of Graham's lap and fanned her face "Why don't we get out of here. Go have some ice cream or something."

"We could ask Duncan and Ingrid to go with us."

Impossible! Phoebe fanned her face a little harder. "You know, I feel a sudden hot flash coming on and if I don't get outside where it's cool, I just might pass out."

Gertie was out the door in five seconds flat, a time Graham couldn't compete with. Why she didn't want to meet his son was beyond him, but he wasn't about to question her. Hell, he just wanted to be with her, no matter what.

When he pushed through the door, he found Gertie standing outside in the dim light from the restaurant. The breeze made her silky dress cling to her legs and breasts and blew her hair wildly behind her. "Feeling better?" he asked, rolling close.

"Much." She stopped fanning her face and smiled. "Mind if we go for a walk."

"Not at all," he answered, happy to finally have her alone.

They headed toward the park, moving slowly side by side.

She was beautiful in the moonlight—warm and charming, and he wanted to know everything about her.

"Have you ever been married?" he asked.

"I came close a couple of times. I suppose I'm too much of a free spirit, and that's frightened a few men away."

"I imagine it would have scared the hell out of me thirty years ago."

"Nothing scared me thirty years ago. Remember, I was crazy enough to dance naked in the mud and rain. What about you?"

"I was in Vietnam—in the mud and rain—writing letters to my wife and wishing I was home with her and our son."

"I was in Berkeley protesting the war."

"I voted for Nixon."

She laughed lightly. "I popped a bottle of champagne when he resigned."

"We don't have a thing in common, do we?"

"That was a long time ago. People change."

"So," he teased, "you're a Republican now?"

"Not in this lifetime," she said, her eyes sparkling.

God, she made him feel good.

They reached the lake and Graham looked out over the water, suddenly uncomfortable with his strong desire for Gertie. "My wife—Jill—was killed in a car accident five years ago," he said twisting his wedding ring. "I don't think I'm quite ready to give her up."

"Okay."

Gertie didn't pry or whine or say she understood. Instead, she sat down in the grass beside his wheelchair.

"That's all? Okay?"

"I don't know you well enough to try to fight for you. Besides, it's hard to fight someone who's been dead for five years."

"You think I should put the wedding ring away and just forget about Jill?"

"Your son's ex-wife is still alive, that gives him reason to hope they'll get back together," she said, wrapping her arms around her knees. "You might be holding on to hope that you'll walk again, and maybe you will. But your wife's dead. All the hoping in the world can't change that."

"Did you ever love someone so much that you wanted to die when you found out that they were gone?"

"Unfortunately, no."

"*Unfortunately?*" How could she look at death as a positive thing?

"Yes, *unfortunately*. I'm forty-eight years old. I've never been married and chances are I might never get married. I've never even been in love, really and truly in love, but do you have any idea how much I've wanted to fall head over heels for someone? Do you have any idea how much I've wanted someone to love me so much that they didn't feel they could go on without me? You've had something awfully special. I can't possibly feel sorry for you."

"I don't want your pity."

"No, but you don't seem to want me, either." She got up from the ground. "I had a great time tonight," she told him, brushing a few blades of grass from her dress. "To be perfectly honest, I probably had the best time I've ever had in my entire life."

He wished he could be more sure of his feelings for her, wished he could ask her to stay, but right this moment he didn't want to deal with the emotions that were driving him mad.

Gertie placed a warm hand against his cheek. "I'm ready for a relationship, Graham. Not only that, but I'm alive. When you decide that you want to live again . . . I hope you'll give me a call."

Cairo leaned against the bathroom wall, trying to ignore the stares of the women walking in and out. Finally, she made a beeline for one of the stalls, locked the door, dropped the lid on the toilet, and sat down.

A jumble of thoughts raced through her

mind, like the fact that Duncan's seductive magnetism was messing with her mind. She didn't want to fall for him again, whether he still loved her or not. She just wanted to tell him about Dylan, make arrangements for visitation, and head for home. If she did anything more than that—like succumbing to temptation—she'd probably end up alone again, and with a broken heart.

So in approximately five minutes she'd just head out to the dance floor and lay everything on the line.

But what could she possibly say?

"You know, Duncan—" That's a good way to start, she decided. "There's a little something I've been meaning to tell you." She'd laugh gaily while they danced. She'd fluff her hair, then smile. "You have a son. A dear little boy who weighed nearly ten pounds at birth. I was in labor for two and a half days. Phoebe tells me I called you a no-good stinking lousy son-of-a-bitch at least a thousand times, and I really meant it. Giving birth to Dylan was pure hell, but having him in my life is absolute heaven. Last night when you told me you took care of your dad after the accident I thought you might have changed, but then you left me this morning without even saying good-bye. That wasn't a nice thing to do."

Cairo took another deep breath, then let her thoughts run wild again. "Anyway," she'd say, "I've decided to let you have visitation rights." And then she'd cap it off with, "Dylan needs a father, but you're not exactly trustworthy so your visits will have to be supervised."

Well . . . that little speech ought to charm him right into a long no-holds-barred court battle.

She buried her face in her hands. Maybe she wouldn't tell him anything. And then she thought of Phoebe. Of Graham. Six billion people on the planet and her aunt had to fall head over heels for Duncan's father. If that relationship continued, pretty soon they'd have to explain to Graham that she wasn't Ingrid Jorgensen, or researching a book on small-town museums, or married to a Viking named Thor, that she was really his ex-daughter-in-law, and that she was the mother of his only grandchild—a kid she'd kept a secret for five years.

Graham was going to hate her just as much as Duncan would.

Someone pounded on the toilet door. "Everything okay in there?"

Cairo unlatched the door and peeked out. "Fine. Just relaxing."

The woman drummed her fingers on the stall. "Mind if I relax a minute, too?"

Cairo smiled. "Not at all." She stood up and

straightened her skirt as she walked out. "Actually, I was beginning to feel a bit claustrophobic."

The woman looked at her as if she'd lost her mind, but Cairo only smiled, went to the mirror and noticed that she really did look like a woman gone mad. Her cheeks were flushed, her hair flew in all different directions, and her eyes were rimmed by smudged mascara.

She turned on the cold water, and splashed a bit on her face. Oh, why did she have to go out and face Duncan now?

After patting her face dry with a paper towel, she took a deep breath and headed out of the bathroom, ready for the confrontation.

He was waiting, one boot heel hitched over the brass rail, his arms folded across his chest. He had on jeans, a white Oxford shirt with just the top button undone, and he looked like every girl's dream come to life.

So why had he been her nightmare?

Duncan beckoned her with an index finger, and like a hypnotized victim, she walked right to him.

"I'm glad you came back."

"Well, I promised and *I* usually keep my promises."

"Touche."

The music began, slow, easy, and she could

feel Duncan's fingers slipping around her waist, pulling her tight, her breasts pressing snugly against his chest. It felt good and dangerous being so close. And she'd never felt so confused.

He dipped his head to the hollow of her throat, and, in spite of her protesting mind, she gave in to temptation the moment his lips touched her skin. All her thoughts about telling him about Dylan fled. She just wanted to concentrate on the sensations floating through her, and on all the things that had gone right between them in the past.

"You look beautiful tonight," he whispered. "You've always been beautiful, even when you were too young for me to admit it even to myself."

"I tried to make you notice me the first time I saw you in Egypt."

"You were a tease back then."

"I was in love."

"You were fifteen. You didn't know the first thing about love."

"I'd been reading romances for years. I used to sneak them out of Phoebe's room and read them under the covers with a flashlight. I knew what love was supposed to feel like, and believe me, I developed every symptom after I met you. You tried to cure me of it, but it didn't work—until you left me."

"I'm here, Cairo. Tonight. I left the biggest find of my life today, because I realized that I'd let the best thing I'd ever found slip through my fingers . . . again." His lips whispered over her skin, along her jaw, and hovered above her mouth. "I'm not going to let you get away again, Cairo. You're far too valuable."

And then he kissed her. She wasn't confused any longer, only hopelessly lost. He wanted her, maybe not forever, but at least he wanted her now. And right now she wanted more than a father for Dylan, more than a tour guide. She wanted Duncan in her arms, in her life.

And, God help her, even if it was just for one night—she'd take it.

"Let's get out of here," he said, his arm fastened so tightly around her waist as he beat a hasty retreat from the dance floor that he nearly carried her.

In less than a moment, they were outside in the cool night air. She could see his eyes darken with well-remembered desire. He wanted her, and she wanted him. She'd *always* wanted him. Maybe giving into passion was wrong, but she needed him now. The world spun around her, and he kissed her like a man gone mad from starvation.

Their tongues touched tentatively, then danced. The kiss deepened, and awakened the passion she'd locked away five years ago.

"I need you," he whispered against her mouth. "There's a lake near here. It's secluded and dark and—"

"Take me there, Duncan." She was probably crazy. But she didn't care.

He didn't say yes, he just dragged her to his truck. He ripped open the door, and nearly threw her inside, his hands all over her thighs and her calves and the backs of her knees until she'd made it to the middle of the seat.

"Hurry," she begged, and Duncan peeled away from the curb. She could have sworn he left half his rear tires on the pavement as he sped out of town. She willed some sense to come back to her, but it couldn't, not when his arm rubbed against her breasts everytime he downshifted.

He'd been right about the grove of trees. It was secluded, and Duncan parked right in the very center, turned off the headlights and engine, and moved toward her. Sanity seemed to have reappeared in his eyes. They were dark and intense and he cupped her cheeks with his hands. "I'm giving you one chance to back out of this."

Surely he must have lost his mind if he thought she was going to run. Leaving him right now was the last thing she planned to do.

"I'm not backing out of anything," she whispered. Her fingers slid over the muscles in his arms, and she tugged his shirt from under his waistband. She slipped her hands under the fabric and over his skin. He was warm and she was hot, and she needed him desperately. "If you want to run, Duncan, too bad. I'm not going to let you go."

"We've still got things to resolve."

"Is that what you want to do right now?" she asked, running her fingers over the zipper of his jeans. "Talk?"

He grinned, and showed her just exactly what he did want to do, exquisite things with his lips and tongue, things she'd dreamed about and wished she could have gotten from the few men she'd seen over the years, but no one could ever compete with Duncan.

His hands were on her arms, trying like hell to push her blouse down. If she'd had an inkling that she'd be with Duncan tonight—in this way—she wouldn't have worn a spandex top that really didn't want to move all that easily. But Duncan was persistent and skilled and, oh, thank God! he finally had the confining thing shoved down almost to her waist, taking her bra right along with it.

Her lips felt abandoned, totally lost when he pushed away from her, and then she saw the intensity of his pale blue eyes staring at her breasts.

"God, Cairo." Suddenly his mouth was on her and she heard a whimper escape her throat as his hand swept down her side and dragged her skirt up her thighs. She tried to help, to make it a little easier for him to send her to paradise, but the gear shift was in the way and the truck was too small and she slammed her knee into the steering wheel and her head banged into the handle on the door and she couldn't help it, but she started to laugh.

Duncan collapsed on top of her, and she could feel the rumble in his chest. Gently he kissed her lips. "I don't have a condom anyway," he said, a grin tilting his mouth. "We could move into the back of the truck and try this all over again, if you've got some kind of protection handy."

Cairo shook her head. "Sorry." She laughed again. "If I'd anticipated something like this, I might have gone to the drugstore beforehand, but, to be perfectly honest, Duncan, you're the last person I ever expected I'd be making love to—again."

"You're not regretting this, are you?"

"No."

He kissed her softly, then helped her tug her skirt down. He tried to help her pull her bra and top up, too, but he was a lot better at taking things off than putting them on and his hands just got in the way. But Cairo refused to push him from her. Instead, she smiled. "This is the best night I've had in a long, long time."

"A little frustrating."

"Maybe it's better to start out slow." She didn't believe that for a second, but it sounded like a good thing to say. "Why don't we have dinner tomorrow night. I'll wear something a little easier to get in and out of, and you can bring a box of condoms—"

One dark eyebrow rose. "An entire box?"

She laughed "Remember our wedding night. You were unstoppable."

"I was younger, too, and as I recall, we didn't bother with any kind of protection."

Oh, God, she'd almost forgotten that little detail. She still needed to tell him about Dylan, but not tonight. Tomorrow would be soon enough. Over dinner and wine. A lot of wine, so he'd be in a good mood and not hate her when she divulged the secret.

He started the truck and she rested her hand on his thigh as he drove the short mile back to town. "I haven't got a clue where you're staying," he said, when they hit Main Street. "I tried every motel in town looking for you—"

"You did?"

"I told you, Cairo. I came back to town to find you. To be with you. Is it that hard for you to believe?"

She smiled and kissed him because she didn't want to ruin the evening by telling him that she still had her doubts about him sticking around forever. Maybe she'd know after tomorrow night.

"Turn here," she told him, guiding him the rest of the way to the Heavenly Haven Inn. He pulled alongside the curb, hopped out of the truck and she slid out after him. He walked her toward the door and she stopped at the foot of the stairs. "Are you going back to the cave tomorrow?" she asked.

"Probably."

"It's a long drive, all the way there and then coming back to have dinner with me."

He tucked a finger under the bottom of her spandex shirt and dragged her toward him. "You're worth it."

"More than finding a city of gold?"

"Where'd you hear about that?"

"The museum."

"It's only a myth, Cairo."

"I don't believe that for one little second. I know you too well. You're looking for a city of gold—the same city of gold you used to talk about in Egypt—and I think you've got a good idea where it is."

He only grinned, refusing to divulge his secrets. "Maybe I've found something even better."

"Now you've piqued my curiosity."

"I thought you weren't interested in archaeology anymore."

"I'm interested in you." She stood on tiptoes and kissed him. "Maybe I can persuade you to divulge all your secrets at dinner tomorrow."

He eyed the front door. "Why don't I come up now and tell you everything you want to know—and maybe more?"

"Because it's late," Cairo said. "Phoebe's probably asleep and I'd hate to wake her." She held onto the newel post and walked backward up the stairs, knowing if she stayed next to Duncan much longer, he'd kiss her, and she couldn't go through that again, not when it couldn't go anywhere tonight.

"You're sure?" he asked, gazing hungrily at her lips.

"Positive."

"Then I'll see you at seven tomorrow."

"Seven," she whispered, and blew him a kiss. A moment later she was inside the house with the door closed, watching Duncan through the lacy curtains as he climbed into his truck. She was feeling kind of dreamy when she walked up the stairs, trailing her fingers along the polished oak banister until she slipped quietly into her room.

Phoebe was waiting up for her when she walked in the door, and Dylan was in her arms.

"Everything okay?" Cairo asked, moving quickly toward her son.

"I think he had too good a time tonight," Phoebe whispered, "and he's having a little trouble getting to sleep."

Cairo smoothed a hand over his cheeks. They were cool, but a little pink, and he woke just long enough to hold his arms out to her. Cairo took him from Phoebe, and his head fell heavily on her shoulder.

Cairo walked the floor with Dylan, humming as he drifted off to sleep. "Did you have a good evening?" she asked her aunt.

"I had a *wonderful* evening. Unfortunately, Graham's not ready for a relationship."

"I'm sorry."

"Don't be. I haven't given up hope. What about you?" Phoebe asked, curling up in a chair. "I saw you drive up with Duncan."

"We're having dinner tomorrow night. We've decided to take things one step at a time and see what happens."

"Did you tell him about Dylan?"

"Not yet."

Phoebe shook her head in annoyance as a light knock sounded at the door.

"Cairo."

A sick feeling hit the pit of Cairo's stomach when she heard the voice. She shot a worried look at her aunt. "It's Duncan!"

Oh, Lord, what was she going to do? She hated to turn loose of Dylan, but she had no other choice.

Phoebe shook her head again and disappeared with Dylan into her bedroom.

Cairo took a deep, calming breath, and walked across the room. She left the safety chain on and opened the door just a few inches. "Is everything okay?" she asked, peeking through the crack.

Duncan nodded. "Can I come in?"

Cairo took a quick look behind her. There were crayons and construction paper scattered on the coffee table. Dylan had kicked off his shoes and they were still in the middle of the room, along with his jacket, a shirt, his underwear, and his Tarzan backpack.

She looked back at Duncan, trying to hide her nervousness. "Phoebe's asleep on the couch. What do you want?"

"I want to show you what's in the cave."

"Now?"

"Tomorrow."

"I can't. I have work to do."

He stuck a hand through the door and cupped her cheek. "Put it off for a couple of days."

"I don't know if I can." She couldn't leave Dylan again, but she heard Phoebe's door open and heard her whisper, "Go with him."

She sighed, thinking about Dylan waking during the night, about his flushed cheeks, about the fact that she'd been away from him too much lately.

"Couldn't it wait a day or two?" she asked.

"It could, but I need to take you there. Just give me tomorrow and the next day and . . . and I'll go to Belize."

His words took her by surprise. Her response did, too. "You don't have to do that, Duncan. I know—"

"I know I don't *have* to do it, but I *want* to do it. So, what's your answer?"

She hesitated for just one moment, then asked, "What time?"

"Six in the morning."

"I can't give you a definite yes, but, if I can get away, I'll be waiting at the curb."

He reached through the crack in the door and swept a callused thumb across her lips. "You won't regret going, Cairo. I promise."

He said it as if he knew for sure that she'd be waiting for him.

Duncan Kincaid knew her all too well.

Twelve

Starting the day on only three hours of sleep was a hell of a thing to do, Duncan thought, especially with the fear gnawing inside that the woman you loved might not be sitting outside on the porch waiting.

Thankfully Cairo was there, leaning against the front bumper of her Dodge. She ambled toward his truck when he pulled up to the curb and damn if he didn't want to put his hands under her arms, haul her through the window, and try the same thing they'd tried last night, right there on Eden Street—in broad daylight—with people looking through their windows.

But he was a grown man, not a horny kid. He could wait a few hours. Right now he was content just watching the way she tilted her baseball cap low on her forehead to block the early morning sun.

"Good morning." Cairo said, as he climbed out of the cab. She threw her arms around his neck, accidentally hitting him in the back with the brown bag she was holding, and planted a scorching kiss on his mouth. She tasted like sugar and chocolate, and he found himself licking her lower lip before she pulled away and wagged a finger at him. "We don't have time for that right now."

"We don't, huh?"

"Not yet," she said with a smile. "But definitely later."

She waved the bag in front of him as he went around to the back of the truck and opened the shell. "I got up early and baked peanut butter cookies. On top of that," she said, as Duncan moved her caving gear from the hood of her four-by-four to the back of his truck, "I've got a thermos of hot chocolate and a pot of Jamaican coffee, because it's a long drive, and I knew you'd be tired, and I know how much you like peanut butter cookies and rich coffee."

Duncan slammed the camper hatch and gripped Cairo by the arms. "You're talking a mile a minute, Cairo. Are you nervous or something?"

She took a deep breath. "I couldn't sleep last night. I lay awake thinking about you and me and whether or not we were doing the right thing or if we were rushing into something crazy—"

He hushed her with a kiss, a hard one, wrapping his arm around her slender waist and pulling her up against his chest so her soft breasts brushed over him. God he loved the feel of her. "Don't think so much," he said, letting her slide back down to the ground before he ushered her into the truck. "Let's just enjoy the day."

She didn't say another word. Instead, she snuggled up close to him, pulled a cookie out of the bag and broke off a piece. "Open wide," she said, and when he did, she popped a chewy morsel into his mouth. Her fingers lingered behind, and he licked each one before she slowly pulled them away. If this kind of thing kept up, they'd never get to his camp or into the cave.

He was heading down the highway leading out of town when Cairo dug an aluminum thermos out of her backpack and poured a cup of cocoa. "Want some?" she asked, and he shook his head.

She took a sip, and he couldn't help but notice the slow, teasing way she licked the chocolate from her lips. "Did you know that you're not the only person looking for Angus Mac-Pherson's city of gold?"

"Half the people in Sanctuary are looking for it," he said. "They're obsessed, but so am I. The first time I came to Sanctuary—"

"Is that when you buried Angus?"

He laughed. "What was left of him. There was a lot of curiosity. People went up to the canyon where I found his body and dug up the area, hoping he might have left some clue to the city. Even his journal was scoured from one end to the other, but they didn't find a thing."

"That's because you didn't give them everything, did you?"

Duncan looked at the sly smile on her face. "What makes you think that?"

"I saw Angus's journal in the museum, and it's smaller than the one you had in Egypt. My guess is you have another one—one that tells the exact location of the city."

"It gives hints, nothing more. That's why I've been out here searching for the past five months."

Duncan concentrated on the road in front of him, following the line down the center when the morning sun blasted over the horizon and hit him in the eyes.

Cairo took another sip of cocoa. "You don't by any chance have Angus's journal with you?"

He smiled. "I take it your curiosity's still piqued."

"My God, Duncan, this could be the biggest find in the last hundred years. Think of the papers you could write—"

"I don't write papers, I just go searching for things."

"Okay, then I could write the papers. But think about the money, the fame—"

"I'm not interested in either."

"Then why the heck are you investing so much time in this?"

"Because, next to having you in my life, it's given me the biggest damn high I've ever had. Because I want to prove that Angus wasn't crazy. Because, *hell*, the city belongs to the people of Sanctuary, not to me. They're the ones who've been searching for a hundred years. Me, I just got lucky."

"You mean you're going to tell them where it is after you find it?"

"And ruin all their fun? No, Cairo, I think I just might give them one or two more clues so they quit looking north of town instead of south."

"I don't understand you, Duncan. You're broke—or pretty close to it. Your reputation as an archaeologist is, well, not exactly sterling, so why not take advantage of this?"

"Because I watched your parents at work. I saw how the hunt for money and glory can consume two people and make them forget everything and everyone around them. I saw what they did to you. Hell, I saw, firsthand, how love can be destroyed when a person's too consumed with their work."

He could see her jaw tighten as she turned to look straight at the road. "I hated you after you left me."

"I assumed that when I found out our marriage had been annulled."

She sighed deeply. "I should have read your letters. I should have given you a chance."

"Yeah, well, I shouldn't have left you, either. We both made mistakes, but we've been given another chance. Let's not blow it this time."

He slid a hand over her thigh, liking the feel of her jeans-clad leg under his palm. "Would you like to see Angus's journal?"

The torment in her eyes disappeared, replaced with curiosity. "I'd love to see it."

"It's under your seat."

Ever since he'd made his decision to share his find with Cairo, he'd thought about the moment when he'd lead her down into the cave and surprise her with the Mayan artifacts. He'd pictured the wonder on her face. But now, with her sitting next to him, he no longer wanted to wait to see her excitement.

It took only a moment for her to find the journal. From the corner of his eye he watched the way she caressed the tooled leather cover, recognizing a priceless, incomparable object. She turned to the first page, and ran her finger over Angus's flamboyant script, carefully turning one page after another, reading his words, mesmerized by all he had to say.

Duncan maneuvered the truck through dry riverbeds, over and around rocks, into canyons and back out of them again for nearly an hour, occasionally catching glimpses of Cairo as she read in silence, not even noticing the bumpy ride.

"It's all so fascinating," she told him when they arrived at camp, "especially the parts where Angus talks about the paintings on the walls in the cavern. It sounds like pictographs in a tomb."

"Is that what you think he found?"

She shook her head as they grabbed their gear from the back of the truck and headed toward the cave. "I don't know. He talks about warriors wearing feathers—"

"American Indian?" Duncan asked, baiting her, wondering if that's the direction her mind was going.

"I don't think so. This is going to sound crazy, but it sounds like he's describing things I've seen in Mayan temples."

"Maya?"

Cairo shot him a look. "You know darn good and well you thought the same thing. It's impossible not to. I mean, what about the way Angus described the carving of a boat filled with monkeys, birds, and dogs, not to mention half-naked men wearing strange, scary looking masks. Those birds were probably parrots, and the masked men were probably the paddler twins from Mayan mythology. My God, Duncan, Angus was describing a Mayan death voyage."

Her enthusiasm and knowledge warmed him, just as it had all those years ago when he'd met her in Egypt. No wonder he'd always wanted her with him.

Without even asking, Cairo grabbed a broken sagebrush branch from the ground and started to wipe away their footprints.

"What are you doing that for?"

"I'm not about to let someone follow us. This could be the find of a lifetime and I don't want to share it with anyone but you."

She didn't waste any time getting to the cave, squeezing between the boulders that had kept it hidden for centuries, and minutes later was crawling on her hands and knees through the tunnel.

Duncan went before her, at last rappelling down into the main cavern.

"Which way?" Cairo asked, the moment her feet touched ground.

He could tell her easily enough, but it was much more fun watching her find the way on her own. "Which way would you go if you were a Maya warrior looking for a new home."

She tilted her head and studied him. "Do you think that's what happened? Do you think a band of Maya left Central America looking for a new place to live?"

"They wouldn't have gone thousands of miles just to hunt."

"Why a cave, though?"

"To escape from the freezing winters," Duncan answered. "Maybe to hide from pursuers."

"If that's the case, they're bound to have left some record in the caves."

She studied the few unblocked tunnels, finally picking the jagged one that the wind rushed through. "If I was looking for a hiding place, I'd go through here."

Duncan smiled. "That was my choice, too."

He followed her into the twisting passage, happy to have her with him, sharing in his discovery.

"If the Maya came here to hide," Cairo said, "what do you think their reasons were?"

"Persecution, maybe. Freedom to form their own government. There could have been hundreds of reasons," Duncan said.

He squeezed through the end of the tunnel right after Cairo, and stepped, once again, into the breathtaking cavern. Cairo's eyes were wide with awe, and he just leaned against the wall to watch her moving from one brightly colored pictograph to the next.

"They're beautiful." She whispered, as if standing in a sacred shrine, not wanting to disturb the peace of the place. Slowly her fingers swept over the drawings of warriors standing hand-in-hand with their women, gods and goddesses, and a tall, golden pyramid, nearly hidden behind stalactites and stalagmites.

"What century do you think these drawings are?" she asked.

"Eighth is my best guess, considering the rulers they've depicted."

Cairo moved closer, exactly what Duncan had done when he'd first seen the pictographs. Her fingers came within a fraction of an inch of touching the faces, and then she knelt down, took out a hand-held flashlight, and shined it on the glyphs at the bottom of one of the drawings. "Have you read these?"

"A few, but you're the expert, not me."

"Come here and look at this." Duncan crouched next to her, their hips and shoulders brushing, and he wanted to concentrate on her instead of the Maya, but still he listened as she interpreted the glyph.

"They were in love. Not just one couple, but many. The women were going to be sacrificed to the gods, so they ran, all of them, and they kept on running for years, afraid of being captured, until they found these caverns where they felt they could be safe."

"Sanctuary," Duncan whispered.

Cairo laughed. "Ironic, isn't it."

She moved about the room, studying other glyphs, other pictographs, things Duncan had barely noticed yesterday because his mind had been filled with thoughts of Cairo.

Just as it was now.

He moved behind her, pulling her against his chest and wrapping his hands about her waist. Lowering his head, he kissed the soft, warm curve of her neck. She moaned softly, and he trailed his lips toward her ear, her cheek, and he was just getting into the swing of things when she pulled away.

"Did you see this?" she asked.

Hell, he didn't want to see anything but her—

naked and in his arms—but he followed her across the cavern.

The wall in front of them was a pictograph collage, where jaguars mingled with bison, and rainforests met high, snow-capped mountains. "They painted a mixture of two worlds," Cairo said, "what they left behind, and what they found that's new and wonderful." She aimed her flashlight at the drawings. "Have you noticed how many women are depicted in their drawings? And children?"

"I've noticed."

"That's unusual for the Maya. They didn't give that much credence to women and children. And I don't see any drawings of the ball game where they paid homage to the sun and moon and where the losers of the game were executed. I don't even see any human sacrifices in these drawings, only animals." Cairo laughed. "I could study these drawings forever, and probably never figure them out."

"Try figuring this one out," he said, taking hold of her fingers and leading her through another tunnel. The next cavern was smaller than the last, but even more colorful. "If you want to be totally baffled by this civilization, take a close look at the drawings in here."

He stepped around her, leaning against an unpainted wall so he could watch her face as she inspected the mural, knowing she'd be even more mystified—floored, really—by what she saw.

She focused in on the very heart of the drawings, her eyes squinting. "There's a sacrificial altar. Did you see it?"

"I saw it. But look closer."

"It's so hard to see anything with all the exotic birds, and the masks, and—"

"And what?"

"That's not a sacrificial altar. It's, oh, my God, there's a man and woman getting ready to make love on top of that thing. You can hardly see them through all the feathers and jade but, Lord, Duncan. They didn't leave anything to the imagination. That guy's huge."

"Wishful thinking on his part, I'm sure."

"Probably, but . . . she's smiling."

"Just a different form of sacrifice, I imagine, but it looks like the victim was more than happy to cooperate."

"Are there more pictures like this?"

Duncan laughed, the sound vibrating through the cavern. "Dozens. This place is like a Mayan *Kama Sutra*, with lessons on making love everywhere you turn. But you're still overlooking the obvious, Cairo. There's more in that collage than you ever could imagine."

It would be so damn easy to point out the

map, but he wanted Cairo to experience the thrill of finding it on her own. "Look at this, Duncan."

He frowned. She was looking in the wrong place. There wasn't anything special in that portion of the drawings. "What am I looking for?"

"You don't see it?"

"What?"

"It's a geyser, like Old Faithful, right in the center of a pool of water."

Duncan looked closer and the clear waters and towering fountain appeared before his eyes. Stalactites hung all about the pool, and a shaft of light beamed down from overhead.

"Do you think there's really a pool down here?" she asked.

"I don't know." He pulled the map he'd drawn from his pocket. Yesterday he'd been so intent on finding the sacrificial altar that he hadn't looked at anything else, but the pool was clearly marked.

"Where'd you get the map?" Cairo asked.

"Right here." He pointed about three feet to the left of where she'd found the pool. It amazed him how things became so clear when they were put right in front of your face—like still having feelings for Cairo. He'd thought he could get over her—but she was back in his life and he wanted her to stay.

Forever.

Again he grabbed her hand. "Come on. Let's go find that pool."

With the map in hand, it took less than fifteen minutes to maneuver through the maze of tunnels. Without the map, they would have been hopelessly lost, and if the diagram wasn't lying, there were booby traps scattered everywhere.

"Hear it?" Cairo asked, as they entered the last passage. "It sounds like rushing water."

A moment later they stepped out of the tunnel and into a room lit by hundreds of beams of light shining down through minuscule holes in the ceiling above. Giant stalactites hung all about. A massive flowstone slide jutted out of the cavern's side and curved right down to the pool of pale, clear blue water.

"It's beautiful," Cairo said.

Duncan went to the edge of the pool. It was shallow for the first fifteen or twenty feet, then darkened toward the center, like the geysers he'd seen in Yellowstone. There was no telling how deep the water went, or how often it drained and then erupted.

He knelt down, and scooped up a handful of liquid, tasting just the smallest amount. Then he drank the rest. "Pure," he said. "Try it."

"I plan to," she said, and her shirt dropped next to him on the limestone floor.

He looked up from the water just as a stream of light shifted and shone down on Cairo's face. She smiled as she reached behind her and unfastened her bra. A second later it lay on top of her shirt. "Am I going in alone," she asked, "or are you going with me?"

A lump formed in his throat. "From now on, we do everything together."

One of the buttons popped off his shirt in his rush to get out of it. Their helmets and flashlights and all of their gear was dropped on top of a table-like boulder, and they sat down together on the limestone to rid themselves of their boots.

When their feet were bare, nothing remained between them but jeans—and those were gone in an instant.

"Damn." Duncan's whispered word echoed throughout the cavern, as he reached out and caressed Cairo's cheek.

"It's been a long time, Cairo."

"Far too long," she agreed. "I haven't forgotten our wedding night and the bathtub . . ." She drew in a deep breath. "I haven't forgotten the water or how good it felt to be in your arms, all wet and slippery."

"I haven't forgotten either," Duncan said, grabbing her hand, tired of talking about all the

sensations when he wanted to feel them instead.

He dragged her into the pool and the water
splashed in their wake.

Cairo laughed, as she ducked under the
warm water and came back up with rivulets
dripping down her face and over her breasts.
Duncan couldn't help himself. He moved close
and lapped a drop off the very tip of her nipple.

"Do that again," she purred, and drew her
shoulders back a little bit so her breasts, her luscious, more-than-a-handful breasts, rose ever so
slightly, beckoning him toward them.

He slid his palms beneath the soft flesh and
lowered his head, taking one rosy crest into his
mouth. He teased her sensitive nipple, flicking
it with his tongue, nipping her lightly with his
teeth. She moaned softly, and he drew his
thumb over the peak of her other breast, loving
the way she jerked at the sensation, her hips
pressing against his, as water splashed about
them.

He felt her hands sliding down his sides, felt
gentle fingers curling about him, squeezing and
rubbing every hard inch of him. He'd nearly
forgotten her touch, but it all came back to him
in an instant. He needed her, he wanted her.

His hand smoothed over her belly. Suddenly
she pulled away, ran out of the water and stood

totally, beautifully naked. Water dripped from her hair, her breasts, the dark blond nest of curls that he'd been dreaming of.

"Something troubling you?" he asked.

"This is crazy," she said, feeling nervous in spite of the bravado she'd shown just minutes ago. She swept her shirt up from the ground and tried to cover herself. "I'm not ready for this."

"I am," he said, and she couldn't help but notice just how ready he was when he walked out of the water.

He plucked the shirt from her fingers and let it fall to the ground. "I remember every inch of you, Cairo. I spent one hell of a night thinking about you—" He tenderly kissed her shoulder. "Wanting you—" His lips trailed along her neck. "Needing you—" He kissed her lips and her arms wove around his neck.

"Say you want me, Cairo."

"I want you."

"Would you do anything for me?"

"Anything," she whispered.

Slowly his fingers trailed over her breasts, her stomach, along the insides of her thighs. Her body quivered, and her need for him seemed stronger than ever.

He knelt before her. Warm hands caressed her legs, the backs of her knees, and she felt like she might crumble. And then he stood in front of her again, a smile on his face and a foil pouch grasped in his fingers. "If I asked you to give yourself to me completely—heart, body, soul— would you do it?"

"I'd give you anything. All you have to do is—"

Her words were stilled, and all the air rushed out of her lungs as Duncan tossed her over his shoulder. He grabbed a flashlight and raced through the tunnel on the right.

"What are you doing?" Cairo asked.

"You're going to be sacrificed."

"I'm what?"

"I've been cursed, remember? I figure offering you to the gods will appease them, and hopefully all my bad luck will end."

"This is insane, Duncan," but she couldn't help laughing as she hung upside down, getting a rather nice, yet somewhat darkened view of Duncan's muscular back and his hard, untanned behind.

After many laugh-filled protests by Cairo, they entered a chamber that was beyond belief. She could just barely see the sculptures in the limestone, the pyramid cut into the wall, and the paintings that surrounded them—but she could see the altar, big as life, especially when Duncan pulled her down from his shoulder and her legs and bottom touched the cold, cold stone.

He looked at her hungrily. "Lie down," he commanded.

She smiled, and obeyed. She could feel her insides sizzling as he circled the sacrificial stone, studying her—every inch of her.

"Put your hands over your head."

She did as he asked and he came close, brushing his knuckles along the sides of her breasts, her nipples, his skin rough and wonderful. This glorious torture was something she could get used to really quickly.

His fingers trailed down the length of her legs, all the way to the very end, to her toes, and he ran them lightly over the sensitive bottoms of her feet. She jerked, a spasm hitting her, and he grabbed her ankle and pulled her leg up and away from the altar.

"What are you going to do?" she asked, her breathing heavy now, labored.

"This is all part of the ritual. You should have looked at all of the pictures, Cairo. The gods were appeased only when the people were happy." He kissed the arch of her foot, her ankle, the inside of her knee. "I want to make you happy," he said.

A low moan escaped from her lips. "I am happy, Duncan. Deliriously happy."

He made slow circles up her ankle and along her calf with the tip of his tongue, and she wondered what delicious torture was going to come next.

"Don't move," he commanded.

That was a complete impossibility, especially when his tongue reached the inside of her thigh, making her hips rise and writhe uncontrollably off the stone.

And then he slid a finger inside her, and she cried out as it twisted and turned and moved in and out and she thought, oh, my God, I can't believe I'm letting him do this to me when a few days ago I thought I despised him.

Hopefully he'd never stop.

When he touched her favorite little pulse point with his thumb, she thought for sure she'd launch right off the altar. And he didn't stop there. Oh, God, she felt his fingers and his tongue and his mouth, doing all sorts of wonderful things that she remembered, memories she'd thought about late at night when she'd lain in bed feeling so lonely she could hardly stand it.

She wasn't feeling lonely any longer. She felt cherished.

"Make love to me," she begged. "Please."

A slow smile touched his lips and she felt his

finger slip from inside her, felt one last loving lap of his tongue, and one more brush of his thumb across that crazy little nub of flesh that had more erotic nerves in it than any other spot on her body. Finally, she heard the rip of a foil packet.

Thank goodness!

And then like an Egyptian god, he rose, ready to accept the woman who was sacrificing herself to him. His pale blue eyes were dark and intense, and he straddled her hips.

Cairo reached out and cradled his face in her hands. "I love you, Duncan."

He smiled, and the rays of light from the flashlight flickered about the room, then dimmed.

"I love you, too," he whispered, and that breath of a sound echoed around them in the cavern that was suddenly blanketed in black.

I love you. I love you. I love you.

She felt him slide inside her, big and powerful and hot. He moved slowly at first, taking his time, giving each of them a chance to know the other all over again, taking time to please her, which he did so very, very much.

As if he could hear what was going on inside her head and understood the needs of her body just by her moans and sighs, he buried himself deep within her. She couldn't remember ever feeling such exquisite pleasure, not just from the wonderful way he was making love to her, but from the depth of his love for her—in spite of all that had happened between them.

He kissed her again, his tongue dancing with hers, and he wrapped his arms tightly around her in this dark and mystical place where the impossible was actually possible.

"I'll never leave you again," he whispered, and she was lost in the sincerity of his words and his strength as he carried her with him to the heavens. Suddenly the stars burst inside her, around her, and the dark cavern seemed to brighten in a radiant flash.

And she knew in her heart that this time the radiance between them would last forever.

Thirteen

"Well..."

Dylan perched on top the sofa, trying to explain to Phoebe how and why he'd broken the ceramic vase that had been sitting in the center of the coffee table. When she'd gone to her room to take a quick shower, it had been filled to overflowing with a beautiful arrangement of lilies that was now nothing but a mass of scattered petals, leaves, and broken stems. There hadn't been a big water spot on the carpeting when she'd left the room either.

"You see, Aunt Phoebe," Dylan continued, "it's like this. Bert, that's Mr. Tibbetts, in case you didn't know, was teaching me some Tae Kwon Do techniques, T-E-C-H-N-I-Q-U-E-S, last night. Did you know that he's a third-dan black belt?"

"Is that good?" Phoebe asked, keeping her temper under control.

"It's not the top, but it's close. And he's really good at it. He was showing me how to do a front kick and a punch and a knife hand."

"A knife hand? What's that?" Phoebe asked, feeling a little uncomfortable with any kind of technique that had the word knife in it.

"Well . . . some people, you know, people who aren't experts at martial arts, call it a karate chop, but it's really a knife hand. I guess it was probably the knife hand that ruined the flowers and it might have been the front kick that broke the vase."

"In other words, the Tae Kwon Do is responsible for all this destruction, not you?"

Dylan drew his little shoulders up almost to his ears. "I wouldn't do anything like that on my own. Besides, I like flowers."

Phoebe massaged the back of her neck. She loved Dylan without question. More than anything, Dylan needed his dad and Cairo needed the man she loved, and the only way that was going to happen was if they spent time together, so Phoebe hadn't minded watching him a few more days.

But right now she had a headache.

A knock sounded at the door and Dylan jumped off the sofa and started to run to answer it.

"Stop right there!" Phoebe called out, and Dylan skidded to a halt. "Since when do you open the door?"

"Since I know Tae Kwon Do."

Phoebe shook her head. "You march right back over to that sofa and sit. It's timeout time. Half an hour at least."

Dylan went back to the sofa and climbed up on the back. He swung his legs back and forth, kicking the floral chintz with his cowboy boots, and Phoebe had the feeling she and Cairo were going to have a pretty hefty repair and reupholstery bill by the time they left the B&B.

Mr. Tibbetts was at the door, bucket and mop in one hand, vacuum cleaner in the other. Phoebe was ready to give him a piece of her mind for teaching Dylan Tae Kwon Do, but he took one look at the mess on the floor and the little boy sitting quietly on the couch, and he spoke up first. "I imagine I'm partially responsible for this little accident."

"It's not your fault, Bert," Dylan chirped. "I already told Aunt Phoebe it was the knife hand and front kick."

Bert attempted to grin, but Phoebe saw his Adam's apple rise and fall heavily. He was feel-

ing pretty darn uncomfortable at the moment—
and, by rights, he should.

"It won't take me but a moment to clean this
up," he said, and immediately started picking
up flowers and broken glass. "And don't worry
about the breakage, or anything else. We won't
be putting it on your bill."

Thank goodness!

Phoebe knelt down next to Bert and picked
up a few bigger chunks of glass. "I have a headache," she informed him, "otherwise, I'd probably laugh at this whole thing."

"I usually confine my teaching to the class-
room or the park, but we were having fun last
night, and Dylan's a quick study."

"Quick to get in trouble, too," Phoebe said
under her breath, just before the phone rang.

"Excuse me a moment."

Dylan was halfway to the phone when
Phoebe gave him a withering glare, and he
slunk back to the sofa.

"Hello," she said, and was surprised to hear
Graham's voice at the other end of the phone.

"Have dinner with me tonight. I cook as well
as I dance."

"Is that another line?"

"I'll let you know after I attempt to cook. Say
yes, Gertie."

Gertie. She'd almost forgotten that's who she

was supposed to be when she was talking to Graham. "I don't know. I'd have to get a babysitter for Dylan—"

"Irene and I can watch him," she heard Mr. Tibbetts say. "I'm not eavesdropping." He grinned. "The room's just small."

Phoebe mouthed a "thank you" to Mr. Tibbetts and told Graham she'd be at his place by seven-thirty, got directions, then nearly melted when he said in that deep timbre of his, "I dragged out some old records. I thought we might be able to dance again."

Phoebe smiled at the thought. Mmm, she definitely liked lap dancing. "Can I bring anything?"

"I have everything I need—except you."

And tonight, she thought, thinking of being in his arms again, *you can have me, too.*

"Ouch!"

"What did you do now?" Duncan asked. "Hit your head, stub your toe, or run into a wall?"

"All three at the same time," Cairo answered, holding onto Duncan's hand as they attempted to find tunnels in the dark, and tried to remember which way they were supposed to turn.

The situation wasn't funny. She was scared to death, just as she'd been when the plane crashed. But fear wouldn't get her back home to Dylan, who wouldn't have a mother *or* a father if she and Duncan didn't survive.

They'd been foolish heading for that sacrificial altar with only one battery-operated lamp. Any good caver knew you didn't go anywhere without at least two sources of light because dark was extremely dark inside a cave, and getting disoriented and lost was remarkably easy when you had no way to judge your bearings.

"The tunnel splits here," Duncan said, and Cairo plowed into his back when he stopped unexpectedly.

"Ouch!"

"What now?" That was the first time his words showed any sign of irritation.

"You stepped on my toe."

"Sorry." She could hear his deep sigh. "Do we go left or right? I can't remember."

"I wish I could help, but I was upside down the last time we came through here and I was concentrating on your bottom instead of the path we were taking."

Finally he laughed. That's what she'd been aiming for, because Duncan was so worried about her safety that he seemed to have lost his adventurous spirit, and that sixth sense that had always kept him safe.

He pulled her close and she was sure he was

trying to kiss her, but he banged his chin into her eye instead. "Ouch!"

"I take it I missed your mouth."

"You were about three inches too high and an inch too far to the right. Want to try again?"

This time she felt his hands cradling her cheeks. She couldn't see a thing, but she could hear the steadiness of his breath, could feel his heart beating hard and strong in his chest, could feel his warmth so very close. He kissed her, and all the worry and fear she was trying to hide by laughing it off seemed to fade away.

She would hold her son again.

She would see Phoebe again.

She and Duncan would get out of here safely, because they were together, and she really did feel, as he was kissing her, like they could conquer the world.

Before she could fully appreciate his kiss, he pulled away. "Left."

"Excuse me?"

"We need to go to the left," he stated. "Come on."

She held back, even when he tugged on her hand. "Is that a *left* as in you're absolutely positive, or is that a *left* as in we have two choices, and left seemed the better of two evils?"

"We have to go one way or the other. I flipped a coin—in my mind—and left won."

"Okay, but if we fall into some deep, fathomless pit and die, I'm blaming it all on you."

Duncan laughed again. "You know, Cairo, if we're going to die, I'm glad we're going to do it together."

"Thanks a heap."

Duncan had no way of knowing how much time passed. It seemed an eternity of bumping into walls, kicking rocks that he didn't remember from before, and worrying about getting out alive.

Trying to move in a pitch-black system of caves and tunnels was pure insanity, but they had only two options: stay put and die, or stumble blindly through the maze and hope not to die.

The second option held the most promise.

The wind whipped about them, and bits of sand and dust pelted their bodies as it howled at their plight.

Damn it, Dunc! You're going the wrong way.

Angus's words came out of nowhere, filling his head with dread.

Stop! Now!

Duncan froze in place. "Don't move," he told Cairo, and she stopped.

"What's wrong?"

"I think we took the wrong turn." He put his hands on her shoulders and could feel the tightness in her muscles. She'd been putting on a good show of not being afraid, but he could feel fear ripping through her. "Don't move even one inch."

"Don't worry. I'm not going anywhere."

He wished he had a rope or string or something to tie around their waists, something to keep them together even if they drifted apart. If they got separated they might never find each other. Even if they called out, the echoes would reverberate through the hollow caverns and it would be far too hard to follow a voice.

He was afraid of losing Cairo, but he was too afraid to let her go any further. He had to do this alone.

"Why don't you sit down," he suggested. "Relax a minute."

He felt her moving, felt her cross her legs and sit on the rocky floor. "Whatever you do, don't move an inch. I need you to act as a directional arrow."

She laughed, the light, nervous sound bouncing off the walls. "You're not going far, are you?"

"I don't know." He kissed her quickly.

"Be careful. Please."

"I'll do my best."

He got on his hands and knees and inched forward, feeling all around him as he moved.

Pebbles slid down from the side of the tunnel. It didn't feel like that much, but it sounded like a landslide.

"Duncan? Are you all right?" Cairo's voice wasn't much more than a whisper, but he could hear her fear.

"I'm fine. I'm probably not more than six feet away from you."

"God, I hate not being able to see."

"We'll get out of here. I promise." He hoped his words sounded more reassuring to Cairo than they did to his own ears. He wasn't sure of anything right now.

Inch after inch he moved, slowly, cautiously.

You've got to go back, Dunc.

"I can't," he whispered, glad that Angus was with him again, as he'd been so often when he was alone.

A sudden gush of air came out of nowhere and wrapped around him like a tornado, dragging him forward. He braced his hands against the limestone floor to keep from moving, and just as suddenly as it had come, it blew away.

That was a close one.

"Damn right!"

Another inch. Another.

He moved his right hand forward and it plummeted through thin air. His elbow hit the edge of a pit, his chin just missed before he regained his balance.

I told you not to go any further.

"You could have been wrong!"

And you could have been dead! Where the hell would that leave Cairo?

For the first time, he wondered if Angus was talking to him or his own subconscious. God, maybe he was just going crazy. The darkness, the closeness of the walls, and the fear he felt for Cairo were eating away at him. He had to get them out of here.

Maybe he could still move forward.

He reached out, hoping for something to touch, but there was absolutely nothing in front of him but a hole. He grasped one of the hard, round pebbles from the floor and dropped it into the pit. He waited to hear it hit bottom, but the sound never reached his ears.

You've got to go back. Try another passage.

"Yeah, I know!" He inched his way back, slowly, cautiously. Not much further, he told himself. You're getting closer. Without warning, his feet touched something soft, and an ear-splitting scream raced through the tunnel and ricocheted through his head.

"It's just me, Cairo."

He turned around and wrapped her in his arms. "I've got a confession to make," she whispered. "I've never been so scared in my life, and I really, really want to get out of here."

"It won't be long. We just made a wrong turn, that's all."

"We *are* going to get out of here, aren't we?"

"I told you I'd get you out of here. I plan on keeping that promise." He kissed her, missing her mouth in the darkness, but loving the feel of her cheek against his lips. "You *are* going to add this to your list of times I've rescued you, aren't you?"

He could feel her smile against his mouth. "I'm going to engrave this one in gold foil."

"I'm going to hold you to that." His arm brushed against Cairo's as he moved past her, heading in the opposite direction of the way she was facing, and together they began their trek back through the tunnel, their movements coordinated so Cairo's hands touched and moved with his feet. The progress was slow, but they had to stay together.

Stinging pain accompanied his raw, scraped knees. Cairo's tender skin probably hurt worse than his, but she never whimpered, never complained, she just followed, touching him every inch of the way, through one tunnel after another. They had no way of knowing if they took the right turn or wrong, but suddenly he saw a dim light.

The temptation to move faster was strong, but it was just one small ray of light, something that could be deceiving, maybe even a hope rather than reality. Still he crawled toward it and at last saw the shards of light beaming down from the ceiling above the pool.

"We made it," he said, breathing a deep sigh of relief.

Cairo crawled up alongside him and smiled. Her face was streaked with dirt and tears and he'd never seen anyone so beautiful in his life.

"Are you okay?"

"Just scared." She rested her head against his chest. "I'm glad you were with me."

He cradled her in his arms, thanking Angus and the gods for keeping them safe. Slowly he stood, lifting her with him, and headed to the crystal clear pool.

Together they swam through the warm water, letting it relieve some of the sting from their cuts and scrapes. Like a relaxing massage, the waves rolled over and around them, lapping gently against sore muscles.

Dirt and blood soaked away and Cairo suddenly felt exhausted. She wanted to sleep, but she wanted to get out of the cave and back home even more.

Duncan held her close, and with gentle hands he washed the remaining grit from her face, and helped her rinse her hair. He kissed her tenderly, then dove deep into the water, coming up again in the center of the pool.

Cairo trudged to the edge of the water and sat down, wrapping her arms around her drawn up knees. For a few minutes she watched Duncan swimming back and forth, his hands knifing hard into the water with each stroke. He seemed to have some nervous energy left inside that needed to burn off.

She, on the other hand, had no energy remaining at all.

Ten minutes must have gone by before he walked from the pool, water dripping from his black hair, beading up on his shoulders and in the soft sprinkling of hair on his chest. Watching him made her body ache, made her heart thunder inside. She held out her hands to him because she didn't need sleep anymore and she didn't want to leave the cave. All she wanted was Duncan.

A sane man would have gotten the hell out of the cavern, Duncan thought, but he knew he wasn't sane. Not now anyway, not with Cairo—naked and beautiful—holding her arms out to him.

He touched her fingers and slid his hands up her arms to her shoulders, and she lay down in the shallow pool and pulled him to her. The water rippled gently around them, but the moment he kissed her, he was consumed by dark blue eyes and the sound of her heart beating beneath him.

Her lips tasted like the water from the pool, fresh, clean, pure. She opened her mouth and their tongues did a slow, sensual dance. A moment later her legs wrapped around his waist. He wanted her so damn bad, but he pushed away from her just long enough to get a condom from his pants. And then he was beside her again, holding her, kissing her hard as he slipped into her warmth. He'd wanted to take things slow and easy because they were both so battered and bruised, but her passion was heated, and her hips rose higher and higher to meet his every thrust.

He couldn't remember lovemaking ever feeling this good and then he realized that he'd felt that way every time he and Cairo were together. She was so incredibly hot and when he thought all his reserves were drained, she'd beg him for more, and he'd suddenly feel rejuvenated again.

"Oh, God," she moaned beneath him. "Oh, God, Duncan, please, don't stop. Don't ever stop."

He kissed her then, her lips and her eyes and the hollow of her neck and she tasted so damn good. He felt her fingernails pressing into his hands, digging harder and harder, begging him to keep right on going.

And then she arched into him, her hips high off the ground, her eyes wide open, sparkling as she whispered, "I love you."

He rose above her, holding her hips while he moved in and out, faster and faster, watching the play of emotion on her face. She was ecstatic, enjoying every moment. She wanted more and more and the more she wanted, the more he needed to give.

Suddenly a smile of pure pleasure curved her lips and he could feel her muscles clenching all around him, over and over again, and then, when he knew she was totally sated and happy, he let himself go, and every nerve ending in his body cried out as he drew her to him and held her tight, and with one last thrust, he exploded from the sheer, all-consuming joy that only Cairo could give him.

Fourteen

The table didn't look half bad, Graham
decided, sitting back and observing his
handiwork. He'd cut a dozen yellow and
pink roses from the neighbor's bushes, which
hung over the fence, and arranged them in a
crystal vase, a wedding present from his in-
laws thirty-four years ago. The china place set-
tings and the wine glasses he'd taken out of a
box in the back bedroom, things he'd thought
about getting rid of, but hadn't had the energy
or courage.

It felt good having china on the table for a
change. He'd gotten tired of paper plates and
beer cans.

He'd found an embroidered white tablecloth

mixed in with all the other linens, thrown it in the washing machine, and managed to get it ironed and spread onto the table. Jill had stitched hundreds of flowers around the border while she was pregnant with Duncan. She'd crocheted blankets and booties and sweaters, too, and he'd watched her for hours because he couldn't take his eyes off of her. He'd loved her something fierce.

Sometime during the night he'd realized that Jill would have liked Gertie, and more than anything, she would have wanted him to be happy.

Tonight was the first step toward finding real happiness—the kind he'd had with Jill—all over again.

Outside he heard footsteps on the porch, he heard a woman humming, and then he heard the doorbell ring.

He took another look at the table and then his eyes trailed to his left hand. Everything new begins with the first step, he told himself. He reached down, twisted off his wedding band, and tucked it into his pocket.

Gertie looked awfully pretty when he opened the door. All those curls of hers were fastened to the top of her head and they sprang out everywhere. She wore a long, flowing dress that was bright screaming green. Her earrings were exactly the same color and dangled almost down to her shoulders.

She had on a pair of Birkenstocks, which she left on the doorstep, and she came into the house barefoot and smiling, holding out a bottle of wine and a corkscrew. "This is already chilled," were the first words out of her mouth. "Would you like some?"

Suddenly he just wanted to get drunk. What the hell was he doing? Gertie had danced naked at Woodstock and he'd made love to only one woman in his entire life. The two of them had no business being together.

My God, she was a Democrat!

"I have to be home by midnight or I turn into a toad," she said, and he looked up from the carpet and into her eyes. Her smile brightened the room.

"I like toads." That was a real idiotic thing to say.

"Good, maybe I'll stay past midnight, but only if you talk to me." She smiled again. "So would you like some wine?"

"Sure." Somehow he managed to laugh. "The wine glasses are on the table."

Gertie almost floated from the small living room to the dining area. She put a finger to her lips and studied his handiwork. "This looks nice. Almost like going to a fancy restaurant."

"Without the waiters getting in the way."

"Don't you hate that?" she said, twisting the screw into the cork then pulling it out with a pop. "I know they mean well and that they're trying to do a good job so they'll get a big tip, but sometimes you just want to have a relaxing conversation. You're not the least bit interested in food, yet the waiters still come by."

She poured wine into two glasses and he took the one she offered. He hoped she didn't expect him to make some kind of lame-brained toast. That wasn't his style. Fortunately, she didn't raise her glass to anything but her mouth, a sweet, pretty, puckery mouth that was naturally red and luscious.

Too luscious.

He downed about half the glass of wine in a couple of swallows. That wasn't the proper way to drink wine, but he was alone with a woman he hardly knew, she looked terribly sure of herself, and he wasn't sure of anything at all.

Except that seeing her flyaway hair and her neon green dress and her luscious lips made him feel awfully good.

She roamed about the room, checking out the pictures on the mantel over the fireplace. "Is this your son?" she asked.

"Duncan," he reminded her, just in case she'd

forgotten. "That was taken when we were in Guatemala a few years ago."

"Do you like to travel?"

"Traveling's my son's passion, not mine. I'd wanted to be an archaeologist once. I wanted to go to Egypt and look for tombs, but I got married instead. It didn't take me long to realize that I'm a homebody. What about you?"

"I'm enjoying this trip—because of you." She smiled, a sweet, sexy kind of smile. "But I'm happiest in Mendocino." She took a sip of wine, and licked her lips. Luscious lips. Red lips.

He licked his lips, too, because they were dryer than hell.

She gazed intently at his mouth and he felt like a teenaged boy catching his first glimpse of a *Playboy* centerfold. Only Gertie was much more beautiful, and sexy because she wasn't airbrushed and she wasn't wearing makeup.

"Did I tell you I'm an artist?"

He had to take a swallow of wine before he could answer. "No."

"I have a studio that overlooks the ocean." She plucked one of the roses from the vase in the center of the table and held it close to her nose. "This smells lovely." She breezed about the room some more, sipping her wine, smelling the rose, looking far too wonderful.

"Do you like the ocean?" she asked.

"More than anyplace else."

One of her slender eyebrows rose. "You must like the prairie, too."

Okay, here's your chance to finally say something coherent. He took a deep breath and another drink of wine. "The prairie's fine, but not my preference. Actually, Sanctuary's just a temporary stop and this house is just a rental."

"Where are you going next?"

"I haven't decided yet."

She sat on the arm of the sofa, crossed one lovely leg over the other, made swirling motions with her foot. "If you love the ocean so much, why are you here?"

"I had a place in Florida, but I sold it a few years ago. I've been tailing Duncan since then. He's good company when he's around, but in the last year, he hasn't been around all that much."

"You get lonely, then?"

"Not exactly. My job keeps me busy."

"What do you do?"

"Come here and I'll show you."

His office took up nearly every square inch of the small and cramped second bedroom, leaving him barely enough room to maneuver the wheelchair, but the desk and bookshelves had been designed to meet his needs. He didn't need anything more.

Except Gertie.

He turned on the computer and listened to the hum of the CPU as it started up.

"I don't know the first thing about computers," Phoebe said from behind his chair, and he wondered if she realized that she had one hand resting on his shoulder and that her fingers were making little circles on his collarbone. God, her touch felt good.

"They're not all that tough to figure out," he told her. "I operated heavy equipment in my last life and a white-collar job was the last thing on my mind. But I needed something new to do when I got out of the hospital and people were just starting to use the Internet. I got interested, took a few classes, bought a good computer, and today I'm building Web pages."

"Show me one," she said, leaning over his shoulder now, her cheek close to his. She smelled like honeysuckle, and she made his blood rush hot through his veins.

"My business is fairly small," he told her, as graphics started appearing on the screen. "Fortunately I've got some fairly big clients who went with me when having a webpage was a new idea. They've stuck around because they like my work."

A swirl of scarlet and white appeared on the monitor while buttons cascaded down the right side. The page was too busy, but he hadn't been able to come up with a better design. "I met a lot of people while I was recovering from the accident," Graham said. "There was a guy in rehab with me who owned a candy company. How the hell we ever got on the subject of marketing is beyond me, but the next thing I knew I was having Duncan bring me all sorts of computer magazines and I was making suggestions about how this guy could grow his business. When I got out of the hospital I put together my first webpage. The guy's business has nearly doubled since then without adding much to his overhead."

"That's great," she said, brushing her cheek against his while she pointed at the screen. "Is there some way you can change the color of this swirl right here. Tone it down just a bit, and change the white to another color? Yellow maybe?"

Graham tilted his head toward her, his lips accidentally brushing her cheek. She turned, too. Their lips came a fraction of an inch from touching, and they just stared at each other for the longest time, and then she smiled and looked back at the screen.

"I don't know what kind of look you're going for, but this is too subtle."

He brought up the working copy of the page

and made some changes. "How about this?"

"The yellow's too bright. And these buttons on the side, can you change them from circles to rectangles, using the same colors that you're putting in the masthead?"

Right now he'd do anything she suggested. When they finished the page he took a long, hard look at it. "I've been agonizing over this page for the longest time because it just didn't work. I thought about trashing the entire layout, but all it needed were a couple of changes to look great. You made it look too easy."

"I like color," she said. "I like different textures and mixing things that look like they'd never go together."

"Kind of like you and me?"

She smiled. "Kind of like that."

She was still close. Her right hand had slid down his chest and her left hand held a wineglass that had long-ago been drained. He reached up and put a hand to her cheek, tilting her face from the screen to look at him. He kissed her, soft, tentative, questioning. He'd only kissed one other woman since he was seventeen years old and he felt like a schoolboy all over again, nervous, unsure.

The tip of his tongue touched hers, and she tasted of red wine and her breasts brushed against his shoulder.

And the timer went off on the oven. "Hell!"

Gertie laughed. "That bad, huh?"

"That good," he admitted. Damn good! "I didn't want to stop."

"We could skip dinner."

"We could, but then neither one of us would know if I was feeding you a line about being a good cook or if I was telling the truth."

Graham had definitely been telling the truth, Phoebe decided. The salad was one of the best she'd ever tasted, with Brie and prosciutto and extra virgin olive oil. He'd roasted a pork loin crusted with peanuts that melted in her mouth, and he served her chilled wine, treating her like a queen. She thought for sure she'd died and gone to heaven, especially when he went to the refrigerator and came back with a slice of white chocolate cheesecake swirled with raspberry sauce and topped with a sprig of mint.

"What do you think?" he asked.

"I think I'm looking forward to learning what else you do so well."

"This was an experiment. Everything to-night's an experiment." She watched his Adam's apple rise up and down in his throat, watched him reach for his wedding band, but it was gone.

"You took it off." Her words were half question, half statement.

"It was time."

"You're sure?"

"Positive. Everything you see here has been in storage for five years because I couldn't bear to look at any of it. Even the meal tonight was a menu my wife had put together for a dinner party she was going to throw if she hadn't died."

"So why did you bring it all out tonight?"

"Because Jill died, not me. Because all the crystal and china and recipes were just the things that surrounded her—they weren't the things that made me love her. Because you and I could have eaten off paper plates and had frozen pizza for dinner tonight, and we'd still be laughing and having a good time and a year from now I wouldn't remember anything but how pretty you looked and how nice you smelled and how much I enjoyed talking to you."

Phoebe hadn't cried in a very long time, but a tear slid out of the corner of her eye. Before she could wipe it away, Graham was beside her. He slid his fingers into her hair and kissed the tear from her cheek. "That's the most wonderful thing anyone has ever said to me."

"I meant every word."

He kissed her nose.

"The last man in my life just said, 'Wow,

that's cool,' and the one before said 'Groovy, baby.' No one has ever strung more than ten words together at a time."

He kissed her lips, and she couldn't remember anything feeling so gentle, so warm, so heavenly. So . . . so . . . short.

He rolled away from her, as if he'd suddenly gotten the fright of his life. This was too fast for him. He wasn't ready.

She was.

At the far end of the room sat an entertainment center and he started to sort through a stack of albums. "What do you want to hear? Let's see, we've got Beatles, Doors, Vanilla Fudge, Cream, Byrds—"

"Stop right there."

"You want to hear the Byrds?"

"I had a crush on David Crosby long before he helped form Crosby, Stills, Nash, and Young. But I never saw him until Woodstock. You know, I even tried to drag him down from the stage, but I guess he didn't go for muddy women."

Graham laughed as he put the album on the turntable. "I should invest in a CD player one of these days."

"Don't. This is much more fun."

The moment she heard the tambourine, she started to dance, slow and easy, suddenly feeling at ease. "Do you have any candles?" she asked.

"Candles, yes. Marijuana, no."

"I gave that up a long time ago, and I'm not into colored light bars anymore, either."

Graham went to the kitchen and came back with a box full of candles in all shapes and sizes.

"Perfect. Now, what about candle holders?"

"They're still packed away."

"That's okay. Plates will do just fine."

She made herself at home, singing along with the music as she took saucers from a cupboard in the kitchen and placed them all over the living room. She could feel Graham's eyes on her, watching her every move.

"Want me to light them?" he asked.

"Please. Then turn out the lights."

She poured more wine and handed a glass to Graham. "You wouldn't by any chance have any Buffalo Springfield, would you?"

"Let me guess. You had a crush on Stephen Stills, too."

"Just his voice. The way I see it, you can't get much better than the voices of Crosby, Stills, Nash, and Young. Perfect harmony."

While he sorted through albums, she took a sketchpad and charcoal pencil from her bag, grabbed two pillows from the couch, tossed them in the center of the living room floor, and sat down.

Graham put a new album on the turntable, and faced her. "Any other requests?"

Phoebe nodded. "Would you take off your shirt?"

"Excuse me?"

"Your shirt. Would you take it off?"

"Why?"

"Because you look awfully good with your shirt on and I did some really nice sketches of you the other night at the restaurant, but now I'd like to sketch what's under it."

"You can't be serious."

"I believe in being brutally honest." Except for lying about her name and Cairo's name.

"I have a few scars," Graham told her.

Phoebe took a sip of her wine. "I'm going through menopause and my breasts aren't quite as perky as they used to be."

"Are you going to show me?"

"More than likely."

Graham laughed, tugged his polo shirt from under his belt, and pulled it over his head.

"Oh, my."

"Oh, my what?"

"You look even better than I imagined."

"Candles have a unique way of deceiving the eye."

"I'm an artist and I'm not easily deceived."

"So, how do you want me to pose?"

"I don't want you to pose at all. I just want you to sit there and drink your wine."

"Can I talk?"

"That would be nice."

"Do you have a particular topic in mind?"

"Whatever makes you happy."

"You."

Phoebe looked up from her sketchpad. Graham's silvery eyes were glistening in the flickering candlelight. "Hold that pose," she said. "It's perfect. Especially your eyes."

She tried to capture what she'd seen, but drawing his eyes didn't have quite the same appeal as looking into the real thing. She'd never had so much trouble concentrating on other male models.

Graham changed albums again, and she caught the flex of muscles in his arms, the strength in his shoulders, the hint of a smile when he turned toward her and the first guitar strum of "In-A-Gadda-Da-Vida" filled the room, bringing back a thousand good memories of parties and dancing and good friends who'd all disappeared when she'd left the sixties and Haight-Ashbury behind. But listening to it now, she formed a new memory—the best she'd ever had.

She dropped her sketchpad and pencil on the floor and went to Graham. "Want to dance?"

He nodded, and she sat in his lap and felt the strength of one arm enfolding her, holding her close to his chest as she rested her cheek against his. He pushed one wheel on his chair and she could feel the rock and sway as her heart beat hard and fast.

His skin was warm, his freshly shaved face smooth, smelling like Old Spice and Irish Spring, scents she remembered from her younger days, scents that never grew old.

He kissed the hollow beneath her ear and trailed many more kisses along her jaw until he reached her lips. "Do you have any idea how good that feels?" she asked him, breathing the words into his mouth.

He took her hand and put it over his heart. "Do you feel that?"

She nodded.

"It hasn't beat that hard in an awfully long time. Not even when I'm pumping iron or playing basketball."

Phoebe took his hand from the wheel and drew it toward her. She kissed his open palm and placed it over her breast. She closed her eyes and breathed deeply, shocked that she'd forgotten how good a simple touch like that, through a bra and silk, could feel.

She wove her hands through his hair and kissed him. She liked the taste of him, the smoothness of his teeth, the way she could feel his breath against her cheek. She wanted him so badly.

His hand trailed from her breast, along her side, to her hip. She could feel her dress sliding up her leg, could feel his fingers on her thigh, inching toward the skimpy little thong she'd bought at Victoria's Secret on a lark because she knew she'd never wear it—but she was wearing it now and she was oh so glad.

Her hand slid down his chest, over his hard, washboard stomach. She clasped his belt buckle with her thumb and index finger, and let the others wander a little further south.

The kissing skidded to a halt. Phoebe felt the snap of elastic on her hip and suddenly Graham's fingers gripped her wrist, pulling her hand from his buckle.

"Is there a problem?" she asked.

"This is moving too fast," Graham stammered, plowing his fingers through his hair. "We need to go back to square one."

"I don't move backward. You can if you want, but that's not my style."

Phoebe scrambled out of his lap, grabbed her sketchpad and pencil from the floor, and shoved them into her bag.

"Where are you going?" Graham asked.

"Home."

"Why?"

She went to the door and opened it. "Because you shut me out of your life the other night and you've just done it again. Because my life might not have been as conventional as yours, but I still get hurt."

"The last thing I want to do is hurt you. But you move too fast for me. You act like it doesn't matter that I'm in a wheelchair."

"It doesn't matter at all."

"Well it bothers the hell out of me!"

"Why?"

"Because you need a man with two good legs."

Phoebe glared at him. "That's the biggest bunch of bull I've ever heard. You're the best man I've ever met, and you make me feel better than any man I've ever known. And I don't care if you have two legs, four legs, or *no* legs."

"You'd care if things went any further between us."

"Well, I guess we'll never know if I care or not, will we?"

She slammed the door and heard the needle slide across "In-A-Gadda-Da-Vida."

She stood on the front porch and started to cry because she'd been so totally foolish. No man had ever wanted to take things slow with her before. And she couldn't remember ever wanting to move so fast. Of course, she'd never been in love—until now.

Fifteen

Cairo lifted her head from Duncan's shoulder and yawned when he pulled to a stop in front of the Heavenly Haven Inn. She'd dozed fitfully for the past hour, while too many thoughts about Duncan and Dylan had rushed through her mind.

Over and over the past few days Duncan had proved his worth and she couldn't think of a good reason not to tell him about Dylan. No, that wasn't true. She had one very good reason right now. If she told him, he'd despise her all over again, and she didn't think she could handle that, not after their perfect day together.

Duncan stretched an arm behind her shoulders and tugged her close. "This is going to sound like a pretty lousy question, since you're battered and bruised, but you wouldn't consider checking out that secluded little park again, would you?"

A grin touched Cairo's lips. "Now?"

He nodded. "You don't have anything better to do, do you?"

"Sleep sounds good. So do a hot bath and a soft bed."

"You weren't quite so anxious to sleep on our wedding night."

"I hadn't been sacrificed to the gods earlier in the day, either."

He rubbed the stubble on his cheeks. "As soon as the tour of Belize is over, I think we should check out the altar again. What do you think?"

"Only if you promise to take extra lights, and"—she rubbed the back of her head "—a pillow might be nice."

"I didn't hear you complaining earlier."

She slipped her fingers into his hair and pulled his mouth close to hers. "I couldn't find one single thing to complain about."

Their lips met, and he tasted so delicious that she wanted to take him up on his offer to head for the park, but she couldn't, not tonight.

It took her a good thirty seconds to drag herself from his embrace, and another thirty seconds to regain her composure. "Thanks for bringing me back tonight," she said, tugging her baseball cap on her head. "I know you wanted me to stick around another day, but I've got so much to do for the trip that—"

"You don't need to explain, Cairo. I know what it takes to plan something half the size of what you're doing."

"You're still going with me, aren't you?"

His eyes darkened. "I made a promise, and contrary to how I handled myself five years ago, I don't break promises."

"You won't change your mind, no matter what?"

He laughed. "No matter what."

Well, that was a big relief. Of course, he had no idea what she planned to tell him tomorrow after she got a good night's sleep and worked up the courage to divulge her secret. Would he still keep his promise after that?

"You look worried about something."

Cairo shook her head. "Just thinking about the trip."

"I've been thinking about something, too." He drew in a deep breath. "I want you to come live with me after Belize."

"Here? In Sanctuary?"

He shook his head. "I don't live in Sanctuary. I live in a tent. I can get a bigger one. I could even get a trailer with a real bed, but—"

Cairo laughed. "Some men promise you diamonds. Leave it to you to promise me a trailer."

"I said I *could* get a trailer, but I prefer a tent." He wove his fingers through hers and drew them to his mouth. He pressed a soft kiss to the back of her hand. "Would you give it some thought?"

Living in a tent with Duncan was impossible. Years ago she would have lived anywhere with him, but too much had changed. She had Dylan to think of now. He needed roots and a good roof over his head. But she couldn't shake the idea completely. "I'll think about it."

He kissed her again. "Just say yes."

She smiled, reached across him and pushed open the door. "Maybe."

Duncan laughed as he climbed out of the truck and pulled her out behind him. "Think I can come up for a little while?"

"It's late," Cairo said. "It's been a long day, Phoebe's probably asleep, and I still have to make some phone calls before going to bed."

"You're a woman with too many excuses, Cairo."

He cradled her face in his hands, and when he lovingly traced her cheekbone with his thumb, she wished she had no excuses, no reason to leave him now. But tonight she had no choice.

"Put something cold on that eye," he whispered.

She'd nearly forgotten about the bruise she'd gotten in the dark. And then he kissed her tender skin, and she thought for sure it would be a hundred percent better in the morning.

"I'm going back to camp tonight, and I'm going to map out a few more tunnels in the morning. I should be back in town by eight. Have dinner with me?"

"I'll wait, no matter how late it is."

He slowly pulled away from her and rested against the truck, folding his arms casually over his chest. "Go on inside. I'll watch you till you're there."

"There's nothing to worry about here. No booby traps, no pits to fall into."

"I'll watch you just the same."

She felt loved, and it was such a good feeling that she practically skipped to the front porch. A moment later she was standing inside, watching through the lacy curtains as Duncan drove away.

The door to the Tibbettses' apartment opened and Irene peeked her head out. "Good evening, Cairo." Mrs. Tibbetts looked terribly worried, and Cairo immediately panicked, fearing something had happened to Dylan or her aunt.

"What's wrong, Irene?"

"You've got a scrape on your cheek and, goodness, is that a black eye?"

Cairo laughed, her worries behind her in an instant. "I had a rough time in a cave today. The light went out—"

"You should always take an extra light with you. I recommend two in addition to the one on your helmet. I've been caving quite a few times and I know from experience that you can never take enough precautions."

"I'll be a little more prepared next time." And I won't let a man carry me off somewhere, stark naked. No, scratch that. She probably would do that again, because she'd loved every moment of it.

"Would you like me to doctor those cuts up a bit?" Irene asked. "I've got an antiseptic lotion that should do wonders."

Before she could answer, Dylan squeezed between the doorjamb and Irene, and when he tilted his head to see her, his eyes widened in horror.

"Are you hurt, Mommy?"

She picked him up and brushed a kiss across his cheek. "I'm fine, honey. Just a few bumps and bruises."

He touched the most painful scrape on her face with his fingertips. "Does it hurt?"

"Not much. It just looks pretty ugly."

"Did someone hit you?"

"Of course not. I ran into a wall in a cave. It was a pretty silly thing to do, and I'll tell you all about it later."

Cairo peered into the Tibbettses' living room, looking for her aunt. "Is Phoebe here?"

"She had a date," Dylan said. "Some guy called her and she got all red in the face afterward. It was a hot flash because she's going through menopause—at least, that's what I heard her telling herself. She was walking around the house trying to figure out what to wear and she had a horrible headache and when her face got red she said she was sick and tired of menopause and hot flashes." Dylan paused just long enough to take a deep breath. "I figured that's what was making her face all red. I haven't looked that word up in the dictionary yet. Can you tell me how to spell it?"

"I'll tell you a little later, honey. Right now, I just want to go upstairs and soak in the tub for a little while."

Irene pinched what looked like a cookie crumb from Dylan's cheek. "Would you like us to watch him for another hour or so?" she asked. "We really do love having him here."

"I hate to impose. Besides, I haven't seen Dylan all day."

"Please, Mommy?"

"It's no trouble," Bert said, joining them in the doorway. "We were having cookies and hot chocolate and Dylan talked us into renting a copy of *The Mummy*. The credits were rolling just as you came in."

"He didn't have his rubber snake with him, did he?"

"Well, yes," Irene admitted. "And, yes, he scared me with it once or twice."

"And you still want him around?"

"Anytime," Irene told her.

Cairo decided that the Tibbettses were saints and she wished she could clone them or send them to Mendocino. Dylan had a bad habit of wearing out babysitters, yet the Tibbettses were asking for more.

Cairo kissed the chocolate stain at the corner of Dylan's mouth. "I won't be long," she said. "And when I tuck you in tonight, I'll tell you about all the wonderful things I saw in the caves."

"And I'll tell you all about the Tae Kwon Do Bert is teaching me. I also have to tell you some more about the vase I broke when I was practicing my front kick and my knife hand, but Bert said it was okay, that we didn't have to pay him a whole lot of extra money because it was really his fault for teaching me."

Cairo cringed as she looked from her son to Bert to Irene. "Was it an expensive vase?"

Irene laughed. "It was a wedding gift from my great aunt Alice. I hated it, that's why it found its way to one of the guest rooms."

"I'm going to owe you big time when we leave here," Cairo said, and Dylan wiggled from her arms and dashed back into the Tibbettses' apartment. "Thanks for watching him. I shouldn't be more than half an hour or so."

"Take your time," Irene said. "When you come back, I have some delicious chamomile tea that will help you sleep. Come in and have a cup."

"Thank you. I just might take you up on that."

Cairo started to walk away, looking forward to the bath, when Irene called out to her one more time. "Would you like to borrow some bubble bath and that antiseptic?"

"That would be lovely."

Irene disappeared in an instant and returned almost as fast. "It's vanilla and smells absolutely delightful. Use as much as you want and enjoy."

Cairo took the bubble bath and walked upstairs. She would have run, but her muscles were starting to ache, and the only thing that could possibly feel better than a nice, long soak in a tub was Duncan soaking in the tub with her.

Duncan had just hit the edge of town when he saw Cairo's backpack sticking out from under the seat. He'd been looking for a reason to go back, some way of getting close to her again and presenting her with a subtle hint that she should duck out of the Heavenly Haven Inn and run off with him to the El Dorado Motel for the night. But he hadn't come up with a good enough reason, until the backpack came into view.

It took less than five minutes for him to whip the truck around, drive across town, and park in front of the white house on Eden Lane.

Grabbing Cairo's backpack, he strolled up the walk. The curtains parted in a window downstairs and a man peered out. The owner, no doubt, probably the kind of guy who was going to make getting into Cairo's room a near impossibility. But he'd been faced with impossible situations before, and he almost always came out the winner.

Opening and closing the front door quietly, he stepped into the lobby. The man from the window was already there. The only thing missing was a shotgun.

"May I help you?" the man asked. His words sounded pleasant enough, but the look on his face said step one foot closer and you'll regret the day you were born.

"I'm a friend of Cairo McKnight," Duncan said, holding her bag in front of him. "She left her backpack in my truck. I thought she might need it tonight or in the morning."

The innkeeper held out his hand. "I'd be happy to give it to her."

"I really am a friend."

"And I really don't allow strangers to visit my guests unless the guest invites them personally, and escorts them to the room—personally."

"Could you call her."

"She's busy."

Duncan scratched the day-old growth of whiskers on his face. Let's see, he had a slash down one side of his cheek, his hands were scraped and his knuckles were bloody. His clothes were covered with dirt and he looked like he'd just escaped from a chain gang. Hell, he wouldn't let himself upstairs either.

"Could I give you a note to slip under her door?"

An attractive woman appeared at the doorway, and Duncan knew that attractive women were usually easier to persuade than men—attractive or otherwise. "Is there a problem?" she asked.

"This man wants to see Cairo."

"Why?"

"Because I'm a friend and because I really would like to return her backpack."

The woman stared at his face, and then she frowned. "Were you caving with her today?"

Duncan nodded, withdrawing his thoughts about persuading anybody. He just wasn't having much luck tonight. "Yes, I'm the one she was caving with. We're old friends."

"And you didn't take an extra flashlight with you?" She rolled her eyes. "I can't believe you'd go caving so unprepared."

"That was a mistake," Duncan admitted. He forced a smile. "I just want to see her again tonight. Isn't there some way you could let her know I'm here?"

The man eyed him up and down and he knew there was no way he was going to say yes, but the woman also eyed him up and down, and then she offered him a half-hearted smile. "She'll be down in half an hour or so for a cup of chamomile tea. You could wait for her in our apartment, if you'd like."

Finally. He stuck out his hand. "By the way, I'm Duncan Kincaid."

The man reluctantly shook it, after staring at the dirt for a moment. "I'm Mr. Tibetts, and this is my wife." Mrs. Tibbetts shook his hand and showed him inside. Mr. Tibbetts followed behind, and Duncan was sure he was being treated to the evil eye.

Duncan stood just inside the door, not knowing what else to do while he waited.

"Wouldn't you like to sit down, Mr. Kincaid?" Mrs. Tibbetts asked.

"I've been caving all day and my clothes are dirty. I'll stand, thanks."

"Would you like some coffee?"

"No, I'm fine. Thanks."

"A brownie? They're delicious."

"No, thanks."

Mrs. Tibbetts was the perfect proprietress for a bed and breakfast, friendly, gracious, and charming. Her husband, on the other hand— hell, he was just doing what he thought was right. Duncan had to give him credit for that.

"Hey, Bert, watch this." A little boy with floppy black hair came charging through a back door and came to a skidding halt in front of Mr. Tibbetts. They didn't look alike. Probably adopted, Duncan guessed.

"Okay, what do you want to show me?" Mr.

Tibbetts asked, his eyes lighting up when he knelt down to eye level with the boy.

"I've been practicing my front kick all night."

The kid wasn't all that big and he wasn't all that coordinated, but he was giving Tae Kwon Do a hell of a try.

Mrs. Tibbetts, seeming immune to the noise around her, sat on the sofa and turned down the sound on the TV. "Is that better?" she asked, looking at Duncan.

"I hadn't even noticed," Duncan told her. "Please, don't turn it down for me."

"It's no bother. It's just a rerun and I've already seen this one two or three times." She folded her hands in her lap. "Have you known Cairo a long time?"

"Ten years."

"Oh, so you really are old friends."

"Pretty old."

Mrs. Tibbetts was nice, but he found himself much more interested in watching the boy. "How long before I can break a board?" he asked Mr. Tibbetts.

"Not long, if you practice."

"I'll practice a whole lot, but I've got to be careful. My mom hates it when I break things."

Duncan laughed and the boy, who seemed to have noticed him for the first time, turned toward him. "Do you know Tae Kwon Do?"

"A little. Definitely not as much as Mr. Tibbetts."

"Bert's a third-dan black belt. That's cool, isn't it?"

"Pretty cool."

"Want to see me do my knife hand?"

Duncan raised his eyes to make sure the question met with Mr. Tibbetts's approval. Tibbetts nodded.

"All right. Let me see your stuff."

"Okay, watch carefully, because I'm really fast."

The little boy slashed to the left and slashed to the right, and then he twisted around and did a kick so high with his right leg that he jerked his left leg out from under him and landed smack on the floor.

Mr. Tibbetts came running, but Duncan got to the boy first, picking him up, smoothing his hair from his eyes. "Are you okay?"

"Yep. That's not the first time I've done that today. I guess I have to practice more."

"I guess so."

Mr. Tibbetts, looking a little dejected, walked to the sofa and sat beside his wife. A second later the kid squirmed out of Duncan's arms and ran to the couch, squeezing right in between the innkeepers.

Tibbetts wrapped his arm around the boy,

then looked at Duncan and grinned, obviously happy that the child had preferred his company to the stranger's.

Duncan, feeling like an unwelcome piece of furniture, moved across the room, standing not far from the TV, and looked at the boy again. There was something terribly familiar about him. His eyes were pale blue. His hair was black, and he had a dimple in his left cheek.

Duncan frowned. He knelt down, his scraped knees rubbing painfully against his jeans, but he gave that little thought. He was more interested in the little boy, and his pale blue eyes.

Mr. Tibbetts pulled the child into his lap. "Why don't you close your eyes, Dylan?"

Dylan? That was his grandfather's name. Dylan Kincaid begat Graham Kincaid who begat Duncan Kincaid who begat . . .

Dylan. Cairo had mentioned that name. *"He's a friend,"* she'd said, but . . .

No, it wasn't possible. It was all a coincidence. He and Cairo had been together only one night—nearly five years ago. Surely she would have let him know if she was pregnant.

Dylan yawned, rubbed his eyes and looked at Bert. "Am I going to spend the night here?"

"No. Your mom's going to get you in just a little while."

"Okay." Dylan yawned again, and snuggled his head into the innkeeper's side.

Mr. Tibbetts stared at Duncan, right straight into his eyes, and then he looked at Dylan as if he'd just recognized the same thing Duncan had.

Same hair color. Same pale blue eyes, the color of eyes he'd never seen before—except in his father.

Rage welled inside him. Pure blind fury.

He might have been an irresponsible fool five years ago, but Cairo had kept his son from him. He'd missed nearly five years of the little boy's life. *His son's life.*

Damn you, Cairo. How could you do that to me?

Sixteen

Cairo combed the tangles out of her freshly washed hair and twisted it into a bun on the back of her head. The bathroom smelled like vanilla, a scent she'd loved since she was little, when Phoebe taught her how to bake. A woman couldn't bake very many tasty items—like peanut butter cookies—living in a tent. It wasn't the most promising environment for a gifted child, either.

There was just too much to think about, so she decided to put her thinking off until tomorrow.

She dabbed antiseptic on her toes, her knees, her hips, elbows, the heels of her hands, and finally her face. By late tomorrow she'd be one big scab, but every abrasion had been worth it.

She walked into the bedroom and stretched, feeling the pull in her muscles. Wouldn't it be nice to have a massage? she thought. Duncan had always been good at giving a massage, his big hands working out the kinks in her shoulders and calves.

Maybe tomorrow night, if everything went well when she told him about Dylan.

She slipped into her best Mickey Mouse PJ's and wrapped up in her Winnie the Pooh robe, things Dylan had insisted she buy when she took him to Disneyland a few months before, and headed down the stairs. Mrs. Tibbetts' chamomile tea would have to wait for another night. She planned to pick up her little boy, settle him down all comfortable and snug in his bed, then climb into her own to spend some quality time dreaming about Duncan.

She knocked lightly on the Tibbettses' door. Inside she could hear footsteps, she saw the knob turn, and the door opened. Dylan hung like a limp teddy bear over Bert's shoulder, his eyes closed, his long black lashes lying sleepily against his skin.

"Thank you so much for watching him," she whispered. "Would you mind putting the babysitting charge on my bill?"

"There's no charge," Bert said, as Cairo gent-

ly pulled Dylan into her arms. His head flopped
down hard on her shoulder and he nestled his
head against her neck. "By the way, a friend of
yours is here to see you."

Duncan stepped into view, and she felt like
the earth had dropped out from under her. His
face was hard with anger, red with rage.

"Hello, Cairo." All the love that had been in
his voice an hour ago had been wiped away in
mere minutes. She no longer needed to worry
how he'd react when she told him about Dylan.

"Hello." There was no way she could work
any humor into her voice. This wasn't the time
for fun and games. "I wasn't expecting you
back tonight."

"You left your backpack in the truck. I
wanted to return it."

She reached for the bag, but Duncan held on
tight. "I'll carry it for you. You've got your arms
full with . . . your son."

Mr. Tibbetts gave her a questioning look, ap-
parently bothered by the tone of Duncan's
voice. "Is everything all right?"

"It's fine," she said, working up a smile.
"Thanks again for watching Dylan."

"You're welcome." Duncan stepped into the
lobby and Bert started to close the door. "If
there's anything we can do, just holler."

"I will. Thanks."

"Goodnight, now."

The door finally closed, and she felt totally alone, with all her guilt closing in on her.

The climb up the stairs seemed to take a lifetime, especially with Duncan behind her, his steps heavy on the uncarpeted stairs. He knew the truth and he'd found out about his son all on his own. He was angry, and she couldn't blame him.

Oh, God, why hadn't she told him before?

Duncan opened the door when she reached her room, and he stepped in behind her. She could hear the door closing, locking, when she carried Dylan into the bedroom they shared. She laid him down softly on one of the twin beds.

She was afraid to look away from her son, afraid to see the hate in Duncan's eyes, when there'd been so much love in them earlier in the day. She started to unbutton Dylan's shirt, then saw Duncan's hands on the boy's belt, loosening it, opening the zipper, and gently removing the tiny pair of jeans. It seemed as if he'd done the same thing a thousand times before, but she knew he hadn't, because she'd never given him the chance.

Once Dylan's pajamas were on, Cairo stood back and let Duncan tuck him in. He pulled the sheet and blanket up to Dylan's neck and caressed an errant lock of baby-soft black hair away from his forehead. His hands looked so big next to Dylan's face, so big and steady and nurturing.

Standing up, he watched Dylan for the longest time, a warm, loving smile on his face. When he turned, she wasn't prepared for the expression on his face.

He despised her.

He walked out of the room and Cairo waited behind, waited for her heart to cease its heavy, rapid beat. She sat on the edge of the bed for a minute, watching her son—their son—sleep. His hair was damp at the back of his ears, his cheeks were cool and pink, and he looked so sweet and innocent. She didn't want him hurt, but she realized she'd hurt him tremendously by keeping him away from his dad.

She smoothed the sheet and blanket over his chest and kissed his forehead. "I love you," she whispered, and then she went into the other room, to face the other man in her life.

Duncan sat on the sofa, knees spread wide with his elbows resting on top. He held one of Dylan's drawings in his hand. "What's this?" he asked.

Cairo sat down across from him and took a quick peek. "Dylan likes to draw pictures of his father. That's just one of many."

Duncan studied the colorful picture. "He's in the jungle, chopping down sky-high ferns with a machete."

"That's because he's lost."

"Is that what Dylan thinks? That his father's lost in some goddamn jungle somewhere?"

Cairo nodded. "I had to tell him something."

"Do you lie to your son about everything?"

"Of course not."

"What about me? Were you going to lie to me if I met Dylan. Try to feed me a goddamn tale about a one-night stand between you and some jungle hero?"

"No." She fought for words but nothing would come.

"Then tell me the truth right now, Cairo. He's my son, isn't he?"

"Yes!"

He sat motionless for the longest time, doing absolutely nothing but glaring, making Cairo wish she could go back and keep this mistake from happening.

Duncan dragged in a deep breath and let it out slowly. He was angry and trying to control his emotions. She wished she'd told him back in the cavern so he could have yelled and screamed and gotten it all out of his system before now.

He rubbed the throbbing in his temple.

"When were you planning to inform me of this little miracle we created?"

"Tomorrow night."

Duncan laughed. "Tomorrow, huh? Why didn't you do it today? Why didn't you do it last night? Why in God's name didn't you do it at some point in the last five years?"

"I tried to tell you."

"When?"

"The other night when I asked you if you'd thought about having a family. But you turned everything around. You thought I wanted you to donate sperm."

"If you'd wanted to tell me badly enough, you would have made me listen. But you didn't. You just let me go on and on, because that was easier than telling me the truth."

"Don't throw all this back on me."

"Why the hell not?" The words seethed through nearly clenched teeth, anger radiating in each syllable.

Cairo knew her words wouldn't appease him, but she spoke them anyway. "Because if you hadn't left me, if you'd lived up to your responsibilities of having a wife, I wouldn't have kept him a secret. But you had better things to do, like running off on some big adventure."

"I told you I was coming back and I would have, but I was in a goddamned jail."

"That was just one more reason for not trusting you."

"You never gave me the chance to explain. Instead, you went out and got a high-priced attorney to annul our marriage—without my permission." He laughed cynically. "Damn it, Cairo, since when can a pregnant woman get an annulment?"

"I didn't know I was pregnant till it was all over and done with. As for getting the annulment before that, all I needed was a good enough reason."

"Yeah, I read all about it in the annulment papers. Let's see, my reasons for marrying you were fraudulent. I wanted your money. You didn't *have* any money and your parents weren't about to give either you *or* me a penny."

"It was an easy way to get out of a bad marriage. I didn't put a lot of thought into it."

"The way I see it, you haven't put much thought into anything for the last five years."

"You have no idea what the last five years have been like for me."

He frowned, his look hateful. "I wasn't given the chance to know what the last five years were like for you! You didn't give me a chance to see my son being born. You didn't give me the opportunity to see him take his first steps, or hear his first words? Maybe I would have liked to teach him Tae Kwon Do or how to ride a goddamned bike."

She stared down at the rug, the swirls of color mixing together into one big ugly mess.

Duncan ran his fingers through his hair and leaned back in the chair, staring at the ceiling. He got up and paced the room, back and forth, back and forth, to the point where she thought she'd go mad.

"Let me get this straight," he said, standing directly in front of her. "You got your feelings hurt so, in retaliation, you got an annulment, you didn't tell me you were pregnant, and then you kept my son—*my* son, Cairo—a secret from me."

"It wasn't retaliation."

"Then what the hell was it?"

A tear escaped from the corner of her eye. She didn't want to cry. She just wanted this whole thing to be over and for Duncan to say he loved her in spite of all she'd done. But she knew that wasn't going to happen. What they'd shared to-day was over. They weren't going to get that back.

"Answer me, Cairo. Why, for God's sake, did you keep me away from that little boy in there?"

"Because I was afraid you'd be the same kind of parent that mine had been to me."

He was silent a moment. Maybe what she'd said would make him understand. But sadly, the anger didn't leave his eyes.

"Have you forgotten that I was there for you when your parents weren't?"

"No."

"Then how could you think I'd be like them? How could you think I'd ignore my own child?"

"Because you ignored me when I needed you the most." A tear raced down her cheek and she wiped it away with the back of her hand. "I didn't want Dylan to have a father—like you— who gallivanted around from country to country. I didn't want you to drop by our place in Mendocino for a day or two just to say hi, to maybe give Dylan a trinket from some foreign country, pat him on the head and ask if he'd been a good little boy for the last year, then leave again on some other stupid expedition."

Duncan stared at her in total disbelief. She wiped even more tears from her eyes with the backs of her hands. Still he said nothing.

He picked up Dylan's treasure box. "Does this belong to Dylan?"

She nodded.

He opened the lid and pushed the items inside around with his index finger. "Are these trinkets what *you* give him when you come back from your tours?"

Anger ripped through her. "Don't accuse me of being a bad mother."

"I've been prejudged. Why shouldn't I have the privilege of doing the same thing to you?"

"You can think anything you want of me, Duncan. I just want you to know that I did what I felt was best for Dylan."

"Best for Dylan . . . or for you?"

"For Dylan."

He laughed and dropped the lid on Dylan's treasure box. "Is my name on Dylan's birth certificate?"

Oh, God, she didn't want to answer that question. If she told him, he'd have every right in the world to Dylan, and she didn't want to give him that.

"Answer me, Cairo."

"Yes! Your name's on his birth certificate."

"Good." He got up from the sofa and walked to the door. "I'll be here at eight o'clock tomorrow morning. I'm taking my son."

"Like hell you are."

"You've had him for five years. I want him for at least the next few days."

"He doesn't know you."

"It's about time he got to know me."

"Then you can do it here. Or you can come to Mendocino and visit him."

"And be a part-time dad? I don't think so. I wasn't raised that way, and I don't intend for my son to spend the rest of his childhood being raised that way."

"You can't just take him, not without him knowing the truth."

"Okay, I'll be here at eight A.M. and you can tell him the truth while we're having breakfast together. Then I'm taking him back to my camp."

"You're not going to take him down in that cave. I won't let you."

"You're not going to stop me, Cairo. That expedition is part of my life, and Dylan's going to become part of my life, too. I don't plan on separating work and family."

"And I'm not going to let you separate him from me."

His next words were calm and spoken with total certainty. "You don't have any choice."

"Yes, I do," she threw back. "I'm going to the cave with you."

She watched the muscles tense in his jaws. "I'll be here at eight, Cairo. Don't run off before I get here, because trust me, if you try to hide my son from me ever again, I'll hunt you down to the ends of the earth, and when I find you, I'll make sure that child becomes mine . . . permanently."

Seventeen

Cairo lay next to Dylan, wrapping her arms around his little body as warm, salty tears flowed freely from her eyes. She couldn't lose him—not now, not ever.

Across the room she heard the door open and saw a stream of light slip over the bed and across Dylan's face. She heard Phoebe's familiar footsteps and felt her comforting hand touch her shoulder, something she'd done many times in the past twenty-six years. She always seemed to be there when Cairo needed her. She was so glad she was here now.

She slipped her fingers over Phoebe's, as if touching them would give her the solace she needed.

But relief didn't come.

Cairo slipped out of Dylan's bed and pulled Phoebe with her out of the room. She closed Dylan's door and started crying all over again.

Phoebe grabbed a tissue and dabbed at Cairo's eyes, then tucked it into her hand.

She picked up a piece of construction paper that had floated to the floor and put it on the coffee table. The movement seemed so normal, but there was nothing at all normal about what was going on right now.

"I saw Duncan outside," Phoebe said.

Cairo curled up in a chair and blew her nose. "Did he say anything to you?"

"No, not a word, but he didn't have to. The moment I saw the anger—and sadness—in his eyes, I knew what had happened."

"He hates me."

Phoebe sat on the coffee table and leaned forward, taking hold of Cairo's hands. "He'll get over it."

"I don't think so, and I don't think he should. I made a mistake, Phoebe. You've told me for years that I was wrong, but I wouldn't listen."

"We all make mistakes, but what happened is in the past and now you've got to move on."

Cairo sniffed back a tear, but it didn't do a bit of good. "He wants to take Dylan away from me."

"That's anger talking."

"What if it isn't anger? What if he tries?"

"You deal with that when it happens. You can't dwell on it now, Cairo. Duncan's hurt, and you should know better than anyone what a person will do or say when they're hurt."

"I'm not going to let him take my son away from me. I'll fight, Phoebe . . . I'll take him to court. I'll run away, if I have to."

"All that will do is perpetuate the problem. What you have to do is talk—when you can do it calmly and reasonably. Tonight wasn't the time for that."

Somehow Cairo managed to work up a smile. "Duncan told me he was taking Dylan back to the caves and I told him I'm going, too."

"Good, then I can have some peace and quiet for a little while."

Cairo studied her aunt's face, saw a touch of sadness behind her sparkling eyes. "Is everything okay? I've been so wrapped up in my troubles that I haven't thought about you. Did you see Graham tonight?"

"I saw him."

"And was it good?"

"It was very good. And then it ended very abruptly."

"I'm sorry."

"Don't be. I have every intention of getting

back together with him. In fact, I've decided I don't want white or off-white for my wedding dress. I'm going to go with red."

"Oh, Phoebe." Cairo threw her arms around her aunt. "I love you so much."

"I love you, too, Cairo. I've seen you go through some pretty tough times, and you've always come out on top. You're going to come out on top this time, too. I have all the faith in the world."

"I've got some great news for you, Dad."

Graham looked up from the computer screen that he'd been staring at for over an hour, and took the beer Duncan held out to him. "I could use some great news."

Duncan sat in the chair next to Graham's desk, and frowned. "Something wrong?"

"Nothing that I need to talk about." He took a drink of beer and turned his chair so he could face his son. "You look like you got beat up in a barroom brawl."

"More like a pitch black cave, and after that, I got kicked in the gut by a woman—the same woman who kicked me in the gut five years ago."

"Cairo?"

"You remember her name?"

"How could I forget. You spent two years

cussing her out and the last three years wishing she'd come back to you. What happened? Did she come back?"

"Oh, yeah. She brought me a present, too." Duncan stared at the beer can, his eyes dark and brooding. "Guess what, Dad. You're a grandfather."

Graham knew he'd misheard something. "What?"

"You've got a grandson. Not only that, but I'm a dad. In fact, I've been a dad for over four years, and I just found out tonight."

Duncan was trying to make it sound light, but Graham could see the pain in his face. "Why is she only telling you now?"

"I don't know. She gave me some big old song and dance about being afraid that I'd be a lousy dad, thinking I was an irresponsible adventurer."

"The entire archaeological community thinks that."

If Graham didn't know better, he could have sworn that Duncan wanted to hit him. Instead, Duncan downed the rest of his beer and crushed the empty can in his hand. "You're right. I don't have a lot of credibility."

"I didn't say that. You're good at what you do, Duncan, and you're honest about what you're doing. You've discovered things other archaeologists would give their own kidneys to find, and then you've handed everything over to one museum or another and refused to take any payment. I don't know anyone else who would do that."

"Yeah, well maybe if I'd been a little more selfish in that department I'd have some money in the bank and a son who actually knows I'm his dad."

"If you lived by someone else's rules, you'd be miserable. What kind of dad would you have been then?"

"I don't know. I wish I'd had a chance to find out."

"Are you going to have that chance now?"

"I'm taking that chance. I'm taking Dylan and Cairo to camp with me tomorrow morning."

Dylan. Graham repeated the name over and over in his mind. "Did you say Dylan?"

"Cairo gave him Grandpa's name. Can you believe that?"

"Cute kid?" Graham asked. "Black hair? Light blue eyes?"

"Yeah."

"Does he think his dad is lost in the Amazon?"

Duncan frowned. "Have you met him?"

"I think so. Is he staying with someone named Gertrude?"

"No. He's with Cairo and her Aunt Phoebe, at the Heavenly Haven Inn."

Graham laughed. "This Phoebe, does she look like a hippie? Curly blond hair? Green eyes."

"I don't know about the eye color, but curly, blond, and hippie sound about right. Why? Do you know her?"

Graham grinned, shaking his head. "I know her, all right. In fact, you're not the only one who got kicked in the gut tonight."

Duncan tilted his beer to his mouth and took a long drink. "What do you say we get drunk and forget all about women?"

Graham put his own beer on the corner of his desk and studied his son's face. It had been years since he'd seen so much torment in Duncan's eyes, and he didn't like seeing it now. "You know I'm not the kind of man to interfere, but how long are you and Cairo going to go on punishing each other?"

"She kept my son a secret. Do you think I should laugh that off?"

"I didn't say that." Graham rubbed the back of his neck, searching for the appropriate words. "I just think you should put yourself in her shoes for awhile, try to understand what was going through her mind when you left her, when you landed in jail."

"I've thought about all that. Yeah, I was wrong, But—"

"Don't make any more excuses, Duncan. Put it behind you and move on because if you don't, you and Cairo are both going to be hurt. If that's not bad enough, you're going to hurt your son, and I don't think either you or Cairo want to do that."

Eighteen

Cairo stood at the bedroom window looking down at the street. Ten more minutes. That's all she had.

Clouds hung heavy in the sky and it felt like all of her troubles were closing in on her. Somehow she had to make Duncan see reason, talk him into taking just occasional visitation rights, so Dylan wouldn't feel like he was being shuttled from family to family, one place to another. No, he'd never agree to that, and she knew she wouldn't ask him to. She'd already taken enough from Duncan. It was time for her to give a little back.

She dropped the curtains and went back to packing for the trip, keeping an eye on her son as he sat on the bedroom floor, struggling to tie his tennis shoes.

Cairo shoved extra clothes for Dylan into her backpack, along with some granola bars and cookies. When she was through, she walked across the room and sat crosslegged on the floor in front of him. "Want some help with that?"

"No, I'm big enough to do it on my own now." He fumbled some more, blew a lock of hair from his eyes, and kept on fumbling. "Where are we going?"

"On the biggest adventure of your lifetime. Mine too."

"Is Aunt Phoebe going with us?"

"No, honey. Aunt Phoebe's not going this time."

"Are we going to Belize? Aunt Phoebe said she'd go anywhere with me—but not there. She says it's humid and hot and that she hates the jungle because it makes her hair all frizzy, but I really think I'd like it there."

"You probably will like it there—when you're bigger. But today we're going caving."

"I thought I had to be bigger to do that, too."

Her eyes traveled from his untied tennis shoes to the top of his head. "You're getting bigger every day, and today you've hit the jack-pot—which means you get to go crawling through some deep, dark, mysterious caves."

"Cool. I bet I got bigger because I learned Tae Kwon Do."

"I'm sure that helped a lot."

"Since I'm bigger now and since I'm going with you, I suppose I should remind you to take extra flashlights. Irene says you should always be prepared for the worst."

"I've already put extra flashlights in my bag, not to mention plenty of rope, reflective tape, and an emergency kit. I've also given Aunt Phoebe and Mr. and Mrs. Tibbetts instructions on how to find us if we're not back in two days."

Dylan stopped fumbling with his shoestrings. His sweet blue eyes narrowed. "We're not going to get lost are we?"

"No, honey. I'm just taking precautions."

He let out a huge sigh of relief. "Good, because I think that would be scary. Sometimes I think my daddy's got to be awfully scared out there in the jungle."

This is your opening, Cairo. Just jump in with both feet.

"Come here." She held out her hands and Dylan gave up on his shoestrings to crawl into her lap. One of these days, far too soon, he'd be too big for her to cuddle this way, and she was going to miss the closeness.

Holding him near, she combed her fingers

through his hair, and tried to push from her mind all thoughts about losing him.

"I have some really special news to tell you."

He tilted his face up to look at her. "You do?"

"Probably the best news of your whole entire life." She took a breath, calming her fears. "Your daddy's not lost anymore."

"Did someone rescue him?" His voice was so calm it almost didn't seem real, as if he'd heard her words but hadn't yet absorbed them.

"He found his own way out of the jungle, because he's big and brave and because he wanted to see you so badly that he just kept hacking away at the brush until he was able to escape."

Dylan stared at his shoes, not saying a thing, and Cairo wished she knew what was going through his young little mind. When he looked up, his eyes were red, on the fringe of tears.

"He wasn't really lost in the jungle, was he, Mommy?"

"What makes you say that?"

"My friend Tommy said you were probably making that up. He said you and Daddy probably got divorced, or that you'd never been married, and you just didn't want me to know." His little eyes narrowed into a frown. "Is that true?"

She had to tell him the truth sometime. The

lie couldn't go on forever. "Your daddy and I *were* married, and we loved each other very much, but . . ." She sighed deeply, wondering if she was making a mistake telling him the truth. When she thought of how her secret had destroyed her new relationship with Duncan, she realized the same thing could eventually happen with Dylan. She had to tell him now. "Things just didn't work out between your father and I. He wanted to travel around the world, and, well, I didn't."

"Didn't he want to see me?"

This was the hardest part of all. "He didn't know about you."

"Why?"

"Because . . . because I never told him about you."

Tears formed at the corners of Dylan's eyes. "Why?"

"For a lot of reasons that probably wouldn't make sense to you, but mostly because I was afraid he wouldn't be a good enough father. I was afraid he might take you away from me. But I know now that that's not true. Your father's a good man, Dylan. He's going to love you very much."

A lone tear slipped from Cairo's eye and Dylan reached up and wiped it away. "Don't cry, Mommy." He wrapped his arms around her neck and held on tight. "I'm not going to leave you. Not ever."

Cairo let the tears fall, until the knock at the door made her jump. Her nerves felt like they'd caught on fire, and she wanted to keep hugging Dylan, afraid, in spite of what he'd said, that he *would* leave her.

The knock came again, and she wiped the salty tears from her eyes. "That's your father," she whispered. "Would you like to answer the door?"

He looked a little frightened, but he nodded, pushed out of her lap, and walked toward the door. He had on a Tarzan sweatshirt and blue jeans that were a size too big. His pant legs were rolled up at the bottom and his shoelaces trailed along behind him. He looked little and precious and she loved him so much.

She stood just outside the bedroom and watched him reach for the doorknob. Slowly, he turned around. His sweet blue eyes sparkled with tears, but somehow he managed to smile, and her heart nearly melted.

And then he opened the door.

Duncan stood in the doorway. From where she stood she could see that his eyes were just as red as Dylan's. He looked down at his son, and she watched his throat work convulsively. His broad shoulders filled the doorway. He was wearing rugged-soled boots, blue jeans and a tan-colored shirt that made him look every bit the hero—a hero who was about to crumble in the face of a four-year-old.

He took a deep breath. "Good morning, Dylan."

Dylan's gaze fastened on the deep scratch and bruised cheekbone on Duncan's face. He didn't move. He didn't say a word.

Duncan reached out to touch his son, and the child bolted, running toward Cairo. He threw his arms around her legs.

Cairo knelt down and gripped his shoulders lovingly. Tears had slipped from his eyes and she kissed them away. "Don't forget what I told you, pumpkin. He loves you, and he wants a chance to show you how much."

"How can he love me? He doesn't even know me."

"You're his son. He'll love you no matter what."

Dylan twisted around and looked at his dad, who'd moved into the room and closed the door. His thumbs were hitched in the back pockets of his jeans, and he made an attempt to smile.

"Why didn't you tell me you were my daddy?" Dylan asked, still standing in the shelter of Cairo's arms.

Duncan looked to Cairo for an answer.

"He wasn't absolutely sure you were his son," Cairo said, and suddenly found it difficult to say anything more.

"I *hoped* you were my son," Duncan added. "I was gone a long time, and I had no idea what you looked like."

"I know you weren't lost in the jungle, so you don't have to tell me a story. My mommy told me everything."

"Did she tell you how much I wanted to get to know you?"

Dylan nodded, and Duncan walked across the room, sitting down on the sofa, right next to the table that held Dylan's treasure box. "I brought you a little something."

Dylan looked up at Cairo, as if seeking permission to accept something from a stranger, and she nodded him toward his dad.

Standing on the other side of the table, he watched Duncan pull something from his pocket. "When I was little, not much older than you, my dad gave me a silver dollar for good luck. It's a tradition in the Kincaid family." Duncan reached across the table and took Dylan's right hand. He pressed a coin into his palm. "This is the one he gave to me. I've carried it in my pocket for nearly thirty years. It's yours now."

Dylan studied the coin, turning it over and over in his hand, and then he tucked it into his pocket. "Thank you."

"You're welcome."

"Would you like to see my treasure box?"

"Sure."

Dylan worked his way toward his dad, and standing close to his knee he pulled his shell-coated box to the edge of the table. "I have a whole lot of things in here that are really special," he said, opening the lid. "This is a nautilus and it's about ten million years old, and this is a fish fossil. It's not quite that old, but close. And this is a feather from my parrot, Zorro. I couldn't bring him with us on this trip because he likes to get me in trouble."

Dylan plucked the feather from the box and held it out to Duncan. "Would you like Zorro's feather?"

Nodding, Duncan took the feather and tucked it into his shirt pocket.

Cairo watched the play of emotions on Duncan's face. She could almost feel his need to take Dylan into his arms and squeeze him tight, but he was holding back, waiting for Dylan to feel that closeness that would only come with time.

"Have you ever been in a cave?" Duncan asked his son.

"No. My mom's sort of particular about what

she'll let me do and what she won't let me do. She's afraid I'll get hurt, but now that Bert has taught me Tae Kwon Do, I think I can take care of myself."

Duncan laughed, which eased some of Cairo's tension.

"Moms have a habit of being a little over-protective at times."

"I can spell that. O-V-E-R-P-R-O-T-E-C-T-I-V-E. I get to learn a new word every day. Aunt Phoebe taught me that one when Mommy wouldn't let me get a science kit."

"Maybe she was afraid you'd accidentally blow up the house."

"I wouldn't blow up the house, but even if I did, the fire department would come real fast because they already know how to get to our house."

"I take it they've been there a lot."

"Well . . . yes. It was Zorro's fault the last time. He's really not bad, he just likes to goof off sometimes. When you come to Mendocino you can meet him."

Cairo hadn't expected that comment. She wanted to say something so Dylan wouldn't get his hopes up too high, but she stayed silent. There were too many details to work out in this new relationship, and all of them would take time.

"My friend Tommy said that he didn't think I had a real dad, but now I can introduce you to him. Boy, is he going to be surprised!"

Duncan shot Cairo a glance over the top of Dylan's head, warning her not to say a word. It was easy to see the workings of Dylan's mind. He had visions of a big family, one where everyone lived together—happily—and they didn't want to take that away from him now.

Dylan moved a little closer to Duncan, putting a hand on his knee. "When are we going to the cave?"

"Now, if you and your mom are ready."

"I'm ready now." Dylan ran across the room and grabbed the heavy bag Cairo had packed for him. He couldn't budge it from the floor, but he made an effort to impress his dad. "Irene—that's Mrs. Tibbetts, you met her last night—gave me a helmet when we told her we were going caving. And she gave me knee pads and elbow pads and a canteen. I think she's being a little overprotective, even though she isn't my mom."

"She just wants to keep you safe," Duncan said. "We all do."

"Okay, well, I'm ready if you're ready."

Dylan dragged the bag across the living room floor while Cairo walked into the bedroom to get her things. She was surprised when she turned around and Duncan stood behind her.

"Thank you for telling him," he said. His eyes were swollen and tired, and she knew that he hadn't slept any more than she had.

"I wasn't going to tell him everything, but I did." She moved toward him and put her hand on his arm, but he pulled away. "I'm sorry for not telling you about Dylan. I was wrong."

"That's history and I'm not going to dwell on it. We have to think about what's best for Dylan now."

"I do that every minute of every day, and I know you'll do it from now on, too. But what about you and me? Can we talk about what's happened, try to get back what we had?"

"I don't know, Cairo." He hoisted the handle of her bag over his shoulder and looked at her with cold, hurt eyes. "I just don't know."

The rain came down in torrents, making it impossible to get to the cave, which was probably the best thing, because Cairo was in no hurry to return to the place where she and Duncan had shared so many happy moments.

Unfortunately, the rain forced them to huddle inside the ten-by-ten tent, where all she could hear was the steady drum of rain on the canvas and the laughter between Duncan and Dylan as they played poker.

She rested on Duncan's cot, staring off and on at the top of the tent and part of the time at the book in her hands. It was an adventure story, something Duncan had dug out of his foot locker. She preferred mystery or romance, but the story was vivid, and it helped her while away the hours.

"Full house," Dylan declared, laying down three jacks and two queens.

Duncan slapped down his own less-than-impressive hand. "How long did you say you've been playing this game?"

Dylan giggled. "You just taught me." He swept the pile of wooden matches from the center of the floor and added them to his growing pile. "Deal again."

"Haven't you had about enough?" Cairo asked, rolling onto her side.

"Just a few more hands. Daddy's still got some matchsticks left, and I really think they should all be mine."

"Okay," she agreed, marveling at the ease with which Dylan had started to call Duncan Daddy. "Five more hands, then you and I switch places, and *you* go to sleep."

"Do I have to?"

Duncan ruffled Dylan's hair. "Yeah, you have to."

"All right."

Duncan dealt five cards to each of them. Dylan had a little trouble getting the cards fanned out, but he had no trouble at all determining what kind of hand he had, what his odds were of drawing the cards he needed, and he seemed to be able to count cards, too. This wasn't exactly how she wanted him to use his gifts, but he was having fun, Duncan was smiling, and everyone seemed happy . . . on the surface. Just like the perfect family.

"Call," Duncan said, when he had just one matchstick left.

"Okay." Dylan laid down a royal flush. "I think this is the best you can get."

Duncan threw his cards up in the air, watched Dylan scoop up the pot, then fell backward on the floor. "I can't believe I've been beaten by a four-year-old."

Dylan climbed across the tent and plopped down on Duncan's stomach. "Would you like me to let you win next time?"

Duncan folded his arms behind his head. "Next time we're playing Fish. Forget this poker stuff. It's much too expensive for my blood." He pulled Dylan against him and hugged him tight. "Now, off to bed with you."

"Can I sleep in my clothes?"

"Everything but your boots," Cairo told him, climbing out of the cot and tucking him under the blankets. She kissed his forehead. "Close your eyes and get some sleep."

Dylan rubbed his eyes and tucked his hands under his cheek. "Are you and Daddy going to play cards now?"

"Maybe."

"How come you two don't talk to each other? My friend Jason's mom and dad talk to each other all the time. They hold hands, too, and Jason said they even sleep in the same bed. I kind of get the feeling that's what moms and dads are supposed to do."

"Jason's mom and dad are married."

"How come you two aren't married?"

"We were, a long time ago," Duncan answered.

"Are you going to get married again?"

Cairo had no idea what to say, but Duncan sat up and tucked the blanket tighter around Dylan's neck. "Your mom and I have a lot of things to talk about. We haven't seen each other in a long time, and we don't know what's going to happen between us."

"Will you at least talk about it?"

Cairo watched Duncan smile. "We've got a long list of things to talk about. Maybe we'll add that to it."

"Okay." He seemed appeased for the moment, and rolled over. Cairo concentrated on her book and Duncan played solitaire until they heard Dylan's light, steady breathing.

"He's fallen in love with you," Cairo said, staring at the blurred lines in her book.

"Does that bother you?"

"A little."

"Why? Because you want him all for yourself?"

His comment angered her. "If I'd wanted that, I never would have come to Montana to look for you."

"If you'd come here because you thought I should have a place in Dylan's life, why the hell did you come up with some cock-and-bull story about needing me to go to Belize?"

"That's not a story. That's true. I told you about the crash. I told you my business was failing, and if that happens, I lose everything I've invested, and then I don't have money for special schooling, or clothes, or anything else for Dylan."

"You're not going to foot the bill for everything anymore, Cairo. He's my responsibility, too. As for Belize—"

"You're not going to back out on me, are you?"

"I can't think of any reason to go, except that I promised. I told you I'd go, and I meant it."

He swept the cards up from the tent floor and

shoved them into their box. "One of these days we're going to have to talk about custody. I don't want just occasional visitation rights."

"I don't want to think about that now."

"I've been thinking about it since last night, ever since I found out I have a son. I have a lot of lost time to make up, and I want him to live with me."

These were words she didn't want to hear. "You'd really take him away from me?"

"Not permanently. Just six months, maybe a year, to begin with. I want him to travel with me, get to know his grandfather."

"I can't let him go that long."

"We can go to court over this, Cairo, and I'd probably stand a good chance of winning. It's not like I've been a derelict dad, someone who abandoned his kid. The only reason I've been out of his life is because I didn't know he existed. At least you were kind enough to put my name on his birth certificate."

Her head hurt from the tension she'd felt all day, tension that was growing stronger by the moment. "I don't want to go to court, Duncan. I can't afford it, and I don't want to drag Dylan through something messy."

He didn't say a thing. Instead, he grabbed a book from his foot locker and laid down on his sleeping bag. "We'll talk about custody when we get back to Sanctuary," he said, staring at the unopened paperback. "I'm sure we can come up with something to make me happy. Nothing's going to make up for five lost years, but I plan on getting a big chunk of the next five, and all the years after that."

Cairo was wide awake, worried about losing her son, fearing Duncan would despise her forever, when headlights flashed across the tent. She jerked up in the sleeping bag at the same time Duncan sat up in his. "Did you see that?" she asked.

"Yeah." He threw back the top cover and peeked through the tent flap. "There's a truck out there."

"What are you going to do?"

"Nothing, unless they get out of the cab and start snooping around."

She crouched next to Duncan and looked out into the night. It had stopped raining, but the clouds were still heavy in the sky. The headlights had been dimmed, and the vehicle sat there for the longest time. Then two men—no, definitely two teenagers—got out, closing the doors quietly. A moment later a roll of toilet paper was launched across Duncan's truck.

"That does it." Duncan pulled on his boots.

"I'm gonna see what the hell those guys think they're doing."

"I'm going too."

Duncan gave her a withering glare. "Stay here, Cairo. Someone's got to watch Dylan."

His gait was heavy, his stride long as he marched through the mud toward his truck. "What the hell's going on?"

One of the guys giggled. "Oops!"

Cairo couldn't help but laugh when Duncan grabbed the boys by the collars. "Don't you have anything better to do than TPing someone's camp?"

"It's summertime. Ain't nothin' else to do."

"You've been drinking, haven't you?"

"One or two beers, that's all."

"How old are you?"

"Twenty-one," they answered in unison.

Duncan pulled their collars up so high it looked like the boys were going to choke. "How old?"

"Sixteen."

"Do your parents know you're out here?"

"What do you think?"

"That you've been out here far too much recently."

"It's a free country, mister."

"You think that gives you the right to mess up my place?"

They just looked at each other and laughed.

"I should haul your sorry butts back to town right now. Ever been in jail?" Duncan asked, his voice filled with anger. "Well, I can tell you what it feels like. It feels like shit. Is that what you want?"

"We didn't do nothing wrong."

"You TPd my camp and I'm getting tired of cleaning up the crap." He shoved both of them toward his truck. "You can clean it up this time."

One of the boys looked at him, teetered a little, then got a silly grin on his face. "You're supposed to laugh about it."

"The first time's funny. The second time's a pain in the butt. The third time makes me angry. We're on the fifth, and I don't think you want to find out just how mad I really am. Now get your butts in gear and clean up that toilet paper."

Duncan opened the door to their truck, pulled out the keys, and grabbed a sixpack.

"Hey, what you doing with our stuff?"

"I'm taking the beer in payment for the trouble you caused. As for the keys, you're not going anywhere till morning when you've sobered up."

"We'll get killed for being out all night."

"Better that your parents do it than some big rig on the highway."

"Hell."

"Clean up your language, too."

"Jeez, you got a bee up your butt or something?"

"You don't want to find out."

Duncan leaned against their truck while they cleaned up the mess. They tossed the trash into their pickup and climbed back into the cab. "You sure we can't have the keys. We're not drunk."

"You smell like beer to me." He tossed the keys in the air, caught them easily, then shoved them in his pocket. "I'll see you bright and early in the morning."

Duncan walked back toward the tent with a smile on his face, but it disappeared the moment he saw her watching him through the open tent flap. He pulled off his muddy boots, left them sitting outside and climbed back into his sleeping bag.

"You don't suppose they'll try following us to the cave tomorrow, do you?" Cairo asked, trying to start some kind of conversation.

"Those two kids aren't into caves, they're into stupidity."

"This trip's become a disaster," Cairo said.

"First the rain, now you getting mad at a couple of crazy boys. This isn't a good sign of things to come."

"Go to sleep, Cairo."

"I think we should go back to Sanctuary in the morning."

"If you're so fired up to leave, hitch a ride with those kids. Dylan's going caving with me."

"I don't feel comfortable letting him go down in those tunnels. He's never been caving, and he's got a bad habit of running off, and—"

"And you're too damn overprotective."

Cairo heard the cot squeak as Dylan rolled over. "Don't argue. Please."

Cairo kissed Dylan's cheek. "We didn't mean to wake you, honey."

"Moms and dads aren't supposed to argue."

She wrapped her arms around him. "We weren't really arguing. We were just talking too loud."

"Tommy Chapman's mom and dad used to argue all the time. Tommy said it scared him— and then they got a divorce."

Duncan smoothed his big hand over Dylan's cheek. "The last thing on earth your mom and I want to do is scare you."

"Promise?"

"Promise," they answered together.

"Okay."

Dylan closed his eyes again, and in only a few moments he was asleep.

"I know you don't have much faith in me," Duncan whispered. "Maybe I never earned your faith, but please don't worry about Dylan. I'll keep him safe. I promise."

I promise. I promise. I promise.

You've broken promises before, Cairo thought, as Duncan's words reverberated in her mind. Please, don't break this one.

Nineteen

Midnight. It was really too late to knock on Graham's door, but it had taken Phoebe all day and most of the evening to plan her strategy. When the cloudburst hit, she knew exactly what she had to do.

She drummed her fingers on the doorjamb, wishing she'd hear the sound of Graham's wheelchair on the hardwood floors inside, but the only thing she heard was the soft pitter-patter of rain hitting the roof.

One minute went by, maybe two, but finally the sound she'd been waiting for came. She heard the click of the lock and saw the knob turning slowly. And then she saw those delicious silvery eyes.

"May I come in?"

"It's late."

"Actually, it's just very early in the morning and I do some of my best talking in the morning."

"Do you have a lot to talk about?"

"Probably enough to keep us going till daybreak . . . or longer."

Graham grinned, and when he rolled his chair backwards she swept right past him. Her red silk dress swished against her legs and the few raindrops that had hit her when she'd rushed from the car to the porch turned the red to a rich, dark burgundy. She rather liked the effect.

When she heard the door close behind her, she took a deep breath and turned, smiling her sweetest, most seductive smile, one she'd been practicing in the bathroom mirror off and on all day.

"I have some confessing to do," she said, sitting down on the arm of the couch and crossing her legs. She let the stiletto on her right foot slide off her heel and dangle from her toes—a very provocative pose, she imagined.

Graham had crossed his arms over his chest. One graying eyebrow rose and she liked the look. She'd have to capture it on paper someday soon.

"So," he said, "what do you want to confess?"

"It's just a silly little thing. I even hesitate to mention it, but I've read somewhere that confession's good for the soul. Do you believe that theory?"

"I believe honesty's the best policy."

"I suppose you're right. If we were all honest, there'd be no need for confession, but then life would be rather dull. And I really dislike boredom."

Graham laughed. "You're not the least bit boring, *Gertie*."

Hmm, he'd put quite a bit of emphasis on that last word. He probably knew the truth already, but it appeared he wanted to hear it straight from her lips.

"I imagine the best place to begin this confession is with the most important thing. My name's Phoebe, not Gertrude."

"That's a big relief."

She frowned. "You don't like Gertie?"

"I liked you. The name didn't matter all that much."

"That's a good answer, Graham. You get points for that."

She smiled a little wider. "For my next confession," she went on, "my friend's name isn't

Ingrid and she's not married to a Viking named Thor."

"No?" He was laughing at her and she liked the way it made his eyes twinkle.

"No. Her name's Cairo, and even though she's my best friend, she's also my niece. On top of that, she was married to your son at one time."

"And here you let me think I was imagining things."

"That wasn't very nice of me, was it?"

"Not exactly."

"There was a very good reason to keep everything a secret from you."

"I don't like secrets, Phoebe."

"I don't either." She took another deep breath. "Do you have some wine?"

"In the refrigerator."

"Would you like some?"

"As long as you're sticking around long enough to drink it with me."

"I'm sticking around for a long time, Graham. Besides, I have one more thing to confess."

Phoebe went into the kitchen, opened the refrigerator and found a bottle of Chardonnay. She popped the cork and filled the two glasses sitting on the countertop. "Were you expecting company?" she asked Graham, who sat in the doorway.

"Yes."

"Oh, dear, I hope I haven't interrupted anything."

"You haven't interrupted a thing. You're the one I was expecting."

She put a hand to her chest in feigned surprise. "Me?"

"You, Phoebe. No one else."

She brushed a quick kiss across his lips as she flitted back into the living room. She wanted a much longer kiss, but that would come later.

Taking a sip of wine, she sat back down on the edge of the sofa and resumed her pose. "This wine's delicious. Thirty years ago I was drinking Annie Green Springs and Ripple."

"I was drinking Red Mountain."

"Oh, that was nasty stuff. The worst hangover I ever had came after I took a few too many swigs off a bottle of Red Mountain."

"I had a few too many hangovers myself back in those days," Graham admitted, "but aren't we getting a little off track? Wasn't there another confession you wanted to make?"

"Actually, this isn't really my confession. I had no part in this at all, it's just something I thought you should know." She took another sip of wine. "You have a grandson."

"Dylan. Cute kid. Looks just like my son did when he was a kid. Of course, I told you that already—when I didn't even know we were related. And you do realize that's a discussion that Duncan and Cairo need to have, not you and me. I raised my son to do the right thing and I try my damnedest not to interfere or make suggestions."

"I make suggestions to Cairo all the time."

"Maybe you do that because you don't have anyone else to share things with."

"I have lots of friends."

"I want you to have just me," Graham told her, and they were just the words she'd wanted to hear.

"If you feel that way, why did you push me away last night?"

"Because . . . uh . . . oh, hell! I haven't had sex in five years and . . . and . . ."

Phoebe listened to him stutter, trying to spit out the words. Finally, she sat down in his lap. "Do I have your permission to be blunt?"

"Since when do you need my permission for that?"

"Well, this might be a delicate subject."

"Spit it out, Phoebe."

"I spent most of last night and all of today wondering why you called such a sudden halt to what was going on between us. And I want you to know that I honestly don't mind if you can't get it up. I mean, I'm an artist and I can think of a lot of creative ways we can please each other."

Graham's laughter was loud and long. "I can't walk, Phoebe, but trust me, I can get it up."

"Then why did you push me away? Why did you spout all that stuff about me needing a man with two good legs?"

"Because I *can* get it up, but what the hell am I going to do with it? I can't do any bumps and grinds. I can't—"

Phoebe silenced his words with a kiss, a deep, soul-searing, I'm-crazy-about-you-kiss. Slowly she pulled away and smiled. "Will you marry me?"

Graham's eyes narrowed. "What?"

"I'm forty-eight years old, I've never had a husband, and my body sags in more than one place, but ever since I saw you the other night, I've thought of at least a thousand and one ways we can please each other, and not one of them included you doing bumps and grinds. I'll show you the first one on our wedding night."

"You're going to make me wait that long?"

Phoebe grinned, walked toward the bag she'd dropped on the floor, and dug around inside. She pulled out two envelopes. "These are airline tickets to Vegas. I've made reservations at the MGM Grand, we can get a license first thing in the morning and be married by noon."

Graham rolled across the room, wrapped an arm around Phoebe, and tugged her back into his lap. "I know Sanctuary's justice of the peace. One call, and he can be here in fifteen minutes— marriage license and all."

Phoebe flipped the airline tickets behind her, leaned into the comfort of Graham's body, and kissed the man of her dreams. "Make the call, Graham. I can hardly wait."

Twenty

♥ Duncan guided Dylan every inch of the
way through the tunnels, listening to him
laugh and chatter and spell out dozens of
words as they crawled and rappelled and hung
together high in the air, looking at stalagmites
and stalactites and listening to the sound of the
wind echoing about them.

Cairo had moved behind, silent, alone, but
somehow smiling whenever Dylan called out to
her or asked a question.

She was being a trooper, and Duncan started
to feel like a jerk.

Hell, how could two people be the best of
friends for years and after one night of marriage
end up being enemies, in spite of a one-day

lapse in judgment when they'd had the best sex ever? It didn't seem fair.

Fair? She'd screwed him out of nearly five years of fatherhood and the way he looked at it, he didn't owe her a thing anymore.

So why was he feeling like a big part of him had died?

"What do you think of this place?" he heard Cairo ask Dylan, as they looped in and out of a row of stalagmites.

"It's pretty cool. Daddy said a mountain man told him how to find this place, and did you know that there's a city of gold somewhere down here?"

Cairo stopped dead in her tracks, and Duncan watched her turn around and get down eye to eye with Dylan. "Your dad's not one-hundred-percent positive that there's a city of gold down here. As far as we know, it's just a myth, so don't get your hopes up."

"He says you should always follow your dream."

Cairo sighed, and ruffled Dylan's hair. "I'm sure he's right."

Damn! All day today, all day yesterday, Cairo had done everything in her power to make him look good in Dylan's eyes. She'd called him a hero. She'd told Dylan about his archaeological exploits and his adventures—the

ones she knew about, anyway. She'd bowed to
his decisions and stepped out of the way so he
could be the one that Dylan ran to at every turn.

Still, he ran to his mom. Dylan's whole life had
been spent with her. He had almost nothing.

What could he possibly have with Dylan if
he took him away from the mother he so obviously loved?

*Quit moaning and groaning, Dunc! Get cracking
and show the kid around.*

Thank goodness Angus was thinking straight
today!

Cairo had been worried about coming into
the cave, and he'd spent a good long time this
morning telling her they had nothing to fear.
Then they'd argued again about Dylan, and
custody, and then Dylan woke up and they'd
both shut up.

It was a hell of a way to live.

He latched onto his son and swung him
around and around. He couldn't get over how
good it felt to do something so simple.

"What's next, Daddy?"

"You know, I've discovered some pretty cool
things in my life, but the things in the next cave
are totally beyond belief."

Dylan's eyes were wide with wonder. "It's
better than this cave?"

"Much better."

"Does the wind howl there, too?"

Duncan nodded. "But there's nothing to be scared of."

Dylan's little chest puffed out. "I'm not scared of the wind. We have this big old tree outside our house in Mendocino and when the wind blows at night the branches scrape against the house and it sounds really, really creepy. I like it to be windy when my friends spend the night, because they don't like it when the tree scratches the house."

"Tell your father why," Cairo urged, looking every bit like a scolding mother instead of the beautiful woman he loved.

Loved? Ah, hell!

"Well . . . you see," Dylan said, taking Duncan's mind off of Cairo for the moment, "Tommy was spending the night and we sneaked out of bed after Mommy was asleep. *Poltergeist* was on TV. Have you ever seen that movie?"

Duncan nodded, having the strangest feeling he knew where this story was going to go. "I saw it once when I was a teenager. It's not exactly a movie for little boys."

"I know. I got chewed out later. But anyway, Tommy and I watched *Poltergeist* and he got grossed out when bugs started crawling out of a piece of meat and when blood started dripping off of some guy's face, and then, well, when the movie was over I got catsup out of the refrigerator and Tommy and I went back up to bed and the wind was blowing something awful and the tree was scraping against the house and Tommy was sort of scared and I told him that one time the tree had broken through the window and the branches grabbed hold of me and pulled me outside and that I got swallowed into the trunk of the tree and that my mom had to hire a witch to come to the house and make the tree give me back. And then when Tommy was really scared, and he was staring at the window where the tree was scratching, I put catsup on my face and screamed, and, well, Tommy peed in the bed and Mommy and Aunt Phoebe came running."

Dylan took a deep breath. "Tommy doesn't come to my house anymore and Mommy fixed the TV so it doesn't work during the middle of the night and I had to do dishes for a week, and on top of that I couldn't play Nintendo. Would you have punished me like that?"

"I probably would have walloped your behind."

Dylan's eyes widened. "You would have hit me?"

Cairo stepped behind her son, her eyes just as wide as Dylan's and shook her head at Duncan. It was a definite warning that spankings were a no-no in her house.

"I might have *thought* about walloping your behind, because that's what my dad would have done to me, but in the end I probably would have decided that a more fitting punishment would be . . ." He had to think back a moment to one of his mom's punishments. What the heck did you do to a kid who was too smart for his own britches. "Well, Dylan, I probably would have made you clean the bathroom for a month."

Dylan's nose wrinkled. "That's disgusting."

"So is scaring your friends so badly that they pee in bed."

"Maybe, but at least you know that I'm not scared of the wind. I'm really not scared of much of anything because I know Tae Kwon Do."

Duncan tried his hardest not to laugh, but he wasn't the least bit successful. Dylan giggled, and even Cairo, with red eyes that looked like they'd been crying all night, managed to laugh.

When their composure finally returned, Duncan grabbed Dylan's hand and dragged him toward the jagged tunnel that led to the chamber of pictographs. He felt like a kid again, leading another kid to a fantastic find. But he wasn't a kid, he was a dad with responsibilities.

He stopped right after stepping into the tunnel and looked back. Cairo was gathering up their bags, the extra flashlights and all the gear that had been sitting on the floor in the main cavern. In his excitement, he'd forgotten their safety equipment, the first aid supplies, all the things they would need if they got stuck in the cave.

But Cairo hadn't forgotten a thing. Cairo, who'd been a flirt and a spoiled kid when he'd first met her had become a mother who recognized her responsibilities. There was a lot he could learn from Cairo about being a grown-up, about being a dad.

Maybe they should give it another try.

For Dylan's sake.

And well . . . for his sake, too.

Holding Dylan's hand, he pulled him out of the tunnel, afraid to let him go anywhere alone, and took two of the packs from Cairo's hands. "I got too caught up in Dylan to think about our gear," he admitted. "I'm glad your head's screwed on tighter than mine."

"I've had more practice at this parenting stuff. If you'd been doing it for five years, you wouldn't have forgotten."

"I'm afraid you're giving me too much credit."

She smiled weakly. Tears had welled up in the corners of her eyes. "You told me to have faith in you. I'm trying."

"You two aren't going to get all lovey and stuff, are you?" Dylan asked, tugging on Duncan's shirt.

Duncan swept his son up in his arm. "Not right now. We're going exploring. But here's your first real lesson. No matter how excited you get about something, don't forget your gear. Your second lesson is, don't go anywhere alone."

"I would never do either of those things. Ever."

"Okay then, let's go exploring."

They ducked into the jagged cave and a moment later entered the chamber that still took Duncan's breath away, even though he'd seen it time and time again.

"Wow. This is cool," Dylan exclaimed, shining his flashlight and the light on his helmet around the cavern.

Duncan crouched beside his son, wrapped an arm around his waist and pulled him to his side. They stood nearly cheek to cheek as they studied the paintings. "What do you think they are?"

"Well . . . they're not Egyptian."

"What makes you say that?"

"Because we're not in Egypt. Besides, my mom's been teaching me all about hieroglyphs and someday she's going to take me to Egypt to see the Sphinx and the pyramids and she said we might even see my grandparents. They're really busy in Egypt so they can't come see me. But, anyway, these aren't Egyptian."

"No, they're definitely not Egyptian, but they *were* made by another ancient people. Have you ever heard of the Maya?"

Dylan's eyes scrunched up as he stared at the pictographs. "I thought they were in Belize. My mom's shown me pictures of some Mayan ruins that she took on one of her trips. I keep telling her I want to go to Belize, too, but she just says 'Someday'. When 'someday' finally comes, will you go, too?"

Duncan looked at Cairo and saw her questioning eyes. Then he turned to his son and smiled. "I'll be going, too."

They stood together for the longest time, while Duncan pointed out the feathered plumes and jade ornamentation worn by ancient Mayan nobles and ear flares that were commonplace in Mayan society. Dylan asked questions about everything he could see—and Duncan hoped his son wouldn't see the pictures of the altars. He wasn't quite ready to explain the birds and the bees.

"Is this a map?" Dylan asked.

Duncan nodded. "As far as I can tell, it shows all the caves and all the tunnels that are linked to this one."

Dylan stood on tiptoes and pointed to a dragon's head. "What does that mean?"

"I imagine there's a booby-trap there, or a pit, or something that makes that part of the caves unsafe."

"Cool, can we go there?"

"No."

"Why?"

"You could get hurt, and there's no need to take chances if you don't have to."

"But I bet it would be fun."

"Maybe, but how do you think your mom would feel if you got hurt?"

"She'd feel really bad. I know because one time when we were talking about you she started to cry. She said she was worried about you, and that she wished—"

"Time for lunch," Cairo called out from across the cavern. She held a bag in one hand and a thermos in the other and he could tell she'd been listening to the entire exchange but hadn't wanted to hear any more.

Duncan and Dylan moved across the cavern to the flat-topped rock where Cairo had spread out their meal. Duncan looked her straight in the eye, and asked, "What did you wish?"

Her voice was low, barely audible in the cave. "That you'd never gone away."

He found himself cradling her cheek in the palm of his hand, loving the feel of her skin against his. Maybe they stood a chance, after all—if they could get over the hurdles that stood in their way.

That, of course, would be a pretty big leap.

He drew his hand away, and pulled Dylan into his lap as he sat on the floor. "What's for lunch?"

"Some sandwiches that Irene made."

"Cool! Irene makes the best sandwiches I've ever eaten. Mommy usually just makes peanut butter and jelly, but Irene puts all sorts of stuff on hers, like chopped up chicken and celery and almonds." Dylan tilted his head up to look at Duncan. "Did you ever have almonds on a sandwich?"

"Once or twice."

"Well, wait until you taste these."

While they ate, Duncan thought that he'd never known a kid who was such a chatterbox, someone who could change subjects without batting an eye. And then he remembered that Cairo had been exactly the same when she was fifteen. Days spent with her had been some of his best times in Egypt. She'd be with him for three months, then go back home to school, and the next nine months would be lonely. When summertime would come once more, he'd repeat the process all over again, every year wanting summer to come faster and faster.

He'd never been happier than the night they'd gotten married. He'd felt like the world belonged to him.

It seemed odd that he had that same kind of feeling now, comfortable after enjoying a meal, reclined against the rock with his legs stretched out and his ankles crossed, Cairo sitting on a rock next to him, and their son playing peacefully in a cavern lit by several battery-operated lamps.

They were surrounded by history, yet the present—Cairo—captured most all his attention.

"Why didn't you go to work for your parents?" Duncan asked. "You worked so hard to become an archaeologist. I don't know anyone who can read ancient Egyptian hieroglyphs the way you can. You know all the dynasties, all the history, you even speak the Egyptian language."

Cairo laughed lightly. "I was a disappointment to my folks."

"Why, because you married me?"

"For starters. After that I disgraced them by

getting pregnant." She was silent a moment, smiling as she looked across the cave at Dylan. "They wanted me to have an abortion and I refused. So, they cut off my money for school, all my living expenses, and, well, what had never been a very good relationship suddenly became no relationship at all."

"You don't sound bitter."

"I'd be working in Egypt right now if they hadn't pushed me away. But you know what? I really do prefer the tourist business." He enjoyed watching the sparkle in her eyes as she continued to talk. "I like the people, the travel, and I'm only gone a week at a time. Then I can go home to be with Dylan, and Phoebe, of course. I don't know what I would have done without her over the years."

"Was she with you when Dylan was born?"

"Every step of the way."

"Was it easy? Hard?"

She laughed. "What do you want, a play-by-play description?"

His good mood plummeted. He sat up and faced her. "No, Cairo, what I want is to go back and live every minute of that time myself. I want to feel Dylan kicking inside you. I want to hold your hand and tell you when to push. But I don't get any of those things. Not one goddamn moment of it."

"Well I can't relive it for you or give it back to you. All I can do is give you the future. That's why I came to Montana, that's why I crawled down in this cave after you, that's why I wanted you to go to Belize with me—so I could find out what kind of father you'd be. I wanted to make sure you had what it took to be a good dad."

"You mean this whole thing was some kind of test? You were checking me out to see if I could be responsible, to see if I'd love my son?"

"That's exactly what I'm telling you."

"Let me tell you something, Cairo, parenthood doesn't work that way. You get what you get—good, bad, indifferent."

"Well, I got stuck with indifferent parents and I didn't want my son to have the same thing."

"No, you chose to give him nothing."

"I gave him *me*. I gave him Phoebe. I gave him everything I had."

"But you didn't give him me."

"And I've felt guilty about it."

"That's supposed to make me feel better?"

"I don't care how you feel. Don't you understand? The only one who matters is Dylan."

"Stop fighting!" Dylan stood across the room, his hands over his ears, tears flowing freely down his cheeks. "Please, don't fight."

And then he ran—down a tunnel that hadn't been explored.

Duncan grabbed a flashlight and rope from the ground and tore off after him.

"Dylan, stop. Please," he heard Cairo calling, as she followed him into the tunnel. He heard the panic in her voice that matched the terror that coursed through his muscles and nerves and veins.

"Dylan," he called out. *"Don't run. Please, stop."*

But he heard nothing. Not a whimper, not a cry, only his own terrified heartbeat.

The tunnel narrowed. It twisted and turned and cold wind howled and slapped at his face as he and Cairo squeezed through passages with jagged rocks that tore at their clothes and skin.

They reached a wide spot, and the tunnel forked in three different directions. He stopped, leaned back against the wall, and drew in a breath.

"Don't stop, Duncan. Please," Cairo urged. "We've got to find him."

"What way do you propose we go? Right? Left? Straight ahead?"

"I don't know. Maybe we should split up."

Duncan clutched her shoulders. "Split up?" He laughed. "Damn it, Cairo, the reason we're going through this right now is because we *did* split up. The only way we're going to make it better is to stay together."

"I just want to find my son."

"Our son, Cairo. *Our* son."

Tears welled from her eyes and he pulled her to him. "We'll find him. I promise. Please, don't fall apart on me, Cairo."

She pulled away and wiped at her tears. "Do you have the map? Maybe we can figure out which way to go."

Duncan drew it from his pocket and studied the many forks in the system of tunnels and caves. "I think we're right here," he said, then ran his finger along one of the tunnels that made a complete circle. "Dylan would have been back here by now if he'd taken that passage," Duncan said, trying to sound calm when every fiber in his body was screaming.

"If he's scared," Cairo said, "he might have just sat down and started to cry."

Duncan put a comforting hand to her cheek. "Don't worry. Please. I'll check out the passage, and you stay here, just in case he comes back."

"You said we shouldn't split up."

"The tunnel comes right back to you, Cairo. It doesn't go anywhere else—if the map is correct." He squeezed her shoulders. "Please, don't go anywhere. I'll rush as fast as I can."

Cairo hated to see Duncan disappear. Hated to be alone in the cavern with her son missing. "Dylan," she called out. "Where are you, honey?"

Her voice echoed around her and rushed through the tunnels. He had to hear her. "Please, Dylan. Answer me. Where are you?"

It seemed as if she called out to her son for hours, when only minutes had gone by. All about her she heard the sounds of dripping water and rushing wind, but never her son. And then off to her right she heard footsteps and her heart slammed against her chest. She saw a light coming from the tunnel. It wasn't Dylan, but it *was* Duncan, and she felt relief and disappointment all at the same time.

"He's not in there," Duncan said, as he taped a reflective X to each entrance.

They studied the map again. "This tunnel heads toward the pool," Duncan said. "This one toward—"

Cairo saw the dragon's head, and remembered the vivid drawing of sharp teeth and vicious jaws on the wall. She looked at Duncan, suddenly more worried than ever. "Dylan spent a lot of time looking at the map on the wall, didn't he?"

"Every inch of it."

"He's got a photographic memory."

"Then he'd remember the pool and head that direction?"

Cairo shook her head. "He likes scary things. I think he'd check out the dragon." A tear slid down her cheek. "He's your son, Duncan. He'll take the adventurous route every time."

"Then let's go find him."

Duncan grabbed her hand. She felt comfort through his fingers, and it warmed her, as they headed through another tunnel.

Unlike the others, this passageway looked inviting. A light breeze floated through the air, the space was wide and high, but they knew it offered a false sense of security—something Dylan wouldn't have understood.

They walked slowly, hand in hand. They were quiet, listening for any noise, no matter how faint. The floor beneath their feet was sprinkled with a powdering of dirt that had filtered down from above, unlike most of the rest of the caves and tunnels, which were hard, solid limestone.

Duncan took one cautious step after another, as if he'd been through this kind of place before. Another step. Another, and his foot plunged through the thin crust of dirt.

Cairo grabbed his arm and steadied him, and he leaned against the wall.

"Oh, God, Duncan. What if—"

"Don't think 'what if.' Just keep thinking that he's safe."

Each step after that was tested first. A little pressure. A little more. It slowed them down. Too slow.

"*Mommy.*"

It was just a whimper, like a little boy calling out in the middle of the night.

"Dylan!" Cairo cried out.

"*Mommy. Help.*"

She wanted to run to him, but Duncan held her back. "We're no good to him if we fall through some hole. We've got to go slow."

"We're coming, Dylan," Duncan hollered.

"Hurry," he cried, his little voice full of fear.

Even though Duncan had told her they had to move slowly, Cairo knew he wasn't being as cautious as he should. He was thinking about Dylan—needing to get to him just as much as she did.

"Daddy. Hurry."

They were close. So close.

The tunnel opened in front of them, a room painted and carved with dragons and monsters, and in the very center a hole, not more than eighteen inches wide.

Duncan quickly tied one end of the rope around his waist and the other around one of the sculptures. "Wrap your arm around the statue and hold on to the rope," he told Cairo, "and don't let go, no matter what."

He got down on his hands and knees and crawled across the floor. The ground gave way beneath his right hand, beneath his left knee, and Cairo wanted to close her eyes to the fear, but she kept them open, watching, praying.

"I'm real close, Dylan," Duncan said, his voice low and calm. "I'll have you out of there in a minute."

"I can't hold on."

"You have to, Dylan. You have to be a big boy and hold on as long as it takes. I don't care how much your arms hurt or how tired you are, you've just got to hold on."

"Okay, Daddy. But hurry."

Duncan was at the edge of the pit, looking down, and bits and pieces of it crumbled away.

Dylan screamed, and Cairo's heart seemed to stop.

Suddenly the whole front half of Duncan's body disappeared into the hole. All she could see were his legs and the toes of his boots digging into the dirt.

And then she heard his voice. "I've got you, son. Put your arms around my neck." Those were the best words she'd ever heard, and the best sight she'd ever seen was Duncan pulling

Dylan out of the hole and into his protective, loving arms. "Keep your arms around my neck," Duncan whispered. "No matter what, just don't let go of me."

"Aren't we safe yet?"

Duncan shook his head. "Remember what I said about booby traps?"

Dylan nodded.

"This place is full of them. So we've got to go slow. We've got to be careful. And we never, ever go off alone. Do you hear me?"

Dylan nodded again, wrapped his arms tightly around Duncan's neck, and buried his face into his shoulder.

Duncan crawled toward Cairo again, trying to follow the same route he'd taken to the center of the room, but even that wasn't safe. His knee crashed through the surface and sent him sprawling down to the floor, but not before he had his arms around Dylan to protect him. And then he moved some more, and kept on moving until he was standing next to Cairo.

She wiped away her tears, but her lips quivered as she smiled. "Thank you," she whispered.

A slow grin pulled at the corner of his mouth. "It was nothing. I do this kind of thing all the time."

And then her tears really flowed. "I know, Duncan. That's what I'm afraid of."

Twenty-one

"Tommy's not going to believe it when I tell him about the dragons and monsters I saw down here. They were really creepy and awful, but they were kind of neat, too. Didn't you think so?" Dylan asked, staring straight at Duncan as he attempted to bandage the minuscule scratch on his son's arm.

"They scared the living daylights out of me." Dylan's running away, his disappearance, and the fear he'd felt had frightened him far more than anything he'd ever experienced in his life. Was this what fatherhood was like, day in, and day out? Would he always worry?

"I bet you've had even scarier adventures, haven't you, Daddy?"

"Each adventure's just a little different than the one before. You never know what's going to happen next, that's why it's an adventure," Duncan said, watching the sparkle of excitement in his son's eyes, mirroring the wonder and awe he'd heard in Dylan's words. He wanted many more moments like this with his son.

"Speaking of adventure," Cairo said. "The only one you're going to have right now is a nap—a good, long nap."

"Naps are for babies," Dylan stated flatly. "Besides, we've got more exploring to do if we're going to find the golden city."

"Sorry, pumpkin." Cairo rose from the limestone floor where she'd stretched out a blanket for Dylan. "One adventure a day is all you get when you're only four years old."

Dylan let out a long-winded sigh. "I bet you'll say the same thing when I'm five."

"I bet you're right."

Cairo smiled, and Duncan hefted his squirming son under his arm and carried him to the makeshift bed, setting him down, then stepping aside so Cairo could take over.

She lay beside Dylan on the blanket, rubbing his back as his head plopped from one side to the other. "The ground's too hard to sleep," he grumbled.

"Just try," she encouraged. "I promise I won't let you sleep through anything exciting."

"Promise?"

"Promise."

Duncan leaned against one of the rock formations in the cavern he'd dubbed the "map room," and watched Cairo coax his son to sleep. She hummed softly, smoothing Dylan's hair from his brow, and Duncan had the oddest feeling that he could watch her for hours, doing nothing more than comforting their child.

He loved her. How could he have ever doubted that?

Slowly she rose, looking down for just a moment at their sleeping son, sprawled across the blanket, and then she moved toward him, with tears glistening in her eyes. "I would have lost him today, if you hadn't been here," she whispered.

"Don't make a hero out of me. None of this would have happened if I hadn't insisted on bringing him with me," Duncan said, throwing out the words that had been eating at him since Dylan first ran off. "I don't know what I was thinking. A four-year-old doesn't have any business in a place like this, and as soon as he wakes up, we're heading out of here. We're not coming back either—none of us."

Cairo sat down beside him, drawing her

knees to her chest and wrapping her arms around them. "I'm not going to let you give up your dream," she said.

"It doesn't seem that important any longer, not when there's a risk of something happening to Dylan . . . or you."

She tilted her head toward him and smiled. "I've spent over four years worrying about Dylan and I imagine I'm going to spend the rest of my life doing the same thing. He's smart, he has his own way of getting in trouble, and that's going to happen whether we're in a cave or safely locked away in our house in Mendocino."

"There are a thousand more dangers down here."

Cairo laughed. "Dylan makes his own danger and he's been doing so since he was nine months old, when he figured out how to crawl out of his crib in the middle of the night. That's the first time he tried climbing up the Christmas tree. At two he rounded up the neighbor's lovable old sheepdog and gave him a buzz, and at three he figured out what a monkey wrench was for and spent the night trying to replumb the bathroom. I don't hold out any hope for things getting easier over the years."

"I wish I'd been there to help you."

"You would have been, if I hadn't kept Dylan away from you."

"Don't apologize. We've both made mistakes, and we've both grown up. It's time to put all the bad stuff behind us and move on."

"You're sure."

"I've never been more positive of anything."

He touched her cheek and tilted her face so he could kiss her. Softly. Tentatively, as if they'd never kissed before. "I've been thinking about us," he said. "I can't begin to tell you the number of times over the years that I've rolled over in the morning and reached for you, only to find that I'd been dreaming, that you were only in my head and heart, and not beside me."

"We must have shared the same dream."

"We always have. Adventure, excitement, quiet nights under the stars. We can have that again—the three of us."

He kissed away the tear that slipped from her eye. "It sounds perfect, Duncan, but I can't live in a tent in the middle of nowhere anymore. I don't even want to settle for a trailer in the middle of nowhere. Dylan needs special schooling, I have a business to run, and I have a home I love."

He laughed. "I haven't spent much time living in a house in a good ten years."

"You'd probably hate it."

"Why?"

"There aren't any bison in Mendocino. There aren't any coyotes or cities of gold or—"

"You and Dylan are in Mendocino. And finding a dream doesn't seem as important as holding on to the one that's already within reach."

"The city of gold could be just around the corner."

Duncan laughed again. "You know, Cairo, I'm sitting here pouring my heart out, stringing together more words at one time than I ever have in my life—all of them leading up to asking you to marry me again. And you keep bringing the discussion back to finding that blasted city of gold."

Another tear slid down her face and again he kissed it away. "Now why are you crying?"

"Do you really want to marry me?"

He nodded. "Just as badly as I did the first time around. Hell, I'll even be a tour guide, if that's what you want."

Finally she smiled, really and truly smiled. "Just promise me one thing. Duncan."

"What's that?"

"That if I say yes, you won't leave me after one night."

He raised his right hand. "I solemnly swear not to leave you. I won't run off on some big adventure, I won't get thrown in jail, and I won't be irresponsible—ever again."

He leaned over and kissed her, not tentatively this time, not softly. This was a kiss meant to seal a promise.

"So, what's your answer?" he asked, the moment he was able to draw himself away from her lips.

She smiled, and wove her arms around his neck. "Yes," she whispered against his mouth. "A thousand times yes."

Dylan had been sleeping for nearly an hour, when Duncan leaned against a stalagmite, watching his wife-to-be study the intricacy of the wall paintings. "How many tunnels do you think are down here?" she asked him. "Twenty? Thirty?"

"More than a hundred, I imagine, considering that most of the passages seem to have half-a-dozen offshoots. It could take someone months, maybe longer, to explore all of them."

"Not someone, Duncan. Us. We're not going to give up this dream, not now, when we could be so close."

"What about Dylan?" he asked. "What about Belize?"

"We just have to be more careful, and we have to make sure Dylan's never out of our sight. And Belize is nearly two weeks away. I still have some things to arrange, but—"

Duncan laughed. She was just as obsessed as he had been, and he loved hearing the sound of her excitement. "Okay, Cairo, since we're not going to give up the dream, for now at least, where do we go from here?"

She put her hands on her hips and stared at the collage painted on the wall. "The key's got to be here somewhere."

"There must be thousands of different pictures to sort through," Duncan said.

"Yes but if there's really a city of gold, do you think the Maya would have built it in a place that's easy to find?"

"No, but I think they may have hidden clues." He pushed away from the wall and walked toward her, draping an arm over her shoulder. "I think they wanted the obvious to be right under your nose, so close that it's hard to see, sort of like they did with the *Kama Sutra*–type drawings."

"I was thinking the same thing," Cairo said. She curled a stray strand of hair behind her ear. "Have you looked closely at these paintings?"

"Not all of them."

She turned, gazing all about the cavern. "Everywhere you turn there are hidden tombs, altars, death boats. But look at the water, Duncan."

It didn't look out of the ordinary, except for the geyser in the center. "What am I supposed to see?"

"The obvious."

"There's nothing obvious, just a lot of animals and birds facing the pool."

"They're not facing it, Duncan. They're lined up, heading *into* the pool."

He moved closer, inspecting the drawing. He could feel himself squinting as he looked at the animals growing smaller and smaller as they moved toward a dark hole at one end of the lake. "It's an underwater tunnel."

It's about time you figured it out!

Duncan laughed to himself. Angus had been far too quiet lately, but he'd suddenly popped back into the picture."

Get cracking, Dunc! You want to find the city, don't you?

Hell, yes, he wanted to find the city.

He grabbed Cairo's hand and dragged her toward Dylan. "Wake up our son and let's get going."

"Where?"

"Exploring. I want to see what's through that tunnel."

"But we don't have any diving gear. We can't—"

Duncan silenced her with a kiss. "We can do

just about anything, Cairo. We're gonna be the best damn team of explorers that ever lived."

It didn't take much more than half an hour to gather their gear and get to the pool. Cairo was right. They didn't have diving equipment and they would definitely need it to make their way through the underwater tunnel. But good fortune seemed to be smiling down on them.

"It's draining," Cairo said, and Duncan could feel her squeezing his fingers as the water rapidly swirled in the lake.

"Wow, this is cool," Dylan said, squirming on top of Duncan's shoulders, wanting to get down. But Duncan held him close, refusing to let him out of his sight, especially now, as the water rushed to the heart of the pool.

"It's like a geyser," Duncan told his son, "a lot like Old Faithful in Yellowstone. All of the water you see here will soon disappear through a hole at the bottom of the pool. I don't know what's underground, possibly a dormant volcano, but more than likely the water will get hot, and the pressure will build up until the water explodes and shoots right back out the hole to fill the pool all over again."

"Does it happen a lot?" Dylan asked.

"I don't know. Some geysers erupt every half hour, some once a year, some every hundred years. I have no way of knowing about this one."

Cairo squeezed his fingers again. "Look," she said, pointing to the far end of the pool. "It's the tunnel. If we're going to go, we'd better do it now."

Duncan shook his head, having second thoughts about this venture. "We can't go in there, Cairo. It's too dangerous."

She looked toward the center of the pool. "The water's deep, Duncan. It could be hours before it's fully drained, and there's no telling how long it will be before the water builds up enough steam to blow. I say we time ourselves. One hour at the most."

"I say we time ourselves too," Dylan added. "If we don't, I'll have to tell Tommy that I was too big a chicken to go into a tunnel, and then he'll tell all the kids at preschool and they'll laugh at me."

Go for it, Dunc!

It seemed unanimous. Still, Duncan looked at Cairo, trying to make the right decision. God, how he wanted to go down that tunnel. But he wasn't alone anymore. He had Cairo to think about, a son to protect. "We're not going," he said flatly. "We're going to Belize in a couple of weeks and when that trip's over, we'll get diving gear and come back."

"Are you out of your mind?" Cairo shouted. "You've spent ten years waiting for this moment. You can't give up now."

"I'm not giving up. I'm just playing it safe."

"You don't like playing it safe. You never have and you never will."

Listen to her, Dunc. For a woman, she makes perfect sense!

Duncan sighed. The water had cleared the base of the tunnel. A pathway seemed to open before them, stretching along the edge of the pool straight to the tunnel. "I'll go by myself," he told them. "No need for all of us to take chances."

"I'm going, too," Dylan stated. "You never know when you might need a Tae Kwon Do expert with you."

"We're *all* going," Cairo said. Duncan could hear a tinge of worry in her voice, but he could also see excitement in her eyes. Just like old times.

He gave it another moment of thought, then said, "Okay, we're all going. But we're giving ourselves just one hour, not a minute more."

He picked up his gear, and tilted his head to see his son. "Do you know how to swim?" he asked.

"Of course I do." Suddenly, Duncan could hear his son's bravado deflate an ounce or two.

"You don't think we're going to drown, do you?"

Duncan clasped Dylan's legs a little tighter. "I wouldn't take you down there if that's what I thought. If the water gets the least bit close to us, we'll run back out of the tunnel. Don't worry, Dylan, nothing in the world is ever going to hurt you."

"Promise?"

"I promise."

They headed into the pool, their boots leaving footprints in the thin coating of silt that covered the bottom. Their flashlights and helmet lights, all of them equipped with brand new batteries, were aimed toward the passageway.

A cool wind blew through the cavern, whistling around the milky white stalactites and stalagmites. A trickle of water dripped over the flowstone falls and rolled toward the larger body of water disappearing slowly into a seemingly bottomless hole.

At last they entered the tunnel, a dark, foreboding passage with thick silt and something that looked a lot like seaweed hanging from the ceiling. Duncan was forced to pull Dylan from his shoulders and carry him in one arm. Dylan grasped Duncan's neck, and they forged ahead, as Duncan pushed aside any obstructions in their path.

"It's kind of scary down here," Dylan whispered, and his voice reverberated all about them.

Cairo laughed. "Just imagine what Tommy's going to say when he hears this story."

"It's going to be so cool. Better than *Poltergeist* any day."

Right now Duncan wished he was watching *Poltergeist* instead of leading an expedition of loved ones through uncharted territory. He rarely got scared when he was by himself. But he wasn't alone this time. The two most important people in his world were with him, and all he could think about was keeping them safe.

The tunnel narrowed, widened, then shrank to the point where Duncan had to put Dylan on the ground and just hold on to his hand, so he could expel all his breath and squeeze through. Finally, they reached carved stepping stones leading up at nearly a forty-five degree angle. These weren't natural. They were hand-made. Someone had definitely been through here before.

A blast of wind whipped about them, whistling as it circled again and again, then disappeared.

Dylan tightened his hand in Duncan's. Except for holding Cairo, touching her and kissing her, holding Dylan's little hand was the most incredible feeling Duncan had ever known. So much faith had been placed in him, and he wouldn't let either Cairo or Dylan down.

One more twist. One more dip. The stairs led down, then up, and just when Duncan was ready to give up, the tunnel split and went in two different directions. *That did it!* He was tired of these Mayan games. Those ancient people thought they could make him quit and turn back, but he refused. He was going forward, no matter what.

That's my boy!

He drew a coin from his pocket. "Heads we go left. Tails we go right."

Cairo laughed softly. "Very scientific decision making."

He tossed it into the air, and all eyes followed the shiny quarter as it slowly tumbled on its way down. Duncan caught it and slapped it onto the back of his left hand. Keeping it covered, he held his hand out to Dylan. "You want the first peek?"

Dylan nodded, and Duncan slowly removed his fingers. "Tails! Okay, let's go right." Dylan started to march off in front of everyone and Duncan latched onto his shoulder and held him still. "You're not old enough to lead."

Dylan sighed, and took his place, hand-in-hand, behind his dad. The stairs in this passage led downward, then up again. "How much longer?" Dylan groaned.

"Not much," Cairo said, and Duncan was immediately reminded of car trips he'd taken with his parents, grumbling when it seemed they'd never reach their destination.

"Oh, my!" Cairo exclaimed, rushing past him when the tunnel widened.

Duncan stopped thinking of the present or future, and immediately thought of the past, when he stepped into a cavern nearly consumed by stalagmites and stalactites. They were everywhere, interspersed with splattermites and popcorn formations, and in between, the room was littered with treasure. Pottery painted with the likenesses of Mayan kings. Clay effigy figures, incense burners, and funerary pots adorned with men wearing owls on their heads, the symbol of the underworld.

"Look at this," Cairo said, holding up a jade mask. "They must have brought this with them from Central America."

Duncan tried to focus on the magnificent mask, but his eyes strayed over Cairo's shoulder to a painted wall, almost hidden by a veil of stalactites. "Take a look at this," he said. Duncan hoisted Dylan on his shoulders again, and together they moved toward the mural.

"It's Copán," Cairo said, reading the glyph

beneath the painting of an ancient Mayan empire. "And these," she said, pointing to five couples, running from the city, "are like the pictures we saw in the other cave. People *did* run from Copán."

Duncan looked at the people escaping from sacrificial altars, their arms laden with treasures of their homeland. They crossed deserts, snow-capped mountains, and grassland, and finally rushed into the mouth of a cave.

"They hid their treasures here," Cairo said, her fingers tracing the glyphs. "I don't have time to read everything, but it looks like the people who first came here were craftsmen, and over the years they tried to create a world similar to the one they'd left."

"Were they homesick?" Dylan asked.

"I would imagine so," Cairo answered. "But they couldn't go back home, because they were afraid of being sacrificed to the gods."

Dylan's eyes widened. "They didn't sacrifice people here, did they?"

"No, honey," Cairo said. "The people who lived here believed that the gods would be happy if they were happy."

"I don't think I'd be very happy living in a cave all the time. I bet you can't get TV down here, and you can't play Nintendo, and—"

"I'm sure they found other ways to pass the

time," Duncan said. "They painted, and sculpted stone—"

"'And built booby traps!" Dylan added.

"They also told stories," Cairo said. "They told their children about their homeland, about the lush vegetation and colorful birds. And when the elders died, their children and grandchildren left this place, wanting to see the paradise their parents had told them about."

"But did they *all* leave?" Duncan asked, curiosity getting the better of him. "Did they make it back to Copán safely?"

Cairo laughed. "I thought the only thing that interested you was the thrill of discovery, that you didn't care to know all the details."

"Let's just say this place has piqued my curiosity." He cradled her cheek in the palm of his hand. "Must have something to do with finding you here."

Cairo stood and slipped her hands around his waist. She looked beautiful in the light of his helmet, her eyes sparkling, her lips tilted into a smile as she stretched up on her tiptoes to give him a—

"Mommy! Daddy!" Dylan shouted. "Look! Over there. It's a whole bunch of toys."

Cairo laughed and her head turned away, following Dylan's pointing finger. Duncan spun around, disappointed that he hadn't had a chance to enjoy Cairo's kiss, but anxious to see Dylan's discovery.

But he saw nothing when he turned around. "I can't see anything."

"You've got to be up high to see it," Dylan stated. "Just start walking and I'll tell you when you're getting close."

They wove through the stalagmites and Mayan treasures and finally, on the far side of the cavern, was a wide expanse of floor covered with carved wooden bison, something resembling a rocking horse, only shaped like a jaguar, not to mention dolls made from shells and bone.

Duncan slid Dylan from his shoulders and let him wander for a few minutes through the vast array of playthings, while Cairo sat down in the middle of all of it, sorting through strings of colorful jade beads and ear flares that were piled high in a wooden basket. "It's beautiful," she said. "I could spend hours going through all of this."

"Unfortunately," Duncan said, looking at his watch, "we don't have hours. Just a few more minutes."

"Ah, gee," Dylan whined, "do we have to go already? We just found the toys and we haven't even started to look for the city of gold."

"We've already stayed longer than we should

have," Duncan said. "Maybe we'll come back someday . . . when you're older."

"You're starting to sound like my mom."

Duncan ruffled his son's hair, then snatched a small stone-carved jaguar from the ground and handed it to Dylan. "I don't normally take souvenirs, but what do you say we hang on to this so we'll have something to remember our journey."

"Oh, all right," Dylan said, latching on to the jaguar.

Duncan hoisted Dylan up on his shoulders. "Ready to go?"

"I suppose."

"How about you, Cairo?"

She didn't answer, and Duncan jerked around, looking everywhere for the woman he loved. Fear raced through him, until her voice—calling his name—echoed through the chamber.

At last he saw her stepping out of a cave that he hadn't noticed before. Its opening was at the top of a staircase, nearly hidden behind half a dozen stalagmites. "I think you'd better come see this," she called out to him.

He was glad to see her, glad she was safe, and he intended to keep her safe. "We've got to go," he said, taking another look at his watch. They'd been gone well over half an hour. "Whatever it is Cairo, it'll have to wait until we come back."

"This can't wait," she yelled.

He knew coming down here had been a mistake, but she seemed determined to get him up those stairs.

Dylan's fingers tightened around his neck as Duncan trudged through the toys, around splattermites and stalagmites, and took the man-made stairs two at a time.

"Look," Cairo said, her eyes sparkling as Duncan reached the entrance.

The light from his helmet shone into the small dark cavern. All around the walls were paintings of jaguar, blue plumed quetzal, snow-covered egret, and keel-billed toucan. And at the very center of the room, on a massive altar, sat a city of gold.

"Cool!" Dylan said.

All the exclamations Duncan could think of were stuck in his throat. The room was magnificent.

He walked into the cave, slowly, almost reverently. Cairo's fingers slipped through his, and they stood in silence, just staring at the splendid creation.

"It's a golden miniature of Copán," he said.

"It's wonderful," Cairo whispered.

Duncan walked around the altar, taking his

time, inspecting every intricate detail: the pyramids, the temples, even the stadium where the Maya played their torturous ball game.

Cairo took Duncan's camera from his pack and snapped one picture after another. "You aren't disappointed, are you?" she asked, her eyes peeking over the top of the camera.

"Not in the least." From all he'd read in Angus's journal, he'd expected to find a golden city that would fill an entire cavern. But he wasn't at all disappointed with this.

"You know," he said, circling the city again, "Angus MacPherson told a lot of wild tales, but I've got the feeling this was the wildest one of all."

I said it was a city of gold. I never said how big it was!

Duncan laughed again, as he pointed out details to his son, knowing that one day in the near future he'd take him to Copán and show him just how magnificent a city the Mayans had really built.

Cairo put the camera away and slipped her fingers around his. "What do we do now?" she asked. "Catalog everything? Call a museum?"

"I don't want to do either. I've got the feeling this is one place that's best left exactly the way it is—as untouched by human hands as possible."

"You're not going to tell anyone?"

"Not a soul."

"Can I tell Tommy?" Dylan asked.

"I think you should keep this story to yourself," Cairo said.

"But I can just see the look on his face when he hears how I discovered this gigantic golden city that was surrounded by man-eating jaguars."

"And I can hear his mother calling me to say that Tommy's having nightmares again and that she doesn't want you hanging around anymore."

Dylan let out a sigh, and squirmed on Duncan's shoulders. "Well, okay, but I'm still going to tell him about the monsters I saw when I fell down that hole."

I kind of like this son of yours, Dunc. Reminds me of myself when I was a kid.

Duncan only grinned, and wrapped an arm around Cairo's shoulders. He kissed her cheek, feeling awfully good about the discoveries he'd made in the past few days.

"What about the people of Sanctuary?" Cairo asked, sliding her fingers about his waist. "Are you going to tell them anything?"

"And spoil all their fun?"

"But they're looking in the wrong place. Don't you even want to give them a hint?"

"I thought about giving them Angus's journal . . .

Don't even think about it, Dunc. You and me still got places to go and things to see.

". . . but, I'm kind of attached to the old guy."

Darn tootin'!

"As for giving them a hint, there are plenty in Angus's other journal. It's just going to take the right person with a good imagination to figure it out." Duncan took another peek at his watch. "Now, what do you say we get out of here?"

Cairo smiled, that beautiful smile that he'd always loved, and when they reached the mouth of the cave they stood side by side and looked back one more time "Was it worth it?" she asked. "All the money invested? All the time, the years of research?"

Duncan's light shone on the golden city. It was magnificent, but it didn't give him the joy he'd imagined. When he felt his son's hands tightening around his neck, when he saw the gleam in Cairo's eyes, he knew where true happiness lay.

He pulled Cairo into his arms, loving the soft warmth of her against him.

"I love you," she whispered.

"You know, Cairo," he said, leaning close to brush a kiss across her lips. "I've been on a lot of expeditions. I've traveled the world, and done just about everything imaginable, but . . ." He took a deep breath, feeling a special warmth in his heart. "Falling in love with you all over again—and getting a son in the bargain—is the greatest adventure of all."

Epilogue

Cairo fluttered around the garden bar in the Tikal Hotel making sure all ten of her not-so-rich American tourists were enjoying themselves. Considering the number of margaritas, mai tais, and daiquiris that had been served, the entire group was having a fabulous time. As well they should. A wedding was supposed to take place in fifteen minutes.

Of course, the groom had yet to arrive.

"When will Duncan Kincaid be arriving?" Mrs. Flores asked. A good dozen gold bracelets jangled on her wrists, big round hoops dragged at her earlobes, and she had her camera poised at the ready as if she expected Duncan to swing into the hotel on a vine, do a Tarzan yell, sweep her off her feet, and carry her away.

Cairo would just settle for him showing up—period. Unfortunately, he was late.

By one entire day.

"I'm expecting him at any time, Mrs. Flores," she said as sweetly as possible, because keeping her clients happy in the extreme heat and sweltering Belize humidity was her number one job at the moment. She had to be a tour guide now. Later she could be a bride—hopefully.

"While we're waiting," she said to Mrs. Flores, "would you like me to take a picture of you and Mr. Flores?" Poor Mr. Flores. He was the only man on the trip and not in very high demand, not even from his wife. Duncan Kincaid seemed to be the man of the hour—and he wasn't even there.

"No, thank you," Mrs. Flores said. "I'll wait until Mr. Kincaid arrives. I hear he's absolutely gorgeous, and Mr. Flores and I are dying to have our picture taken with him."

Mr. Flores rolled his eyes, and Cairo buzzed over to another guest. "How's your margarita, Mrs. Russell?"

"Delicious, thank you." Mrs. Russell put a hand on Cairo's arm before she could buzz away. "I was so excited to get that special invitation in my tour packet. I just love weddings, especially rather secretive ones. Couldn't you give me just one little hint who's getting married?"

Nobody, maybe, but Cairo couldn't say that. "I'm afraid it wouldn't be fair for me to tell you and no one else, Mrs. Russell."

"Oh, I suppose not. It *is* going to take place, isn't it?"

"Of course," she said, and kept her hopes up high. "Everything's ready and in fifteen minutes, somebody in our tour group will be getting married." Even if she had to drag Mr. and Mrs. Flores out of their seats, stick them in front of the justice of the peace, and insist that they repeat their vows because, after all, that would be terribly romantic.

Suddenly Phoebe was standing next to her, looking positively perfect in screaming purple silk. "You're going to pass out from heat and worry if you don't sit down and take it easy."

"I can't sit down. I'm anxious and scared."

"Duncan's fine."

"What if he's not?"

"Don't even let your mind wander in that direction. Instead, think about the fact that as soon as this tour is over, you'll be taking your long-awaited honeymoon. And if for some reason you'd rather not think about endless nights making love to the man of your dreams, you could think about preparations for *my* wedding."

"But you're already married."

"Of course I am," Phoebe said, admiring the plain gold band on her left hand. "As wonderful as my first wedding was, it lacked everything but a charming husband and a justice of the peace. Now, my idea of a *real* wedding is Pacific Ocean breezes blowing through the redwoods, a white gazebo, roses strewn everywhere, and forty-eight years' worth of friends sitting around in chairs watching me finally get hitched. I don't mind getting gifts from them, either."

Phoebe was doing a great job taking Cairo's mind off her worries, and she'd worked terribly hard to make this day special. "Thanks for the twinkling lights," Cairo said, looking at thousands of them strewn through the ceiling-high ferns and artificial trees. "And thank you for the dress, Phoeb." It was a frothy concoction of lavender silk that Phoebe had finished the day before Cairo had left the States. And just this afternoon she'd woven white and lavender orchids into a crown which sat in the refrigerator behind the bar, waiting—like Cairo—for the groom.

"Oh, Cairo!" Miss David, the only woman on

the trip under the age of sixty, waved at Cairo from her table.

"I've got to run," Cairo told her aunt, glad for another distraction.

"Why don't you let me handle this one?"

"No, I really do like being with the people, or I never would have started this business. Besides, you've got a husband and a nephew hanging around somewhere. Why don't you keep them company until Duncan shows up?"

Phoebe brushed a quick kiss across her cheek. "You're a lovely bride, Cairo."

"And you're the best aunt a girl could ever have." She squeezed Phoebe's fingers and ran off again.

"I'm beginning to think Duncan Kincaid doesn't really exist." Miss David whispered as if she didn't want anyone to hear her speaking such blasphemy.

"He's not a myth," Cairo assured the woman.

Mrs. London spun around in her chair, and came to Cairo's aid. "He's definitely not a myth. I've seen pictures of him, and the stories I've read are absolutely incredible. Why, did you know he rescued an infant from the mouth of a crocodile while he was in the Amazon?"

Cairo slapped a hand to her chest. "No, I hadn't heard that story. Do you know others?"

"Oh, many, many more." Mrs. London giggled. "Did you know he has a fan club on the Internet? There's even a picture of him without his shirt on, and—" Mrs. London fanned her face. "He's gorgeous."

This was fascinating news, and Cairo would have pulled up a chair to hear more, but suddenly she heard gasps from at least nine out of the ten women in the room—the tenth being herself—because an absolutely gorgeous man strolled into the room—one day late.

Mr. I-have-a-fan-club-on-the-Internet was attired in safari khaki, he'd somehow come up with an Indiana Jones hat that looked downright sexy tilted low on his brow, and he had a keel-billed toucan on his shoulder. The baby boa constrictor wrapped around one arm was a little over the top, Cairo thought, but Duncan Kincaid had promised her he'd make a spectacular entrance for the people on the tour, and he'd done it to the max—one day late.

"Good evening, ladies—and gentleman." He caught Cairo's eye and winked. "Sorry I couldn't get here sooner."

"Oh, Duncan!" Mrs. London's hand waved wildly in the air. "We're just thrilled that you're finally here. Please, tell us, are the stories true about you and the crocodile?"

"Actually," he said, closing ranks on Mrs. London, looking like he was going to swallow her whole, "it was a jaguar right here in Belize. You don't see them all that often, but occasionally they sneak right up on an unsuspecting person—like you, for instance—and when you least expect it—" he paused for effect "—*pounce!*" A gasp rose in the bar and Duncan wrapped strong, caring fingers around Mrs. London's arm. He smiled, and Mrs. London and all the other women seemed to melt under the heat of his pale blue eyes. "Don't worry, Mrs.—" he looked at her name badge "—Mrs. London, or may I call you Edna."

"Edna's just fine."

"Cairo and I aren't going to let anything happen to you on this trip. Our plan is to make it as enjoyable as possible."

He was laying it on a little thick, but the women were oohing and aahing and Cairo was oohing and aahing herself.

"Mr. Flores." Duncan lifted the toucan from his shoulder. "Would you mind holding a friend of mine?"

Mr. Flores eyed Duncan suspiciously.

"He's safe. I named him Fruit Loop. Not very original, but fitting."

"He won't bite?" Mr. Flores asked.

"He won't do anything. I've already lectured him on wedding decorum and he's agreed to be a perfect gentleman."

Mr. Flores grinned. "All right." Duncan set the bird on Mr. Flores's shoulder, and suddenly Mrs. Flores turned her attention on her husband, snapping one photo after another.

"Now, who would like the boa constrictor?"

"Me, Daddy! Me!"

Cairo had the feeling that her emotions were ready to burst, because a fat tear rolled down her cheek when Dylan came running into the bar and launched himself into his father's arms.

"Daddy?" Miss David exclaimed to no one in particular. "Hmm, this *is* an interesting turn of events."

"May I hold the boa?" Dylan asked, his eyes wide as he looked at the snake wrapped around his dad's arm.

"Why don't we ask your mom?"

"Do we have to? She'll say 'When you're bigger!'"

"That's her prerogative," Duncan told him. Dylan rolled his eyes, and Duncan chuckled. "Well, Mom, what do you think?" Duncan asked, looking at Cairo.

"*Mom!?*" Miss David wasn't the least bit pleased with the newest turn of events, and Cairo mentally struck Miss David's name off the list of future clients. Then she looked at the boa. She looked at her son and his dad, two of a kind for sure, and said, "Just be careful."

Duncan put the snake in his son's hands, showed him the right way to hold it, then ushered him toward Graham and Phoebe. "Watch him, will you? I've got a little something to tell Cairo before the wedding starts."

Finally, after a long day and a half of worrying, she watched Duncan saunter toward her, every woman's fantasy come true.

And then right out loud, in front of everyone, he said, "We're still getting married, aren't we?"

"*You're not married?*" Miss David cried out.

"Well . . ." Cairo might have explained, but Duncan wrapped a hand around her waist and swept her to a secluded spot behind palms and ferns. A pair of scarlet macaws stared at them from their perch in an artificial tree, and twinkling lights flashed down on them.

"I was worried about you," Cairo whispered. "I called everywhere I could think of—"

"You wouldn't have thought about calling the place I went, and before you ask me why I didn't call—"

"I don't care where you've been or why, I'm just glad you're here."

He smiled and kissed her, and she found herself leaning into the comfort of his embrace. "I have a wedding present for you," he whispered, his mouth trailing to the hollow beneath her ear, sending little shivers of delight all through her body.

"Mmm, that's nice," she said, barely listening to his words because she was far too busy with his lips.

"It's a rather special present." He lightly nipped the very tip of her earlobe. "Something unique. Almost a one-of-a-kind gift."

"Mmm, that's nice."

A gentle breath and a soft, light kiss, touched her ear. "Would you like to know what it is?"

"Mmm, sure."

Once again he kissed her. "Look at me, Cairo," he said, his voice mesmerizing, and when she opened her eyes and looked into his pale blue ones, she was caught in his spell.

"I went to see an attorney yesterday."

She frowned. "Is something wrong? Is it about the city of gold?"

"No, Cairo, it's about us. One hundred percent about us."

"What? Do you want me to sign a prenuptial agreement, or something?"

"It's a little too late for that. We were married five years ago."

Cairo laughed lightly. "You seem to forget. I, unfortunately, had that annulled."

"And I filed papers yesterday to have that decision reversed."

Had she heard him correctly? "*Reversed*? Is that even possible?"

"If it was originally granted for the wrong reasons, and if one party wasn't too happy with the whole idea and wasn't given an opportunity to contest, it's definitely possible. Our annulment meets both those conditions."

"Does that mean you don't want to get married tonight?" She looked about her, at the orchids strewn through the ferns, at the twinkling lights that reminded her of that star-filled Egyptian night when she'd first kissed Duncan, and she wanted to repeat those vows she'd made five years ago.

"Oh, we're definitely getting married—again. This time, though, I want a bride for more than just one night."

"Anything your heart desires." Cairo stretched up to kiss him. "I'm afraid I didn't have time to get a gift for you."

"I already have everything I need, Cairo. Just you and Dylan."

Duncan swept her up in his arms and spun her around and around. "Do you know how much I love you?" he asked.

"If it's one-tenth as much as I love you, it's enough to last forever."

One more time he kissed her, and she could hear all the women sighing in the background.

She was sighing, too, right into a pair of terribly sexy lips. All too soon Cairo heard music begin to play, and together they walked past their group of travelers, awestruck women, one bewildered man, toward their family and a minister who was patiently waiting to marry them— again.

Phoebe was in her husband's lap, looking gloriously happy. Graham's silvery eyes sparkled with love. And Dylan . . .

"Dearly beloved," the minister began.

A scream pierced the hush, and all heads jerked around. Miss David had horror written all over her face, and Dylan climbed out from beneath her chair holding a boa constrictor high in the air.

"Dylan!" Cairo struggled to keep her voice as calm and controlled as possible. After all, she *was* at a wedding. *Her* wedding! "What on earth are you doing?"

"Well . . . I just wanted to see if a real snake could scare a person as easily as a rubber snake and . . ."

Duncan squeezed Cairo's hand, and her heart swelled with love. This was truly the way life was meant to be—one wonderful and exciting adventure following another.

Coming next month
HOW TO TRAP A TYCOON
By
Elizabeth Bevarly
An Avon contemporary romance

It's the book with all the answers . . .

Dorsey MacGuinness wrote *How to Trap a Tycoon*, never dreaming she'd just penned a runaway bestseller—using a different name, of course—that all the women were wild about . . . and all the men were nervous about. So when sexy millionaire Adam Darien declares war on its author, Dorsey doesn't know what to do . . .

Because she's fallen head over heels for *this* tycoon—but what will happen when he uncovers the truth about Dorsey?

Dear Reader,

Next month is June, and romance—and weddings!—are in the air. So if you've enjoyed the Avon romance you've just finished, then you won't want to miss any of next month's delicious Avon love stories, guaranteed to fulfill all of your most romantic dreams.

Love and romance in the old west is the theme of Susan Kay Law's sensuous, spectacular Treasure *THE MOST WANTED BACHELOR*. The richest man in town knows he has to take a bride, but he'll be darned if he'll marry someone who's just after his money! Then a pert young gal catches his eye—could it be that the most eligible man in town is about to marry?

Every now and then you can't help but wonder what it would be like to marry a millionaire. In Elizabeth Bevarly's contemporary *HOW TO TRAP A TYCOON*, Dorsey MacGuinness has written a bestseller that's become a handbook for single gals across the nation. But sexy Adam Darien isn't about to succumb to some gold-digging female . . .

Historical fans will be thrilled—Danelle Harmon's de Monteforte men are back! This time, *THE DEFIANT ONE*, Lord Andrew de Monteforte, meets his match in sexy Lady Celsie Blake, and when they're caught in a compromising position wedding bells ring . . .

Lady Margery Welles has the uncommon privilege of choosing her own husband, but she's in no hurry to wed. So she selects dashing knight Gareth Beaumont to pose as her suitor in Gayle Callen's *MY LADY'S GUARDIAN*.

Yes, June is the month for weddings—and none are more romantic, more beautiful, more sensuous than the ones you'll find here at Avon Romance.

Enjoy!

Lucia Macro

Lucia Macro
Senior Editor

AEL 0500

Discover Contemporary Romances
at Their Sizzling Hot Best
from Avon Books

A CHANCE ON LOVIN' YOU   *by Eboni Snoe*
79563-9/$5.99 US/$7.99 Can

ALL NIGHT LONG   *by Michelle Jerott*
81066-2/$5.99 US/$7.99 Can

SLEEPLESS IN MONTANA   *by Cait London*
80038-1/$5.99 US/$7.99 Can

A KISS TO DREAM ON   *by Neesa Hart*
80787-4/$5.99 US/$7.99 Can

CATCHING KELLY   *by Sue Civil-Brown*
80061-6/$5.99 US/$7.99 Can

WISH YOU WERE HERE   *by Christie Ridgway*
81255-X/$5.99 US/$7.99 Can

IT MUST BE LOVE   *by Rachel Gibson*
80715-7/$5.99 US/$7.99 Can

ONE SUMMER'S NIGHT   *by Mary Alice Kruesi*
79887-5/$5.99 US/$7.99 Can

BRIDE FOR A NIGHT   *by Patti Berg*
80736-X/$5.99 US/$7.99 Can

Avon Romances—
the best in exceptional authors and unforgettable novels!